# PICO

A Novel about Corporate Greed and Humiliation

**Derek Wheeler©**

First published in 2024

Cover Photo by *Mukul Kumar*

**Information is power. Disinformation is abuse of power**.

*Newton Lee*

# 1

The evening tube train squeals into the station and after an expectant pause, slides its many mouths open to regurgitate the humanity it had previously digested. Husbands, wives, mothers, fathers, sons, daughters and lovers rush along the platform and then upwards towards the cold night air. Only George Patterson impedes the flow. His shuffling pace creates an island of obstruction in the fast-moving stream, forcing turbulent eddies of irritated humans to form around him before leaving him in their wake. George is a slightly overweight, late middle-aged gent wrapped in misery and a badly buttoned raincoat. His shock of black hair is just beginning to show ashen tips and the empty briefcase he carries has seen better days. He is miserable because he is going home – but then, he's been miserable all day at work. His workday journey between the two places of gloom is rapidly coming to an end as he finally reaches the bottom of the up escalator, and he finds himself wishing that the ride would go on for ever – better that than to arrive at his next destination.

Waiting for him at home is his wife, Penny Patterson, or Pee-Pee as she used to be known by her friends – when she had any. She is sitting on a high kitchen stool, expertly cooking the evening meal without having to put her feet on the floor. She does this

by surrounding herself with strategically placed pots and pans within easy reach. Her feet are swathed, as usual, in thick socks and pensioners' soft, furry slippers so that when she eventually has to stand, it won't be too painful.

Usually, Penny hasn't a great deal to be cheerful about, but on this particular evening she is buoyed up by a guilty secret. Secret from George that is. A rare but distorted pleasure is to be had as she contemplates, in her confused and distorted mind, a victory over her husband and a hefty blow by which she will unthinkingly widen the wedge which is separating them in their marriage. But she has an itch that cannot be ignored, and which desperately needs to be scratched even through the scratching makes it worse. It is impossible to understand the desperate need that it engenders without having experienced it personally. No sufferer will ever be able to find the words to describe its all-consuming intensity to those who have never felt it. And with it comes guilt. A guilt too great to bear alone.

George opens the front gate and hesitates before walking up the short garden path to his front door. He just wants a moment to remember the Penny he *used* to know rather than the one he is about to encounter.

It's a 1960s disco and a blonde girl with beautiful legs and wearing high-heeled shoes is dancing. She has no partner, but she doesn't seem to care as she sways rhythmically to the music. George seeks anonymity in the shadows furthest from the dance area. Even from his distant position he is mesmerised by the blond girl and her uninhibited performance. He tries to visualize what she would look like naked.

The music has stopped, and the DJ is jabbering incoherently into a microphone. The girl has vanished. George looks vaguely around, expecting to see nothing interesting, and *finding* nothing interesting, heads towards the bar which is in another room. As he gets to the door, he feels a sharp push in his back and turns quickly and instinctively to catch a falling figure. The figure bends low to pick something up from the ground. A flashing light momentarily illuminates the face – it is the blonde girl, hopping on one foot and holding up a broken high heel shoe in triumphal justification for her sudden impact and present proximity. She is laughing and George realizes that he is still holding her tightly. It seems the most natural thing in the world to offer to buy her a drink and how could she possibly refuse such an offer from her saviour? Her name is Penny. Disappointingly, she doesn't drink alcohol. An orange will do fine.

On their wedding day Penny permits herself to sample a small glass of sweet white wine. It is the first time that alcohol has ever passed her lips. The effect is immediate and apparent: the usually bubbly blonde girl explodes with the energy of a popping champagne cork. She momentarily forgets the pain that she felt when she put her shoes on that morning.

Now, after nearly twenty years of marriage and two major operations on her ruined feet she is capable of drinking a whole bottle, not just of wine, but of spirit in a single evening if she could get her hands on one. And George's task is to ensure that she can't. Alcohol and shoes have caused the transformation. How she had loved shoes! Birthdays and Christmas: new shoes always did the trick. Shoes for shopping, shoes for parties, shoes for dancing – the higher the better. Never mind the pain just look at the effect. Her long legs made longer with those beautiful, stupid, foolhardy, ridiculous, fatal shoes. And when she could stand the pain no longer, she found that she could hardly walk with or without them.

George opens his front door. Penny is waiting for him in the hall.

George: 'Hi.'

Pause.

Penny: 'Dinner is on.' Then looking more closely, 'Why are you wearing mascara and smelling of perfume George?'

It isn't a question. She *knows* why - it's because they're difficult to remove. She used to joke about it. She is being provocative.

The routine 'How are you, Pen?' is lost as she turns her back on him and hobbles painfully into the kitchen diner to throw plates noisily out onto the table. This is the signal that George has been dreading. She has been drinking.

With a sinking feeling he moves into the front room, kneels before the sideboard and recovers the key from deep in his inside jacket pocket. The sideboard door opens too easily. Penny is watching him, arms folded from the doorway as he carefully examines the contents. Bottle of gin still unopened, brandy still in its pristine sealed box, whisky decanter still full of acetone nail polish remover, vodka … where's the bottle of vodka?

'Where's the bloody vodka Penny? How did you get into the sideboard?'

She smiles and restricts her reply to a slightly slurred, 'Ah ha! Wouldn't you like to know?'

'What is happening to you, Penny? What the hell is happening to *us*? Why are you acting like a child?'

'Glad you mentioned "child", George. We got one, remember? He doesn't live with us – couldn't wait to get away. He's somewhere else in some godforsaken college wasting his time and our money doing a dead-end course in art app..appp…GODDAMIT *appreciation*! What kind of a job will he get with that? What kind of a life, eh

George? And it's all *your* fault. I'm not taking the blame for it. You've ruined his life just like you've ruined mine!'

George is shocked. He's heard this before but not with such vehemence.

'Penny this is the alcohol talking. You'd never say these things if you were sober. This is why I try to keep you away from the booze – look what it does to you. Simon will be fine. He's just finding his feet in life, meeting new people, bumping into new ideas. I tell you, he may not be the brightest, but he will be OK.'

Penny gives a snigger, sits down at the dining table and shakes her head in apparent disbelief at her husband.

'You just don't understand, do you? You've just got no fucking idea what you've done. *You* who gave me my first alcoholic drink. *You* who promised help but still keep a locked cupboard filled with booze. *You* who professed love for me but who failed miserably to stop me drinking when we both knew I shouldn't have during pregnancy. You who professed love for our new-born son but still refuses to accept your part in his instant rejection of me at birth – screaming every time I picked him up because of what I did to him in the womb. I can't bear all the guilt for Simon's failures on my own. His stupid failure of a father has got to take the blame.'

The telephone rings and George reaches gratefully and unthinkingly to answer it. This has provoked Penny into alcoholic fury.

'That's right! Pick up the fucking phone, why don't you? Never mind listening to me. What use am I? There's bound to be someone more interesting to listen to than me on the fucking phone.'

She staggers towards the drink's cabinet, falling to her knees and ripping the door off of its hinges.

'I hate you George Patterson!'

'Hello?' says a voice on the phone. 'Hello. Is that you George? Listen, mate. We've got a few major decisions to make over finances. Gus wants us all in first thing in the morning…'

George dimly recognised the Australian accent but Penny has grabbed hold of something from within the cabinet and she throws it with all her fury-enhanced strength at George's head.

As the glass decanter flies towards him George clearly understands two things. Firstly, that Penny had managed to get to the vodka by removing the pins from the hinges of the cabinet and secondly, he knows that the decanter, when it hits him, is going to hurt a great deal. He is right on both counts. He feels the excruciating pain of acetone from the nail polish remover as it pours into the deep cuts in his face made by a thousand glass shards from the smashed decanter. Without uttering a sound, he lets the telephone receiver slip from his hand where it falls on the freshly red-spotted carpet. Then he follows suit.

# 2

George is chief chemist at Keynote Cosmetics Ltd. In fact, he is the company's *only* chemist. This accounts for his tendency to wear mascara and eyeshadow and lipstick and to smell of perfume and to keep nail polish remover in glass decanters. (You have to test the products you're making if you are a cosmetic chemist – just remember to remove them before going to the pub at lunch time).

Keynote is a small company and it has no cosmetic products of its own. It makes a meagre living either by providing extra production facilities for well-known cosmetic companies, or by inventing and manufacturing products for companies which have cosmetic brands but no factories or formulation facilities of their own.

Although cosmetic science doesn't rate highly on the scale of technical complexity, it does require considerable chemical and creative skills. Since George is the only Keynote employee able to provide these skills, and since he has now been completely missing from work for a week, the board of directors are more than a bit perturbed. They are having a board meeting to decide what to do. It's probably going to be the most focused board meeting they've had since they took over the Company less than a year ago.

The meeting is taking place in the large office of the Italian Managing Director and company owner, Mr Giovanni 'Gus' Volante. Gus considers himself to be an international businessman and takes care to behave accordingly. This involves expensive suits, personalised business stationary, expensive cars and an elitist attitude designed to strike fear and awe into his employees. In reality he can afford none of these luxuries. His main asset, in his mid-fifties, is his appearance – a serious, intense face with greasy, swept-back hair greying at the temples and a set of musical stave lines that appear across his forehead whenever he becomes concerned or angry, which he frequently does. At the moment this is imprinted with the music to *Mars, the Bringer of War.*

Gus is a mystery man. He arrived on British soil from Somewhere-in-Italy carrying nothing but a shed load of mysterious money. By happenstance, he had contacted the commercial arm of an estate agency where Beverley Curtis was employed, perched and primed and ready to leap onto the first rich investor that came her way.

Miss Beverly Curtis, Company Secretary and Assistant to Mr Volante is much younger than Gus and has short black hair, spectacles, a black trousered business suit and a complete absence of make-up. Her face is *also* contorted. This is because she is swearing vehemently at the third director, the Australian, Mr. Brett Kander. This is something she does with monotonous regularity. At the time of Gus's mysterious entry into the

UK Beverly was employed by Beaufort Business Brokers as a part of the junior staff dealing with customers who were looking for businesses to purchase. She had correctly assumed that this would bring her into direct contact with wealthy businessmen, and her plan was to use these contacts to her own financial advantage. She did not have a clear plan of how to do this but was prepared to place her trust in fate, her business-like appearance and a knowing, slightly superior smile. Beverly wears her anti-feminine dress and her foul-mouthed aggression as a danger signal, like the bright stripes of an angry wasp. As with all narcissists she is in perpetual competition with the lesser mortals around her. Lesser mortals such as Brett. She's not going to let "being a woman" get in her way.

Gus Volante, when he first encountered Beverly, was quite specific about what he wanted: a small to medium-sized perfumery company. Unfortunately, a hunt through the Beaufort records revealed no such companies for sale. However, there *was* a small cosmetics company available in East London that included facilities for making alcohol-based products. Giovanni demanded to be taken to see it and Beverly was happy to oblige. As he took his time over the inspection of the premises Beverly grew more impatient. On the way back in her car, she took the opportunity to halt at traffic lights and turn to her potential customer.

'Well, are you going to buy the fucking place or are you just pissing me about?'

Gus appeared to be unmoved. Turning back to her with an expressionless face he uttered the immortal words 'Only if you come as my secretary.'

It was a match made in some kind of heaven.

Brett Kander, the third member of the trio, is a stocky, full-faced Australian with almost blond hair and cinematic high cheek bones that give him a permanent grin. Having travelled to England some time ago to escape his wife and family, he is a left-over from the previous company that owned Keynote and was happy to continue to serve the new owner as Sales and Marketing Director.

...

The meeting has commenced. The agenda is easily the clearest so far tabled by the young company:

1. Where the fuck is George Patterson?
2. What the fuck are we going to do?
3. AOB

Even though the discussion of these agenda items is destined to get a little blurred from time to time, this is likely to be the very best Board Meeting that Keynote has ever had, both in terms of focus and direction.

Beverly is the first to talk.

'You fucking smiling at Brett? Bin round to his fucking house again have you, you twat? Or don't you know where he lives?'

Practice makes perfect. This enables Brett to reply as though she has made a polite request.

'Yes Bev. Been to his house, several times, day and night as a matter of fact. Shut and barred. No lights, no sign of life.'

'Ok. So, you checked with his neighbours? Surely, they must have seen something. Anything, for fuck's sake?'

'Neighbours have no idea where he or his wife are. Lady at Number 16 across the road has agreed to phone me the moment anyone turns up.'

Gus intervenes.

'Ok. Ok. *Sta' zitto!* Listen! We in *big* shit without Patterson. A week now. Huh? So now I need to know. How big?' He picks up a large paper knife from the desk. 'When do I cut my throat, huh?'

'Money wise,' says Bev, 'we're already in fucking trouble. At the end of the month, we've got the payroll and a bank loan instalment to make. I was hoping for a payment to cover it but nothing's been delivered. Nothing to invoice. What going on Brett? We need something to fucking invoice.'

Brett appears to be genuinely apologetic.

'I'm sorry Bev, but we've got production and formulation problems all over the place. There will be nothing going out until we fix them, but without George it's not looking good.'

'Come on Brett,' says Gus. 'You been here longer than us. You a clever guy. You got the – what's it – the knowhow, yes? So why the hell you can't fix things huh?'

Bev agrees. 'At least you could try. Its only cosmetics for fuck's sake. What's so fucking difficult?'

Brett produces an A4 writing pad, consults the scribble on it and carefully reads through the list of problems. These are continuing to pile up. A batch of shampoo which is too thick, pressed eyeshadow production where the rejection rate is over 50 percent, a batch of lipstick being off-shade, a backlog of twelve new colours to match against cloth samples - by the end of the month.

'Either of you two have colour-matching skills? I'm sorry but I've no idea how to do any of it. Sorry.'

'So, what the fuck are we going to do?'

'Wadda we do? It's simple,' suggests Gus waving the paper knife in the air. 'Please don't make a mess on my beautiful table with your blood.' He lays a trembling, liver-spotted hand down on its surface in a token gesture of protection.

Brett is a very different animal. He is an arranger, not a doer. As a conversationalist and a lover of poetry, he finds himself to be surprisingly well-suited to the handling of customers. He loves the taking of orders on the telephone from a comfortable chair and treating favoured customers to an occasional lunch at the local

Indian or Chinese. But Brett is not a problem-solver. Presently, he is out of his depth.

'If anyone should have his wrists cut its fucking George Patterson,' Beverley retorts with vehemence.

Gus joins in.

'We getting nowhere. We need Patterson fast. So, I ask again Brett. You been to his house, yes? You check with neighbours?'

'Yes. I've already said Gus.'

'All of them? Not just next door huh? Along the damn road? Three doors? Four doors? Whole damn street?'

'Yes Gus. Whole damn street.'

'And nobody see the guy even leave – his wife as well. Nobody?'

'Nobody Gus. Not a bloody soul.'

'No car, no van, no *ambulancia*? Jesus! But you try the hospitals? Huh? No record – man and wife together? Mr Patterson and wife?'

Brett hesitates.

Bev: 'Don't tell me you didn't check with the fucking Hospitals?'

'As far as possible – yes. They don't like giving you information unless you are a relative.'

'Didn't you tell them that you've lost a chemist?'

Brett doesn't answer but comes up with a suggestion.

'Do you think he might have been - kidnapped?'

He regretted saying it as soon as the words were out of his mouth. George Patterson kidnapped? George

Patterson - quiet, white coated, clever, industrious, mundane, unobtrusive. A character who brings his own sandwiches for lunch presumably made by his miserable alcoholic wife. Kidnapped? Whisked away in the dead of night?

There's a pause while they contemplate this possible explanation.

'Maybe he making drugs? Yes? Is making them from home maybe? *È un dannato chimico* – damned chemist. Huh?'

'Look Gus,' ventures Brett hesitantly, 'I really don't think that's likely. But let's face it, the obvious thing to do is... well... to report his disappearance to the police. He is a missing person for God's sake.'

One of the mysteries which surround Gus is his strong aversion to the police or anything associated with them. In normal times this didn't seem important but now with Patterson's disappearance together with the possibility that their jobs might follow the same path, it has *become* a problem.

'You go to police and I kill you. No police. You hear me?'

'Well in that case what do we do?'

'Ok. Then the answer she's simple. Hand me the bloody knife.'

'That's really fucking helpful Gus,' snorts Beverly. 'It's made me feel a lot better already - I don't think.'

The telephone on Gus's desk burbles into life with a flashing red light that demands attention. The new telephone system is the only major investment made in Keynote since the new owner took over. Now Brett can automatically switch through to the company receptionist and record any conversation automatically if needed.

Still slightly shaken from the violence of Gus's outburst Brett hesitates and then presses the still flashing answer button.

'What is it Lynne? I thought I told you we were not to be disturbed.'

As he listens, his face, changes from irritation to surprise.

'Hold on, Lynne, I'm going to put you on speaker. Repeat what you just told me.'

The crystal-clear voice of Lynne Cooper, the receptionist, can be heard over the telephone speaker system.

'It's a bloke from the local newspaper. He wants to talk to someone about an article they are going to publish about Keynote.'

A surprised silence is broken by Bev.

'Fucking hell. How did they find out?'

'Find out what Beverley?' asks Brett thoughtfully putting his hand over the telephone receiver in the mistaken belief that Lynne's sensitive ears need to be protected.

Gus, still with anger in his system: 'You think?'

'What else can it be?' Looking around. 'This is not good. Bad. Very bad. The last thing we need right now.'

'So, what do we say guys? We can't keep holding him on the line.'

Getting no response, Brett tells the receptionist to put him on while the others remain silent.

'Hello?' says the caller, clearly. 'This is Mike Davis from the *East London News*. Who am I talking to please?'

'Hi Mike, this is Brett Kander. How can I help you?'

'Would that be Mr Brett Kander? Sales director of Keynote Cosmetics?'

'The very same, Mike.'

'Oh, good afternoon, sir. Thank you for taking my call. Just a courtesy call really. We're thinking of doing a piece on Keynote in next week's edition and I thought you ought to have a heads-up and a chance to comment on it before we publish. Is that alright?'

'Well, this is a bit of a surprise Mike – not to say shock. We don't normally figure much in the local news. What's the proposed story about? Do we get to see it before you go into print?'

'Yes, I'm very happy to discuss it with you which is why I'm grateful for this initial response. In fact, I was rather hoping we could have a face to face to make sure we've got all our facts straight. What do you think?'

Pause while the trio exchange grimaces and shoulder shrugs.

'You still haven't said what the story is about Mike.'

'OK. Well, the word is going around that one of your senior employees, your chemist Mr – or is it Dr? - Patterson has gone missing. Can you confirm that?'

'Where did you hear that from?'

'Oh, just local gossip, you know. I pick up all sorts of weird things in this job. Is it true?'

Another pause.

'Why should that be of interest to a newspaper like yours Mike. Pretty mundane stuff. Bloke doesn't turn up to work for a few days. Hardly headline news I would have thought.'

'Yes, you're quite right – normally.'

'So, why the call?'

'Well sir there's another bit to the story. You see we seem to have evidence that he has been putting bits of animal into your cosmetics – bits of pig in fact. Is that true?'

...

It's safe to say that none of the three directors had a clue about what went into their cosmetics. The production guys did of course but they only added ingredients following a production formula and instructions given to them by George Patterson. However, what George got up to in his tiny laboratory was anyone's guess. For all they knew he *could* have been playing with bits of animals as ingredients. If he was and if the local newspaper had not only discovered it but were about to publish it – probably on their front page - that was going to be a major embarrassment and problem. Putting bits of pig into their cosmetics would not go down well with Keynote's customers or the local community with which they already had a love-hate relationship.

Keynote Cosmetics occupied a somewhat dilapidated corner site in a refurbished area of East London. The building having survived the bombing raids of the second World War had also managed to resist being swept away by the wave of new council flats and small terraced houses which now surrounded it, leaving it as incongruous and unlikely as a lamb chop in the centre of a wedding cake. It's relationship with the local population vacillated between complaints about the nightmare of heavy delivery lorries squeezing along the narrow roads on one hand and the benefit of valuable employment for local unskilled females (who were needed to fill, cap, label and pack cosmetics and toiletries on the company's production lines) on the other. For some years Keynote had survived calls for its demolition but to date, with some support from the local workforce and their families it had survived relatively unscathed. But a news story of the kind now envisaged could easily provide the protesters with enough extra ammunition to shoot the company down. Who wants a company that puts bits of farm animals in their products? Mike Davis's telephone call had consequently stunned the Keynote board. They clearly couldn't ignore it and a face-to-face meeting with the reporter seemed to be the obvious next step. But where? Not at the factory where there might be some evidence to be found. Thus, it was agreed to meet with him on neutral ground: the White Horse pub, less than half a mile down the road from Keynote.

# 3

When Gus Volante purchased Keynote from its previous owners, he inherited not only the building and equipment but also a number of existing employees. Brett Kadar was one of these, and so was Miss Lynne Cooper who occupied the reception desk just inside the front entrance to Keynote. Once impressive, the entrance now comprised a row of badly tiled and damaged exterior steps leading up to a double set of doors. Behind these, the reception area was replete with a few IKEA chairs and a cheap blue carpet. This was Lynne's workplace, seated uncomfortably behind her desk, and she is to play an important part in our story.

As a young girl Lynne had been quiet and withdrawn, shy in company and with few friends. A classic introvert. A loner. Expert physiologists agree that to change a person from being introverted to extroverted is nigh on impossible and would, in any event, take a lifetime of careful treatment to achieve. In fact, it took Lynne Cooper less than thirty seconds.

It happened while Lynne, at the age of seventeen, was being transported to her convent school in the back of her parents' car. Looking out of the window she read these words on the side of a lorry in the next traffic lane:

*'There's only one life. Live it.'*

The blinding truth of this brief homily hit her with a force so powerful that all the physiologists in the world would collectively be unable to explain it. In that inspirational moment she saw herself curled up in a corner watching life pass by and not participating in it. One life, and she was missing it. The jolt she received from that realization switched something in her brain from negative to positive in an instant. She felt the dead weight of her accumulated unspoken opinions, her suppressed feelings and her neglected girlish instincts rise up inside her like boiling milk bubbling over and rushing to fill her consciousness. What a fool to waste what she'd been given!

The girl who emerged from the back of that car was the alter ego of the one who had entered it just a few miles before. And her parents never forgave her.

To be fair, it was some time before Lynne came to terms with her new sense of freedom but as her self-doubts disappeared, she gradually found the courage to cast her inhibitions aside. And when she did - what a relief! Of course. Only one life! And she intended to live it. To the full!

Her first move was to change her magazine reading habits: she started to buy copies of *More* and *Heat* and read about how to achieve an orgasm – a major change from reading her mother's more restrained magazines which, if they mentioned orgasms at all merely told you how to knit one. Then, with experimentation she discovered several ways of actually doing it and liked them sufficiently to keep trying to improve her technique. Several likely lads of her acquaintance also benefited from this learning experience.

By now she had also changed her appearance and this was beneficial to the pursuit of her new taste for sexual adventure. A very shapely figure emerged like a butterfly from the chrysalis of the now abandoned loose fitting garments of her pre-revelation era. She favoured short tight skirts and even tighter tops and blouses often with open fronts to reveal an ample amount of cleavage. This transformation was completed by shoulder-length blonde hair and a face, already attractive, enhanced by skilful use of make-up. Sheer stockings provided the finishing touch together with high heeled shoes that often vied with her lipstick to produce the brightest colour. In a word Lynne was making unambiguous use of what life had provided, in a relentless pursuit of what she interpreted as life's own ultimate objectives.

Initially Lynne had opted for a thespian career but her mediocre performances in local amateur theatre productions anticipated her failure to get into RADA. A brief period as a photographic model followed, providing a satisfactory solution to her twin objectives of earning a living and meeting interesting men. This came to an abrupt end when her father inexplicably discovered her as the centre fold in a soft porn magazine and threatened to cut her off from the family fortune if she didn't get 'a decent job.' Whilst Lynne was uncertain about the possible size of any inheritance, she decided to take no chances, especially as she was not getting on too well with the ego-centric males who dominated the porn business.

So, after a series of office jobs (most of which she lost by reason of her embarrassingly eccentric behaviour) she applied for and obtained the job of receptionist at Keynote Cosmetics.

To her surprise and pleasure the world of cosmetics turned out to be male dominated. There were far more men than women who came through Keynote's doors as sales representatives – and these were often of a character and disposition likely to comply with Lynne's ideas on how to live life. Since the change of ownership, the Keynote management had left her pretty much alone to get on with it. Only when copious use of the photocopier to provide images of various parts of the human anatomy were discovered was she called upon to explain herself. Her obvious (and successful) defence was that she was not the only person using the machine and anyway, she couldn't keep her eye on it all the time. The outcome was a strict instruction that henceforth, only Lynne herself had permission to use the copier. She promptly rewarded her employer's trust by displaying the following notice in large letters on the wall:

'PLEASE DO NOT INTERFERE WITH THE RECEPTIONIST'S REPRODUCTION EQUIPMENT WITHOUT HER PERMISSION.'

This served to fuel Beverly Curtis's jealous fury. 'Now perhaps we can get rid of this fucking tart.' But the loyal Brett managed to restrain his co-director and hastily removed the poster before Gus saw it. He then gave a severe lecture to its slightly amused originator, whose response was, 'Sorry Mr Kander. Bad choice of phrasing now you come to mention it.'

# 4

Three weeks before Mike Davis's fatal telephone call, Keynote's evening cleaning lady, Mrs Disha Patel had handed in her notice, and Lynne was given the job of finding a replacement. Hopefully, someone from the surrounding population. This proved not to be difficult since Mrs Patel had highly recommended her bingo partner and friend Mrs Edna Beresford for the job. On paper Mrs Beresford seemed an ideal candidate.

'You should apply,' she had told Mrs B. 'Just two hours in evening from five to seven. Very easy work. You clean and dust offices and laboratory only. Finish in time for bingo on Thursdays, yes?' Mrs Beresford smiled. It was not a sensation she was used to. The creases in the face that she had owned for some fifty-seven years came mainly from muscles involved with frowning and grimacing. Smiling had played a very minor part in their formation - but then, she had had very little to smile about. Since Mrs Beresford is another lady destined to play an important part in our story, she deserves some background attention, Over the years, Fate had dealt her a seemingly endless series of losing hands and having thus been frowned upon Mrs B had frowned right back and she had plenty of chubby face to work with. Close inspection of her top lip and chin revealed a growth of soft grey hair which would probably become more visible as age played its trick of progressively disarranging her hormone balance. Her face also sported a pair of brown squinting eyes and crowned by grey hair. This had been moulded into a neat and unspectacular shape by the frequent attention of a hair net coupled with infrequent attention by the mobile stylist who 'tidied it up' once every few weeks. As to the rest of her, her body could also be described as chubby and aging. She favoured the long, flowery, loose-fitting, shapeless dresses of the kind that were not inclined to emphasize her amble bosom or a generous girth at the hip. She wore sensible shoes with little or no heel and these did little to raise her above her natural five-and-a-half-foot stature.

At the time of her marriage to Mr Beresford life had been full of hope and ambition and devoid of grimaces. Like most females of her generation, she had expected to fulfil the dual role of loving wife and mother. Fate stepped in soon after the marriage ceremony however when Mr Beresford – Sid to his numerous friends – inexplicably joined the merchant navy and went to sea leaving his wife with her ambitions intact but with no legitimate means of achieving them until he returned home to port. Of course, the young Mrs B did her utmost to produce the patter of tiny Beresford feet whenever the wind blew Sid back into her arms but Fate had decided otherwise. And by the time he eventually retired from the navy, her husband had apparently lost all interest in the act of procreation – although Mrs B was to be given evidence to the contrary sometime later.

As Sid settled down as a landlubber his wife began to focus her unrequited maternal instincts onto things small and furry. It started with cats, of course. Sid would not countenance dogs – not in their two-bedroom council flat with no garden – and especially since dogs reputedly needed to be taken for walks. Cats and similarly-sized furry animals however were allowable and Mrs B threw herself into the task of saving abandoned and otherwise fallen cats with an enthusiasm that surprised and dismayed her husband in equal measure. Ragged felines from local farms or cat sanctuaries began to appear, hiss, urinate, defecate, give birth, shed hairs and shred both furniture and exposed flesh with alarming rapidity. After some months of wholly admirable restraint Mr Beresford finally announced that the either the cats or he would have to go. It was a tough decision. But when one of the chinchillas finally chewed through the electricity supply cable fusing both the lights and the poor creature's brain, they jointly agreed that domestic pets would have to be banned. In any case, by this time Mrs B had come to recognise that cats did not provide the kind of helpless dependence that she was craving. Robbed of maternal love and then deprived of creatures to love and care for at home she turned towards the welfare of animals in general. She joined societies. She signed letters of protest. She delivered leaflets. She collected money. She became particularly incensed by the cruelties imposed on animals, especially chickens and pigs, by factory farming methods. This caused her to grimace rather a lot. It also caused her to take on the countenance and demeanour of a protester. She joined societies that placed no value on any person who did not agree with them and she learned how to use the apparatus of protest and dissent including the exploitation of the local press.

It was too good to last. Fate struck again. One evening, she returned home to find her husband, Sid, in a state of partial undress lying in front of the television and quite dead. It was the first time – but not the last – that a slightly fuzzy photographic image of Mrs B would appear in the local newspaper, the *East London News*. According to the news item (a copy of which she kept folded up in the back of her purse) Mr B had died from a sudden heart attack. What the item failed to mention was that when he was found the television had been showing a pornographic video of a most explicit kind – a fact that the coroner must have undoubtedly taken into account when drawing his conclusion about the cause of death. Mrs Beresford prepared to mount a campaign against the local video rental store for erroneously and incompetently hiring out a vile video to her innocent husband. Before she could take further action however, she answered the doorbell to find two of Sid's security colleagues offering their sincere condolences on the death of her Sid and politely requesting the return of the video they had lent him.

Released from the restraints imposed by her demised husband she used her new found freedom to pursue her animal campaigning with renewed vigour and also to join her local Bingo club, which is where she made the acquaintance of Mrs Disha Patel. Mrs Patel was also widowed but lived with her son, who was doing well enough to enable him to fund his mother's retirement and enable her to return to their family home in Mumbai. Hence the vacancy for a cleaning lady at the factory. When her friend offered to help her get the job, Mrs B was unsure... but she badly needed the money. The job seemed to be real enough, and the money would be a godsend. Disha would arrange it - all Mrs B had to do was turn up on the appointed day at the appointed time and ask for the receptionist.

## 5

The trio of Keynote directors had arrived early at The White Horse pub for their meeting with Mike Davis. They sat huddled together for safety and comfort in the corner of the pub's back room. This was a location usually reserved for live music but on Tuesday afternoon it was empty, just as Mike Davis promised it would be. All three directors had fortified themselves with large whiskies as they awaited the reporter's arrival. Brett was sick with apprehension. Beverly was straining to fully engage her aggressive and affronted frame of mind. Gus was slightly bewildered and struggling to find a way to exert the privilege of authority that his money clearly owed him. Who was this local rag reporter and what the hell did he know about cosmetics or even business for that matter? What the hell was he talking about – bits of pig in their cosmetics? Rubbish surely. Patterson wouldn't do a stupid thing like that would he? Would he?

'Truth is,' Brett had said, 'we have absolutely no idea about what he gets up to in his laboratory.' They had made a careful inspection of his deserted lab of course and the raw material section of the warehouse. Animal bits were nowhere to be seen, thank goodness.

'Do you really think that he's been putting pig into cosmetics? Even if he was, whose cosmetics? Good God.

Suppose he has! Think of the legal actions we'd get. We could all end up in prison!'

'You no idea what he was doing Brett?' asked Gus.

'Look, none of us do. I haven't a clue. He could have been using rat poison for all I know.'

'We deny it of course.' Beverly.

'Sure, then newspaper man shows us his proof, yes? I brought the knife along, ready.'

Brett is not impressed. 'Not helpful Gus. Anyone got other ideas? If it's true, how do we justify it and how do we explain why our chemist is missing?'

By the time Mike Davis arrived they had managed to transform mere trepidation into something so close to panic that they didn't notice him until he spoke.

'Good afternoon, lady and gents. May I join you?'

Gus's reaction was an Italian glare but Brett, who was used to being nice to people he didn't like, forced a smile and stood up to shake the newcomer's hand.

Bev scowled at the enemy sizing him up. Youngish. Slim. Bespectacled and looking like a secondary school teacher.

'Hi Mike. Fancy a drink?'

The reporter, glancing round the table and assessing the demeanour of the three occupants, liked what he saw.

'Sure. I'll have a pint please. Thanks very much.'

As the Marketing Director briefly disappeared to order the round Mike sat down opposite Gus Volante ignoring the presence of Beverly Curtis.

'Nice to meet you Mr Volante. I believe you are the owner of Keynote?'

Gus's scowl deepened. 'So?'

'So how is business?'

'You want I should give you a balance sheet?'

Mike smiled and shrugged his shoulders. Beverly took the opportunity to open her account.

'Mr..er..Davis. You asked us to meet you here to discuss something you are going to put in your newspaper, not to make small talk. We are all busy people...'

Mike turned and looked directly into her eyes. 'Forgive me I've not had the pleasure. You are Miss Curtis, I take it? Well Miss Curtis, whether or not I put this "something" in my newspaper is going to depend on what you tell me this afternoon. The front page is on hold at the moment so I'm going to have to make my mind up pretty quickly.'

'Front page?' gasped Gus in alarm. 'Is it that important?'

'You tell me Mr Volante. Let me ask you directly. Do you mash up animals to put into your cosmetics?'

The silence that followed this simple question was due partly to the time needed to absorb it, partly due to fevered calculations about which reply was the least damaging, but mainly due to the terrible thought that the truthful answer could be 'yes'.

It was Brett, returning from his drinks-ordering duties, who replied. He decided to play for time.

'Come on Mike. What makes you think that we would do such a thing? What possible motive would we have for putting bits of animals in our cosmetics?'

'Again - you tell me.'

Gus was shaking. 'This some kinda joke yes? April fool fun huh?'

'No Mr. Volante. It's not April and it's no joke. We have a witness.'

Gus was bubbling with native Italian aggression but Brett managed to silence him by raising an urgent hand.

'Look. Let me get this straight Mike. Strewth! You're telling us that you have a witness? Someone who has seen us putting animal bits into our cosmetics? Is that right? Actually *seen* us do it?'

The barman appeared with a tray of drinks and advanced slowly towards the table.

Mike backed off a little.

'Not actually seen, no. But I have – evidence.'

'Evidence that we put bits of animal into our products?'

'Correct.'

'And again, why would we do that?'

Mike gave a weary shake of the head.

'As I've already said I'm hoping you will be able to tell me – just so we get the story right.'

'Bits of animals – all kinds of animals?'

'No. Just pigs. Bits of mashed-up pigs.'

The barman placed the drinks on the table and casually made newspaper history with an off-hand remark.

'I've got a cousin in America who puts pig fat on his face and body regular,' he said helpfully. 'Swears it keeps him fit and healthy. Seems to work, too. He's ninety-three and as lively as a forty-year-old.'

Then giving the table a superficial and ineffective wipe, he made his way back to the bar next door without any idea about what he had just done.

Brett was ready to react.

'This is unbelievable Mike. You need to be very careful about what you print. I can't imagine what sort of proof you think you have but you should understand that if we have to, we would be prepared to take matters further – in court if needed. Bad publicity from unsubstantiated claims of this kind could ruin our company and that would mean substantial damages for your paper. You're certainly going to need some pretty convincing evidence.'

'Then you deny it – you specifically deny putting bits of animal into your cosmetic products?'

'Where's your evidence?'

Mike was unfazed. 'You want to see it?'

He opened his holdall, extracted two sheets of A4 paper and laid them out on the table.

The shock of this revelation could clearly be seen on all their faces. After a long, stunned silence, Beverly was the first to react.

'And just where did you get this – "evidence" from Mr Davis?'

'This came directly out of your chemist's laboratory. Before you ask, I'm not at liberty to reveal how I obtained it Miss Curtis, although you should be assured that it is a very reliable source which will stand up to any degree of scrutiny.'

'Indeed. But you claim that this so-called "evidence" came from our chemist's laboratory – a highly confidential area in private premises? Have you heard of industrial espionage Mr Davis?'

'Have you heard of health and safety regulations and the European Cosmetics Directive Miss Curtis?' Mike countered. 'Have you heard of animal rights?'

To the clear astonishment of her two co-directors, Beverly smiled serenely and knowingly.

'It seems to me that your – informant – has already committed a crime by stealing confidential information from us. We, on the other hand have not transgressed any laws or regulations since we have not put any cosmetics containing the "additives" your "proof" refers to onto the market.'

'By "additives" you mean piggy bits Miss Curtis?'

Beverly smiled.

'So,' Mike continued. 'You now admit that such "additives" do exist and you *could* be planning to put cosmetics containing them into the market?'

'We're admitting nothing Mr Davis.' She looked at her dumbstruck colleagues who were wondering where she was going and how long the prison sentence towards which she was leading them was going to be.

'I don't suppose,' she continued, standing up and encircling the table for effect, 'that you have ever heard of our brilliant chemist Mr George Patterson?'

'Not apart from the fact that he seems to be missing.'

'No. You obviously don't move in elite scientific circles.'

'I'm a reporter Miss Curtis not a chemist.'

'More's the pity because if you where you would know that he has an international reputation as a master cosmetic scientist and a gifted inventor.'

Brett's feeble attempt to interject was brought to a premature end by a wave of Beverly's finger in his direction.

Mike took a swig from his glass of beer and then retrieved a pen from his pocket and a pad from his case.

'I have a feeling you may be about to tell me something my readers might be interested in.'

'That depends on whether your readers can handle the truth.'

Beverly was beginning to enjoy herself which is more than could be said of Brett, who could resist the urge to speak no longer.

'Look Mike. Before this goes any further, I think we, as responsible directors of the company, need to have a bit of a private chat. Company secrets and all that. Could we call you first thing in the morning?'

Mike sighed resignedly and slowly got to his feet.

'Sure – but you've only got until midday to respond. That's when the paper goes into print.' And so saying, he gathered up his papers and headed for the exit. 'Thanks for the chat and the beer. I'm sure we will be in touch again - very soon.'

When he had gone, Gus exploded.

'Beverly you crazy? What the hell?'

'You've as good as told him we put bits of pig in our cosmetics for chrissake,' Brett informed her vehemently. 'That'll be headline news on Thursday followed closely by the obituary of Keynote – and us with it.'

'Calm down. I have a plan.'

Gus was on his feet.

'A plan? That's nice. Maybe we all emigrate to Russia Beverly? Is that it? Maybe you have uncle in the KGB? You're right. Working in slave camp probably better than being bombed by animal rights. *Mi piace!*'

'Calm down Gus. Hear me out before you blow your fucking mind!'

'It'll better be a rip snorter Beverly,' warned Brett, holding his head in his hands, 'because personally, I can't see a bloody way out of all this.'

'Sit down for fuck's sake. Now let's just have a recap, OK? Firstly, Keynote's virtually bankrupt and we've lost our chemist which means we're up the fucking creek.'

'Up to our armpits,' suggested Brett, the need for contextual consistency having escaped him in this particular moment.

'Further than that,' agreed Beverly, adding to the confusion. 'So it would be fucking useful if we could turn it into a source of money – preferably a lot of fucking money. Agreed?'

This suggestion did not go down well.

'*Geniale*!' cried Gus leaping to his feet and striking his forehead with the palm of his hand in a moment of mock revelation. 'Now I see it all! We just need to find source of money! Beverly Curtis you are brilliant!' Then fake comprehension stuck him and his face changed to wide-eyed deliberation. 'But wait a minute - I see a tiny flaw in your plan. Where we gonna find da money? You think we get it by selling that *sciattona* in reception who probably told the newspaper? When I finished with her nobody will want to buy!'

'Whoa!' cried Brett standing in front of Gus and stretching out both arms out to arrest the latter's progress towards the shaken object of his fury. 'We need to calm down a bit Gus.'

Brett turned his back on Gus to face Beverly.

'Come on Bev. This had better be bloody good!'

Beverly had understandably been backing away from the table.

'Look, I got the idea from what the barman said. We admit that we've been working on putting bits of goddam pig in cosmetics – at least, our chemist has. Trust me – just go along with what I say.'

Beverly Curtis was an opportunist not a calculator or planner. Never had she had greater need for this gift than at this moment. She clearly felt that a possible way out of the cul-de-sac they had been herded into had opened up. But she needed time to work it out in more detail. To the surprise of her startled companions, she suddenly became very calm – almost relaxed.

'As I said, I have a plan.'

'*Mi piace*!'

'Hear me out Gus. Ok. This is about Patterson. He's made a major fucking breakthrough and discovered how to stop – no, reverse – the aging process. Proved it in secret experiments with creams containing extracts of pig. However somehow the secret's got out. It's so fucking valuable that he's afraid of being kidnapped and made to reveal the secret. So he's hidden himself away somewhere he can't be found. Only he knows the secret – but he won't reveal it to anyone unless…'

'Unless what?'

'Unless someone buys the company. If someone wants the secret, they have to buy the whole goddam company and him with it! Not shares, the whole company.'

'And then?'

'Then we take the money and dissafuckingpear! What do you think?'

Bret had returned his head to their now familiar position between his hands. Silence followed.

'Come on,' insisted Beverly. 'What else have we got? You want me to show him my tits?'

'Beverly. That would be an even worse idea – even if you had any. I think your plan is just about the worst load of complete pitiful rubbish that I've ever heard. Even a ten-year-old kid would not believe such infantile crap. And you know what makes it worse? You're right. It's all we've bloody got.'

# 6

A few days earlier the appointed time had come and Mrs B stood at the bottom of the steps of Keynote Cosmetics for the very first time, shaking slightly with apprehension. Then suddenly above her the main doors miraculously opened and humanity rushed out to meet her. It was as though the pent-up excitement generated in anticipation of her arrival had proven too great for the building to contain. Human beings in a variety of shapes and sizes clutching bags umbrellas and briefcases hurled themselves down the steps towards her. In fact, Keynote Cosmetics closed at 5.00 pm and the workers were performing a passable copy of a St Trinian's' end of term escape exodus. Too late, Mrs B realized that it was impossible to dodge this apparent greeting frenzy.

Lynne Cooper, sheltering from the homeward rush behind her reception desk, glanced unnecessarily at her wristwatch. She realized that the new cleaning lady would not be able to get up the steps until the usual idiotic stampede had subsided. Still, punctuality was something she expected and it was already three minutes past the appointed hour. This new woman Mrs - she looked down at her notes - Mrs Beresford would have to learn.

In fact, Mrs B *was* learning, fast. She had adopted the frozen rabbit position that had served her so well at animal rights protest meetings when confronted by similar oncoming hoards. This technique involved standing very still, closing the eyes and holding the breath for as long as possible in the hope that she would not be thrown to the ground and trampled underfoot. Her reaction to such threats and provocations had become instinctive.

Lynne on the other hand was becoming impatient. By kneeling on her chair and leaning forward (as she often did when male salesmen caught her attention) she could just about see out of the main doors and down the front steps. Thus positioned, she could make out the head and shoulders of a middle-aged woman wearing a plastic rain hat and a grim expression. The woman was now slowly advancing up the steps and as she did so a more complete picture gradually came into view, step by step. First the generous bosom and then plump waistline and, as she made it to the top of the steps, the heavily stockinged legs peeping out from under the brown raincoat and ending in flat well-worn shoes.

Mrs B, on the other hand, was too pre-occupied with the slippery and slightly uneven steps to have experienced a reciprocal revelation of Lynne Cooper. Having finally arrived at the top however, her first forward glance revealed a vision of blonde hair, red lips and a generously exposed bosom hanging out of a skimpy black lace bra. She was not impressed. The two women were clearly approaching each other from opposite ends of the compatibility scale. Under normal circumstances people as mismatched as these would not even have spoken except for a casual 'excuse me' or similar politeness, should the need arise. Mrs B would certainly not have had any desire to talk with such a "painted, over sexed tart" and it goes without saying that Lynne would have avoided such an "old, fat, passed-it slob" who had "let herself go" (in spite of, or maybe because of the fact that this description accurately fitted her mother). However, present circumstances had decreed that the two of them must meet and communicate. Lynne must welcome and instruct Mrs B as to her duties and Mrs B must be suitably receptive and compliant. It made for an interesting exchange.

Lynne: 'Hello. Are you Mrs Beresford?'

Mrs B: 'Yes.'

Lynne: 'The new cleaning Lady?'

Mrs B: 'Yes.'

Lynne: (holding out a hand) 'I'm Lynne the receptionist.'

The only response from Mrs B was a slight nod.

Lynne: (withdrawing her hand) 'Have you done cleaning before?'

A look of dark anger from Mrs B.

Lynne: (realizing that she's made a tactical error) 'Mrs Patel highly recommended you.'

Mrs B: (looking around at the shiny office gadgets) 'Will I 'ave to dust all these?'

Lynne: (trying to lighten up and not be intimidated by this stupid old bag) 'No. No need to touch these, I look after them myself. You just need to clean the offices. All your cleaning stuff and overalls are kept in a cupboard, over here...' (pointing).

On the way to the cupboard Mrs B suddenly stopped and looked with a strange intensity at a framed print on the wall. It depicted a large dog with a gerbil on his back and a chinchilla nestling contentedly between his two front paws. 'Gawd!' she proclaimed in a loud voice.

Lynne was irritated. She was already late and this silly woman was delaying her further. She turned back with a sigh.

Lynne: 'Something wrong Mrs Beresford?'

Mrs B: 'That's my picture!'

Lynne: 'I don't think so. Bought it myself a couple of weeks ago – the shop framed it for me.'

Mrs B: (quietly) 'I 'ad it on the wall in the kitchen when my Sid was alive. Stupid, he used to call it. He reckoned you'd never get them animals to sit tergether like that - not in real life.'

Lynne: 'It's only a print Mrs Beresford. It's not a photo. What happened to your copy?'

Mrs B: (dejectedly) 'Lost. Lot of my stuff disappeared when Sid died. (Pause). I used to love that picture.'

Mrs B's hardened exterior, although honed and perfected by battles too numerous to relate, had a chink in it. The picture found it and hit home. A look of wistful, helpless sadness came over her. It was a look intense enough to cut through human prejudice. Lynne reacted to it in spite of herself because she had no choice. She reached for the print and took it off the wall. Returning to her desk with it, she turned it over to remove the print from the frame with the help of a letter opener. Mrs B watched in bewilderment as Lynne laid the print face down on the photocopier. She dialled *1234* on a keyboard and then pushed a large blue button; the machine sprang into life and a copy appeared together with a slight whiff of ozone. The copier was Lynne's favourite piece of office equipment. She was happy to demonstrate it to the incredulous Mrs B. But she was not happy with the copy – it was too dark. Lynne pushed more buttons, and the photocopier produced another copy. This had to be repeated twice more before Lynne was happy with it and handed the final version to an awestruck Mrs B with a smile.

'It's for you Mrs Beresford. You can keep it.'

Such a simple thing, a picture. But like music, it can have evocative powers quite beyond the realm of human understanding. Mrs B accepted the picture with the wordless and guileless manner of a person totally unused to be given gifts of any kind. The expression on her face however, as she gazed at the picture in front of her provided sufficient thanks to satisfy Lynne.

From that moment onwards Mrs B was content to follow meekly in Lynne's footsteps as she demonstrated the areas that needed to be cleaned and the methods by which cleaning had to be done.

They finished in the laboratory – a room with white, kitchen-like benches around the walls on which stood glass beakers many of which were filled with mysterious coloured liquids. Between the beakers were stirrers of various kinds, scraps of paper with scribbled notes on them and plastic pots with powders or more yellow liquids in them. Higher up on the walls were shelves with more plastic containers. Some of these were translucent and their highly coloured contents could clearly be seen through the container walls. Mrs B's attention was directed to the floor which was the only surface she was obliged to clean by swabbing with a mop and detergent. The benches were not to be touched under any circumstance. Mr Patterson the chemist would look after those.

All in all, Mrs B concluded that this was not a bad job, but that laboratory floor would need some attention to get rid of all those greasy stains.

...

The very next evening, Mrs B marched into Keynote's cosmetic laboratory for the second time, now armed with mop and bucket and a determination to clean the badly stained floor. The task proved to be more difficult than she expected. The stains were stubborn and some of them appeared to consist of coloured waxy films that needed to be scraped off rather than just rinsed off the floor surface. Nevertheless, Mrs B was determined to repay the tarty receptionist for her unexpected gift so she laboured long and hard, emptying buckets of mysteriously dark coloured water down the sink and replenishing the bucket with fresh water from the tap to which she added a generous quantity of foaming abrasive floor cleaner. When at last she was satisfied that she had performed as good a service as possible she rested and took time to look more closely around the laboratory.

She had never been much interested in cosmetics and had long ago abandoned their use entirely. The last to be given up was lipstick. This had been considered essential in her younger days but now she regarded it as a waste of money. Nevertheless, beneath the hardened and grim exterior of the campaigner that she had become, there resided a feminine beating heart that could not be entirely quenched by contact with mundane, unromantic reality. She had been prepared to treat the laboratory with great circumspection and with dread arising from her deep mistrust of "chemicals." But she was not expecting anything like this. She sensed that she was a place where dreams are manufactured – half empty beakers full of delicately coloured creams. Glass bottles containing highly fragranced liquids and shelves full of jars with intensely coloured contents but with no obvious purpose or function. In spite of her protective instincts, her curiosity was stimulated to the point at which she was prepared to disobey her strict instruction not to touch anything on the benches or shelves. Of particular interest were some semi-transparent plastic flasks that sat high on the topmost shelves on one of the walls. There were a number of these containing intensely red liquids, each one a slightly different shade of red. These ranged from pillar box through purplish and then through reddish orange and finally pink. What were they? If there had not been a small set of steps available outside the laboratory door, she might never have found out. Mrs B had found the steps in the lab and had moved them in order to clean the floor. Now she made use of them in the manner for which they were undoubtedly intended. Positioning them close to the mysterious shelves she heaved her not inconsiderable bulk slowly up them until on the top step she could just - barely - reach the magic jars. She prodded the nearest with her fingertip to separate it from its neighbour in order to get a better grasp, and as she did so the jar toppled sideways and forwards bringing both it and its neighbour crashing down onto the bench below. Mrs B glanced apprehensively down to see what damage she may have wreaked on the beakers and trays on the bench surface below – but what she saw had such a traumatic effect on her that all such concerns were immediately abandoned as being irrelevant. One of the plastic containers was lying sideways on the bench with its label uppermost and clearly visible. The print was large and clear and even without her glasses Mrs B had no trouble reading it. But the enormity of its message was such that it took a few moments to register and its implications to sink in. Then trembling, she dismounted the steps and clung to them for support for a few moments more. A voice inside told her that she must be mistaken. She re-read the label. Good God! Against all her instincts she picked up the plastic container and examined it. It had a screw top which she had absolutely no intention of undoing. Instead, she surveyed the contents through the semi-transparent container walls. It was only three-quarters full and was able to see how the liquid inside flowed like thickened blood as she tilted the jar. Shuddering, she stood it back on the bench and picked up the second jar. The contents, a slimy-looking viscous liquid of a slightly bluer red colour behaved in the same way. It had an almost identical but equally vile disgusting label. She placed it next to the first monstrosity and stared at both of them. She had to do something – but what?

Her first thought was to contact her animal rights group, *Justice for Animals*. But no! That would have to wait. She had a much better idea. She would talk to the local paper. Herself. Directly. Mr Davis needed to be contacted, but how could she get him to take it seriously? The last time she called him (was it about the number of large dogs being kept in council flats?) he didn't seem very co-operative. In fact, he was almost rude to her. But she was certain that he would be interested in this story if only she could convince him of the importance of it. Certainly, he would require evidence, and how was she going to provide that? Her word against the Keynote company's. She no longer cared about being branded a weirdo, she'd got used to that a long time ago, but this was too important to be dismissed as just another fabricated gimmick to get publicity for the animal rights cause. She needed proof. She possessed no camera, the working of which would, in any case, have been beyond her comprehension. In frustration she stormed out of the laboratory and down the stairs towards the ladies' toilet and as she hurried by, she glanced up at the print on the wall. The large dog, the gerbil and the chinchilla. The effect on Mrs B was instantaneous. She stopped dead in her tracks. Slowly a smile passed over her face. She retraced her steps to the laboratory, collected the two hideous containers and headed back towards Lynne's reception desk – and the photocopier.

...

The Mile End offices of the *East London News* were comfortable without being flashy. Miranda Stevens, when she was appointed Editor-in-Chief, had inherited an ageing local newspaper clinging on to WI articles about local restaurants and knitting circles for copy. During her five years as chief, she had brought about a modest transformation. This included a change from broadsheet to tabloid format and the employment of a number of younger, ambitious reporters who between them found more exciting content without alienating the traditionalist readers. Mike Davis was one of this new breed. His habit of wearing of a suit and tie to work in preference to the prevailing open neck or t-shirts of his colleagues endeared him to many of the older readers of the *News* and certainly helped cement his relationship with Mrs Beresford. For this reason, Mrs B had adopted him and made him the target for her reporting of any perceived detriment to the health of cats, dogs and other animals in the local territory. Mike considered her a pain in the neck but out of politeness and the fact that she occasionally came up with something worth reporting he tolerated her frequent visits and telephone calls. However, when Mrs B turned up at the office on this particular morning, she was in an agitated state of a kind that he had not seen before. She even brushed aside the offer of her usual cup of tea and came straight to the point.

'Wicked people are putting animals into cosmetics!'

'Whoa – steady on Mrs Beresford. I can see you're in a kerfuffle but I don't quite understand. You mean someone is putting cosmetics *on* animals?'

'No. They're putting animals INTO cosmetics!'

'What - you mean they're using ingredients that come from animals. Fish oils, that sort of thing?'

'No!' shouted Mrs B, frustration adding impetus to her anger. 'I mean they're chopping up animals into bits and putting 'em INTO their cosmetics.'

Mike felt his initial scepticism growing.

'You mean raw chopped-up animals?'

'Yes. Pigs.'

Mike had had dealings with many animal rights enthusiasts over the years, Mrs Beresford among them, but what he was hearing made the usual complaints about dogs trapped in cars and ill-fed ponies and factory farming pale into insignificance.

'I find that very difficult to believe Mrs Beresford. Are you certain?'

'As sure as I'm standin' here. Seen it meself.' Then, triumphantly, 'I got proof!'

She dived into her bag and produced the two sheets of A4 paper. These were the very same sheets that Mike would soon show to the Keynote Board. After a quick look at these, he called the Editor-in-Chief and asked her to join them immediately. Together they re-examined the two sheets of paper laid out on the table in front of them. They were obviously photocopied images of two semi-transparent plastic storage bottles, each containing a red liquid. Innocuous enough - if it hadn't been for the labels firmly attached to them.

| PIGS IN CASTOR OIL | PIGS IN CASTOR OIL |
|---|---|
| R6:20-001BTR | R7:10-001BTR |

# 7

The story didn't even make the front page of the *News*. It rated one small column on page three next to stories about a local radio mast causing skin to itch and a bishop's visit to a local primary school.

### A Pig of a Problem

The chief chemist at local cosmetics firm Keynote Cosmetics has apparently disappeared after reputedly putting bits of ground up pig into some of his company's skin creams. According to the company, he had discovered its remarkable effects on skin aging. They believe that the chemist, Mr George Patterson may have vanished to a secret hideout, together with his wife, in order to keep his valuable, secret recipe safe from prying eyes.

The company's owner and chief executive, Mr Giovanni Volante, defended his chemist's actions. 'George is a very special person. He is a remarkable chemist as he has now proven with this ground-breaking new cosmetic cream, for which the results are truly amazing.' When asked about the ethics of putting bits of pig into cosmetics, Mr Volante replied 'Look, animal parts have been used in cosmetics for many years. If the stuff works, where's the problem?' Others, of course, may disagree.

...

Many miles distant from East London in one of the sleepier areas of Brighton, Ralph Ellis was sitting in the front room of his large and slightly crumbling two story flat above his paper shop. He was contemplating life and the cup of tea he had just carefully brewed. Upstairs on the very top floor, his wife Mary was working at her computer busily writing some nonsense for a so-called "celebrity" to pretend to have written for himself. As usual, she had taken the main pages of the *Daily Informer*, Britain's largest broadsheet newspaper with her 'for background reading' leaving Ralph with only the sports pages, girly supplements, advertisements for holidays and the letters page. He took a sip of the tea and savoured its perfection. It was good. A work of art. However, the old enemy, boredom, was beginning to set in. It took him less than a minute to flick through the five television channels looking for those most likely one to have something interesting on for evening viewing, but to no avail. Who wants to watch another re-run of *Only Fools and Horses* which he had almost certainly seen twice before. In desperation he returned to the last page Mary had left him with and began perusing "letters to the editor." A cursory glance revealed the usual plethora of poor jokes about the performance of this or that politician, but the last letter caught his eye. It was entitled "Power to the Pigs?"

Sir

My wife, like many others, is increasingly concerned about the appearance of wrinkles around her eyes. The best advice she has received so far is to place a slice of cucumber over each eye for twenty minutes each morning. However, I read in a recent article

(East London News, November 19) that bits of pig added to cosmetics may supply us with the secret of prolonged life. Should I advise her to replace the cucumber with slices of bacon?

Name and address supplied.

Ralph smiled and reached into a kitchen drawer for a red pen. One of the things that he still shared with Mary was a sense of humour. He drew a red ring around the letter with an arrow directing attention to the margin where he scrawled the message '*Funny*!' Having thus exhausted all readily available sources of amusement, Ralph donned his overall and set off downstairs to open up his newspaper shop – the embodiment of his life savings.

Mary was a free spirit as well as a moderately successful freelance journalist. At present she was spending one of her infrequent periods of co-habitation with her husband, but she didn't spot the red ringed letter until later in the morning, having descended to make herself a cup of coffee. She too smiled at it – but her natural curiosity had been aroused. What *was* the article that the letter referred to? She was pretty sure that the *East London News* was one of the locals owned by the *GLOCOM* conglomerate, in which case it was in the same group as the *Informer*. Having often worked for that paper, it was no effort for Mary to call the sub-editor to request a copy of *East London's* November 19th article. He sounded curiously hesitant on the phone.

'Can I ask you why you want it?'

'Just curiosity. I saw it referred to in another article and it sounded interesting,' she replied. 'Is there a problem?'

'No – no, not at all, I'll have the article faxed over to you,' he replied and disconnected.

An instinct for the unusual is something which good journalists have hard-wired into them and Mary was a very good journalist. This was apparent when later, in the middle of reading the newly faxed article, the telephone rang and she heard the croaky voice of Monty Meyer. This caused her to be surprised and a little apprehensive.

'Hi Mary, it's Monty.'

'This is an honour Mr Meyer,' replied Mary with false deference, having known him since he was a cub reporter.

'Yeah, well us gods sometimes have to communicate with you mortals. Keep you in your place.'

'And you do that so well. It took you three months to pay me for the last morsel I wrote for you.'

'Not me Mary. Love you to bits. Those dammed accountants…'

Monty Meyer's clipped vocal style was at odds with his reputation as an outstanding journalist. His position as executive editor of the *Daily Informer* had been via his earned reputation as a brilliant investigator with an infallible strategic instinct that had enabled him to increase the sales of every paper that he had ever worked on.

'Thanks for the apology. So, what can I do for you?'

'My minions tell me you asked for a copy of an article.'

'Shock horror! Did I neglect to pay for it? Is the paper doing so badly that any bad debt needs to be reported immediately to the editor? Or perhaps my status within the industry is so high that any request from me sends excited shockwaves through the whole of the editorial staff. I'm very flattered.'

'Dear old Mary. You know - any excuse to talk to you. Anyhow, turns out that that article you requested is special. Boss himself has demanded that we massage it into something bigger. Says there's potential in it. However, nobody here keen. Still, the Boss has a good track record. Good at smelling out a good story.'

'I'm not sure that "smelling" is quite the way to put it Monty but I personally think he might be onto something - if my opinion has any relevance. Women, cosmetics, animals, ethics, missing chemist – quite a heady mixture I would think.'

'Glad to hear you say that Mary old love. Happy to take it on then?'

Mary paused. Steady. This was going too fast. This could be an interesting assignment. On the other hand, if the Boss, aka Sir David Corbet was pushing for this and she fouled up, it wouldn't do her career prospects much good.

'Whoa just a minute. Exactly what am I happy to take on Monty?'

'Simple enough - professional like you. Just a nice controversial article. Cause chaos among the cat-loving tree huggers, vegetarians, animal rights brigade, cosmetic scientists and other assorted weirdoes. Bring 'em all out into the open. A good free-for-all.'

'Wow. I don't know Monty...'

'Good. Come and see me – we'll do lunch. Tuesday, Ok?'

There was no resisting Monty when he was in this mood.

### Pigs, Cosmetics and Animal Rights
#### By Mary Ellis

We humans, curious and thinking creatures that we are, have a number of difficult problems we would like answers to. Is there a God? What are we doing here? How did it all begin? Can killing ever be morally justified? Do animals have rights? The first three of these have a fundamental origin beyond the intervention of humankind but the last two contain an element of human judgment.

The issue of our relationship as humans with other animals has been the subject of intense, robust and even violent debate. In truth, no universal agreement over the rights or otherwise of animals is on the horizon. Grossly simplified, the arguments follow the following divergent paths.

For: *Human* animals have rights. There is no morally relevant difference between human animals and adult non-human mammals. Animals therefore have the same rights as people.

Against: Animals don't think, are not really conscious, have no souls, don't behave morally, are not members of the 'moral community' and lack the capacity for free moral judgment. They should not be treated as humans.

At one end of this spectrum, people argue that animal rights teach us there are things we should not do to animals as a matter of principle, no matter what the cost to humanity of not doing them. For example: if animals have a right not to be bred and killed for food then we shouldn't do it. But although killing animals for food infringes their God-given rights, these same rights are not infringed when they are hunted and killed for food by other animals. And here the real difficulties start.

The arguments for and against animal husbandry, hunting, factory farming and laboratory experimentation on animals have been rehearsed many times and need not be repeated at length here. But recently, a less publicized aspect of human-animal relations has found its way into the spotlight in the form of an article published in our sister newspaper, *The East London News*. It has attracted much attention and not a little fury.

The article relates to the experimental use of pig extracts in cosmetic creams. The use of these is claimed to reduce the signs of aging to a remarkable degree in users. Those of us who have struggled in vain to justify the skin rejuvenating claims made by cosmetic companies are obviously interested – but are we prepared, ethically, to put piggy bits on our faces for the sole purpose of vanity? We might ask whether the pigs are especially bred to produce whatever chemicals are doing the trick. We may not object to the ethics quite so much if they are only using bits of offal that had little use anyway and might otherwise have been thrown away. On the other hand, we may feel more comfortable with the idea that special, hand reared pigs have been used — a kind of super, *Channel* or *Dior* pig whose bits are a cut above the average. To put these on our faces might make face creams worthy of the price which we would undoubtedly have to pay for them. But apart from our reservations about piggy health and wholesomeness and fitness for use on our delicate skins, some of us might return to a consideration of our moral right to use animals — some might say, dumb animals - in this way. Would we do the same if the animal used was a domestic pet? Would we be prepared to put bits of cats or dogs in our creams rather than bits of a farmyard animal? If not, why not? Does the close association of man and domestic pet somehow confer rights on the cat or dog not enjoyed by the equally intelligent pig? An interesting dilemma, don't you think?

Of course, it is true that raw materials obtained from animals have always been used in cosmetics. Even common old toilet soap is made from animal tallow. And which of us hasn't benefited from the luxurious moisturising properties conferred by added lanolin without giving a moment's consideration to its animal origin? For some reason, however, the revelation that 'piggy bits' were found in laboratory jars, which seems to be the case here, has engendered feelings of revulsion and hostility from people who have never before concerned themselves with animal ingredients in cosmetics and toiletries. The fact that the cosmetic chemist concerned, George Patterson, has apparently disappeared has increased the interest over the discovery. According to the local newspaper, his discovery has remarkable effects on skin aging, requiring him to vanish into a secret hideout together with his wife in order to keep his secret recipe safe from prying eyes. Perhaps he will be able to defend himself once he has been found but meanwhile, there has been a remarkable absence of scientists ready to rush to his aid. However, after much searching, I was able to get an opinion from just such an expert, Professor James Locke, a consultant dermatologist from Kings College, London.

'I am not familiar with Mr Patterson's work I'm afraid. He does not seem to have published anything,' said the professor. 'However, it is well-known that pigs are very closely related to humans – that is, their skin is very similar to human skin - so it makes a certain amount of sense.'

Not to everyone professor. Inevitably, however, the Money Men have cottoned on to the potential value of this discovery, should it turn out to be as good as the company involved, Keynote Cosmetics, implies. So now the search is on in earnest for the mysterious Mr – or is it Dr? - Patterson.

Only one thing is certain: this story still has a very long way to run.

'Brilliant,' said Monty putting the typescript down. 'Bit of editing needed but we'll run it in our Sunday edition, Centre page. Should get things moving nicely. Well done Mary Old Sport! By the way, The Boss has spoken again – I've had to get one of our less talented hacks to come up with a version for one of our red tops.'

'Sounds like you're exploiting me as usual. Bet I only get paid for the one article?'

'Yes. Sorry. Your style is a bit too erudite for our lovely red top readers, sweetheart. It's destined for folk less able to string more than a few sentences together.'

'Tsk tsk Monty. That's elitist talk.'

'Isn't it just? The Boss himself has overseen the version we've cobbled together for the *Daily Buzz*. He actually had a hand in it! He's insisting headline and centre page. And he's putting some cash into it too. Whoa, exciting stuff.'

Mary sighed.

'Just one thing,' she replied. 'If you *do* manage to get hold of any of this cream ...'

'Yes?'

'You *will* let me have a pot to try, won't you?'

It was almost possible to hear the grin over the phone.

...

Mary could hardly wait – and nor could Ralph. As soon as it arrived, he dashed upstairs with a copy of *the Daily Buzz* and spread it out on Mary's desktop.

> **MISSING CHEMIST DUE TO PIG-OUT ON HIS INVENTION BUT WHERE IS HE?**
>
> The search is on for a cosmetic chemist who is rumoured to have invented a wonder cream. There are only two problems – it contains bits of pig and he has disappeared. Even his employer, Keynote Cosmetics, don't know where he is – or do they? *Continued on page 7...*

The centre pages had what looked like a passport photograph of the missing George.

> ... This is George Patterson. If you spot him, you could be in the money. According to the cosmetics company he works for, he's invented a cream that slows or stops skin from aging. Can you imagine how much that would be worth? Is George living it up an exotic private island or on his luxury yacht? Well, probably not, because he has vanished. And so far, neither his bosses at Keynote Cosmetics, nor the chasing public hoping to cash in have managed to find him. The theory is that he has gone into hiding to avoid publicity. None of the large cosmetic companies we've spoken to are getting too excited at the moment. A representative from one major beauty company said that while they would certainly be interested if Mr Patterson could demonstrate that his cream really works, they are not actively seeking him presently. The pull of huge potential profits, however, means that there is no shortage of other people looking for him.
>
> Not everyone is happy because rumour has it that it contains bits of chopped up pig. Animal rights campaigner Stephen Henshaw from *Farming Without Tears* told the *Buzz* 'This is another example of the slippery slope we are on. What's next? Intensive breeding of animals for use in cosmetics? Pigs this time, but who knows what other animals are in the evil sights of the beauty industry? It's totally morally and ethically abhorrent.'
>
> *PIG MAIL-ON*
>
> Let us know your thoughts on whether it is ever acceptable to put bits of pig into cosmetic skin creams. The Daily is offering a £250 prize for the best reply.

'I'm a bit confused,' confessed Ralph. 'Why all this fuss about an anonymous chemist from an obscure cosmetic company obviously trying to sell snake oil? What is Corbet up to?'

'I'm not sure Ralph. It may have less to do with this magic cream's alleged properties and more to do with the fact that it contains bits of pig. Sir David obviously sees some value in this story but it's more related to the making of a healthy profit than concern over animal welfare. Monty agrees. In any event, Corbet certainly seems intent on creating a witch hunt for this poor chemist.'

'I've heard of *testing* cosmetics *on* animals.'

'Testing, yes. But putting mashed up bits of a well-known animal *into* creams? That's another step altogether. I can see that the animal rights mob and the moral crusaders coming out in force over that.'

'Not to mention the vegan and vegetarian establishment. And how many of you ladies are likely to want to put them on your face? Could lead to a cosmetics industry backlash I suppose.'

'I guess the answer is watch this space. From what Monty tells me, this is far from over.'

# 8

Simon Patterson sat alone and lonely in the refectory of *Bath Centrum University*. A half-eaten and half-forgotten sandwich lay curling up on the table in front of him together with the remains of a warm tin of coke. Another dreary day of *History of Art* awaited him – what was it first thing? "The life and works of *Bellini.*" As if he cared! But he really needed to avoid nodding off in mid lecture, and this was becoming more difficult as the sleepless nights accumulated. What was the point anyway? It wouldn't make any difference. Lectures on art? Just a box-ticking exercise. If you failed to turn up nobody complained. *Bath Centrum* had reluctantly agreed to educate Simon. It was making feeble efforts to impart sufficient knowledge to him to justify some kind of paper qualification. He had been accepted as a student, even though he had only managed to achieve one A level (in art), and a doubtful certificate in technical drawing. In fact, this was considerably less than the minimum qualifications needed according to the University's published regulations. However, the desperate need to fill the student roster had obviously influenced the Dean's generosity. In practice, as long as you've produced the course fee, the Art Department at *Bath Centrum* left you pretty much alone. Alone and very much frustrated.

So here he was. A pointless life with no future prospects and no self-belief. How had that happened? Simple. He was a feeble runaway, not strong enough to lend support to his pathetic father and too weak to withstand the erratic behaviour of his alcoholic mother. He'd grown up believing that she preferred alcohol to him, anyway. And now he despised them both almost as much as he despised himself. Useless parents with a useless son. He couldn't wait to get away from them but now that he had, he really couldn't see the point in anything anymore. He had been contaminated at conception with Patterson genes and was pre-programmed for failure. He hadn't spoken to his parents since the beginning of the term and he didn't expect to. He had blocked his father's telephone number as effectively as he had blocked most of his childhood memories. Cut off as he was from family, and having no close friends or even acquaintances who knew where he was, he remained totally ignorant about what was going on outside his gloomy little bubble. Was there room in his life for anything more failure? Had he finally reached the bottom and if not, what next? Ah yes, there *was* something else. He was a complete failure with the opposite sex. No real girlfriend – no friends at all, in spite of the fact that he was in full possession of all the sexual urges of a nineteen-year-old male. He was primed with a ready-to-use sex cocktail of adrenalin, dopamine, serotonin, testosterone, but he had no means of opening the cocktail shaker lid to release them. There were plenty of girls at *Bath Centrum*, some of them drab and colourless as only art students can be, but also others of the wriggling, giggling mini-skirted kind who could frequently be seen clustering in small groups. Simon had hungered after them, but his lack of confidence and his bumbling, inept attempts to interest them had only met with failure. Cupid's poisoned arrow had plunged into Simon with unerring accuracy – but alas his sexual urges were unable to be brought to fruition. So, having no real lover, in desperation, he invented one. Lisa. Beautiful but imaginary. A fantasy princess who asked no questions and willingly showed her love, lying side by side with him in his small bed with her golden hair spread wide on the pillow. His imagination had perfected every detail of her firm body and angelic face – especially her clear blue liquid eyes and soft sensuous mouth beneath a pert nose worthy a Botticelli painting. Lisa was never far from his mind. At night, she was with him at every waking moment and often in his dreams. Even now at the refectory table, closing his eyes, he could imagine her on the other side of the table; so real that he was tempted to reach out to touch her. But alas, the joy was only momentary. Once he came back to reality his need to pretend served only to reiterate his own pathetic inadequacies.

The casual visitor to the refectory could easily have mistaken Simon's inert and quiet demeanour for deep thought. In reality he had simply retreated into his bubble. Eventually, he was awakened from his day-dream by the noise created by two individuals standing at the distant vending machine; a man and a woman. They seemed to be having problems. The female, with her back to Simon, was continuing to punch the buttons whilst her companion had seemingly given up and was looking around the refectory. Simon's instinctive reaction was to lower his head over the table and appear to study the cigarette burn etched into its plastic centre in the hope that they wouldn't come over to start a conversation. Too late. Damn! It looked like they *were* coming over. *Keep your head down Simon, pretend you are too busy to talk.* He bent over and studied the table top with a fierce intensity, but then came the sound that he was dreading: a female voice.

'Excuse me, I wonder if you could help us?'

Simon slowly and reluctantly raised his head and looked straight into the perfect face of Lisa!

She was identical in every way. The same sparkling blue eyes, the flawless lips and mouth, the delightful nose, the slightly slanted perfect smile, the long blonde hair cascading over her shoulders. She was perfect in every detail, exactly as Simon had always imagined her. And there she was standing in front of him!

Simon stood up suddenly and violently in a state of shock, pushing his chair over onto its back.

Lisa spoke again.

'Sorry... I didn't mean to startle you. We're only after a bit of help with the vending machine over there. Can't seem to make it work, even though it's full of cans.'

That smile. Those eyes.

'My name's Sophie by the way – and this is Marc.'

Simon was hardly able to move, desperately trying to squeeze his brain to make room for reality. Was this real - or was he still dreaming or hallucinating? Then suddenly, curiously, unexpectedly, he was overcome with an even stronger emotion. An intense jealousy that tore at his gut. Simon looked at her companion. He was ugly, skinny, gawky and bespectacled. What was such an inadequate male specimen doing with his Lisa? How could he bear the fact that this imperfect creature had usurped the affections of his golden idol? It was more than flesh and blood could stand.

Lisa/Sophie spoke.

'Are you alright? So sorry to have startled you – you seem a bit shocked!'

Shocked wasn't even close. But Simon had recovered sufficiently to speak.

'S.. s.. sorry, it's just that – you look like someone I know – I wasn't expecting…'

She smiled again. Simon's heart melted at the sight.

'Well I don't think we've met before. Have we? As I said, my name is Sophie and this is Marc. Pleased to meet you.'

Sophie/Lisa held out a beautiful hand and Simon hesitatingly reached and touched it: it was warm flesh and blood, proof that this creature was real – she really *did* exist. Too much. *I can't cope with this. I need to get out. I need to think!*

'Look I'm really sorry but I have a lecture in a couple of… I need to go. Sorry.'

'Hold on – we only wanted a chat,' laughed Marc. 'We're not going to rob you! If I could figure out how to get a drink out of that blasted machine, I'd buy you one.'

Still in panic mode, Simon searched frantically through his pockets grabbing a few metal coins which he threw on the table.

'Tokens…'

'Pardon?'

'The machine doesn't take money – you need tokens.' pointing to them on the table.

'Oh, I see. No wonder. Can I borrow of few of these? Enough for three cans, I hope? Yours is a Coke, isn't it?'

'I'll go,' said Sophie/Lisa, picking up the tokens. 'Back in a mo.'

No. This was wrong. She should stay with me, and her ugly boyfriend should go. *Don't leave me alone with him.* The realisation that this totally inferior suitor could achieve success way beyond Simon's wildest expectations had become almost unbearable. What further proof of his own pathetic inadequacies was needed?

'Don't even know your name.'

'Simon. Sorry.'

'Well I have to say this place is a bit of a dump, Simon. No wonder there are so few people around. Were you studying when we interrupted you?'

'No.'

'In that case I'm glad we came over. Tell me to mind my own business, but here you are sitting all alone. I guess most of the other students could be out on the town or in the bar. Don't you drink?'

'No.'

'Well here comes some Cokes anyway.'

Lisa/Sophie had returned cradling three cans.

'Hey sis, this is Simon. And he's here on his own.'

'Pleased to meet you, Simon. To be honest you look as though you could do with a bit of company.' She began sharing the cans around and dropped excess tokens on the table. Simon observed, to his surprise, that he was now sitting. He had an all-consuming, burning question that he needed to ask but couldn't bring himself to ask it in case it was the wrong answer. He squeezed a single word out.

'Sis?'

Marc was momentary puzzled but then the penny dropped.

'Sis ... yes. She's my sister.'

'As a matter of fact, we're twins,' said Sophie/Lisa laughing, 'though it's hard to believe, isn't it?'

'In our last year at school, she was voted prettiest student and I was voted the ugliest.' Marc has joined in the laughter and Simon can feel colour coming back into his cheeks. He even manages a weak smile. 'I had no idea that you were…brother and sister.'

'You thought he was my boyfriend?' said Sophie, pretending to be aghast at the thought. 'Do you honestly think I would go out with a bloke as ugly as him? Come on Simon – I'm almost offended.'

Now he knew that Marc was not a competitor, to his amazement, found himself talking.

'You asked why I was on my own. Well, to be honest, I'm not a very sociable person. Bit of a loner and if I'm honest, a bit depressed.'

'Come on Simon, that's no way to talk.'

'I have to apologise for my patronising brother Simon,' said Sophie. 'He's under the illusion that he's some kind of superior person. But I'm sure that chatting can help. What about your parents? It'll soon be the end of term, I should think. Going home might be an answer – shoulder to cry on and all that.'

*Why am I allowing the conversation to go in this direction? I never discuss my feelings with anyone.*

'I don't talk much to my parents. We…don't get on.'

'You mean you don't even '

telephone them Simon?' asked Sophie.' Just to find out how they are?'

'Or where they are?'

A curious remark.

'I *know* where they are, Marc – they're at home in Wanstead. *How* they are, I couldn't tell you.'

'That's sad Simon. When was the last time you spoke to them?' This was Sophie.

'To be honest I can't remember. Can we change the subject?'

There was a small silence before Marc answered.

'Look we haven't told you what we're doing here. We're not students – at least, not art students – we're just a couple of would-be journalists trying to become cub reporters and we're in Bath because a big newspaper boss is going to present some major art prizes tomorrow at the Exhibition Hall and, well - we've managed to scrounge a couple of invites.'

'And since there's an Art School here at the *Centrum* we thought we'd pop in and try to get some arty background in advance.'

'Are you thinking what I'm thinking, sis?'

'I hate to admit it but yes. Simon is the only art expert we've managed to contact…'

Sophie smiled and sat down at the table.

'Simon it looks like you're our only hope. Please help us. You have to come with us - as our art consultant.'

'You'd really enjoy it. Famous people, free booze and grub – and the art is not too bad as well!'

This was too much too quickly.

'Kind of you, but….'

Sophie reached over and put her hand on Simon's arm.

'Please come Simon. We'd really would love you to.'

The look in her eye seemed genuine. This was a real invitation.

Marc dived into the inside pocket of his jacket and produced a slightly crumpled envelope.

'Look here's a pamphlet which will tell you a bit more about it. We're not going to take 'no' for an answer.'

'No. Look, it's kind of you but…'

'It's tomorrow night. Have you got anything planned? Are you doing something else?'

Simon could lie and say that he was. But for some reason he felt that that kind of dishonesty was not called for. After all, these were two friendly people who were only trying to help. And there was also the opportunity of spending some more time in Lisa/Sophie's company. Temptation to agree to go with them was beginning to grow.

'Come on Simon. Tomorrow night,' said Sophie, giving his arm another squeeze. 'We'll be waiting at the entrance to the refectory at 7.30. Yes?'

*Yes, Sophie, yes!* The squeeze did it! Simon will follow you to the ends of the earth.

…

The leaflet fluttered face up on the bed as Simon shook the envelope to expel its contents. A 'Compliments' slip followed to which was attached a glossy, ticket-sized Invitation.

The leaflet revealed itself to be a communication from the Southwest Area of the Arts Council.

### *'MANCHESTER ART GALLERY TO HOST CORBET AWARD FOR YOUNG ARTISTS'*

*The Corbet Award is held every two years and the prize of £25,000 is provided by the sponsor, Sir David Corbet, the head of GLO<u>COM</u>, the global media corporation. Bath will host this prestigious award this year. The Hon Duncan Webb, Head of the Bath School of Art and a leading authority on the History of European Painting, will present it to the winning artist. It is hoped that Sir David will attend himself. Twenty-seven young artists will have their admissions exhibited from an entry of over 200. The winning entry will be chosen by the artist Mr Sheraton Brown, famous for his remarkable watercolour still life paintings.*

*Sir David, who is a keen supporter of young artists, has outlined the reason for the Award. 'We need people who think and work creatively, whether it's by writing, playing music or painting and sculpture. Arts education provides young people with the skills needed for a happy and purposeful life. I see many examples in my own company of ordinary youngsters who, given encouragement, demonstrate remarkable problem-solving and communication skills, prove to be creative and innovative, and strive for excellence. We need to recognise and encourage such young people, and this is what the Award is for.'*

*Admittance to the award ceremony and the exhibition is by invitation only.*

Simon had, of course, heard of David Corbet, since he was rarely out of the news but had never bothered to research his background. The university library and *Who's Who* had the information he needed.

*Sir David Francis Corbet CBE (born 4 March 1942) is a global media proprietor and the Chairman and CEO of GLOCOM, one of the world's largest media conglomerates.*

*Corbet became a director of Newsfeed Limited in 1971 having worked as a reporter, then editor-in-chief of Newscast Daily, taking it from a small regional newspaper to the largest selling daily paper in the UK. He became managing director of Newsfeed in 1973 and under his direction, the Newsfeed Group expanded rapidly by acquiring a number of troubled newspapers and magazines, including G Local, a large group of local papers which was threatened with closure in 1980. On March 15th, 1982, Newsfeed Limited became a division of GLOCOM, Corbet's newly formed global news and communication holding company. GLOCOM now has interests in radio, TV and the Internet and also owns Johnson*

*Distribution, a leading publisher of trade and lifestyle magazines in the UK and North America.*

*Sir David is divorced but has two children from his marriage to Kathleen Carpenter, the author and broadcaster. He is a keen and generous supporter of the arts and has a particular interest in the discovery and promotion of new young artists and painters. He was listed as number 85 in the latest edition of Forbes 'The World's Richest People.'*

After a quick glance at the media mogul's smiling image, Simon read no more and began to give some serious thought about what he would be expected to wear for the event. Luckily, frugal living had ensured that he still had some of his grant money left.

Yes, thanks to his newfound twin friends, he was beginning to see some point in getting out of bed tomorrow morning…

…

The exhibition invitees were generally well spread out, with little groups of two or three people collectively scrutinizing each of the exhibits. There was also a much larger bunch which was moving around the gallery like a giant amoeba under the guidance of a gentleman with copious white hair and beard.

'Sheraton Brown,' whispered Sophie, answering Simon's unasked question. 'He's doing the judging – though heaven knows why.'

Simon hadn't heard of him. 'No good then?'

'Bloody useless,' suggested Mark. 'But, as you can see, he has something of a following.'

Sophie had collected glasses of champagne and the three of them stood in the centre of the gallery forming a drinking huddle.

'Hadn't we better start looking at some of the paintings?' asked Simon, glancing furtively around the gallery walls on which they were hung.

Before he could get a reply there was a sudden, excited movement at the far end of the gallery signalling a new happening. A small crowd appeared, proudly headed by an elderly gentleman with a balding, slightly bowed head and eyeglasses - the Chancellor of the *Bath School of Art*. Then after a discreet gap an even more distinguished figure appeared following in the Chancellor's solemn and eminent footsteps. This figure was instantly recognisable by the invited guests who moved deferentially aside to allow the Great Man easier access to the main body of the gallery. Sir David Corbet's newspaper image didn't do him justice. His distinguished appearance and commanding demeanour accurately reflected the fact that here was one of the most powerful men on the planet. Sir David Corbet, a man who was courted by senior politicians and heads of state and honoured by Royalty. As he passed along the gallery, pausing frequently but briefly to look at some of the exhibits, Sir David's path took him ever closer to where the Simon and his two new friends stood. As the Great Man got almost within touching distance the awestruck Simon instinctively retreated so as not to contaminate greatness with his own ordinariness.

Sophie, however, reacted quite differently. She handed her glass to her brother and running forward she threw her arms around Sir David's neck.

'Daddy!' she cried.

Smiling, the Great Man pushed his daughter away to arm's length.

'Not now Sophie. We'll meet up later.'

# 9

Mrs Edna Beresford turned the envelope over in her hands. She was darkly suspicious and more than a little concerned. Should she open it? Mrs B wrote letters only infrequently and used her telephone hardly at all. She was used to incoming mail with her name and address typed and revealed through a little transparent window in the envelope. The gas and electricity bills came in those. Sometimes there was no window and her name and address were neatly typed on the envelope - a white or brown envelope. She had learned to deal with these over the years, often with the help of her friend Mrs Patel. At Christmas she received cards from her few remaining acquaintances and on those, her address was written by hand, and the envelope always had an ordinary stamp on it in the corner. But this letter was odd. It was thicker than most letters, and the address was typed, yet it had a stamp on it. A second-class stamp. This was a new combination: typed address but with an ordinary stamp. What could it be? Until recently she would have asked Mrs Patel whether she should open it. There were lots of people on the telly advising people to be careful about opening letters and getting cheated out of money – not that she had any to be cheated out of. But it might be important. Perhaps someone she knew had died – better take a chance. She lifted the corner of the envelope flap and carefully eased the two surfaces apart as though she was diffusing an unexploded bomb. At last, she could gingerly open the flap and peer inside. There was a single sheet of folded paper – a letter - and a folded envelope. She prised out the letter and unfolded it. Having found her reading glasses she brought the type-written message into view.

*Dear Mrs Beresford,*

*I hope you don't mind me sending you this letter. You'll remember me, I was the receptionist at the cosmetics factory when you started as cleaning lady. They gave me the sack because they thought that I reported the pigs in cosmetic thing to the local newspaper, but it wasn't me. I think it may have been you. More power to your elbow! I would have done it myself if I had discovered those dreadful bottles.*

*Anyway, it seems like it's all over the newspapers now, and I'm a bit worried about you in case you start getting calls from reporters and the like. I think we should meet up so we can discuss it. If you think you would like to, please tell me by sending back the SAE. When I get it, I will phone you on Wednesday evening next week at 8 o'clock in the evening so you'll know it's me and answer the phone.*

*Yours sincerely*
*Lynne Cooper.*

Mrs Beresford's heart sank. Not because of the letter contents but because of the identity of the sender. Of course she remembered Lynne Cooper. She remembered her distaste at the way she dressed and the unexpected kindness she had shown in copying her lost picture, which was looking down on her from the kitchen wall. She felt a powerful wave of regret and conscience at being the cause of Lynne losing her job. The feeling was so intense that she felt the need to sit down to recover. After a few moments she picked the letter up from the kitchen table where she had dropped it and with a slightly shaking hand, she carefully re-read it. Then she read it again. Her strong instinct was not to get involved. There was no denying Mrs B's commitment to the animal cause; she had shown many times how a passionate belief could overcome her natural reluctance to put herself forward in the cause of animal welfare. After all, it was her hatred of animal exploitation that made her report the laboratory samples in the first place. But it wasn't the idea of animals being bred to produce bits of cosmetics that had bothered her. She suspected that that didn't happen. No, it was a much deeper feeling of revulsion about the idea of animal bodies being used to beautify human beings. This had really aroused her anger and her determination to stop it in any way she could think of. But Lynne Cooper – that was another problem. How could she repay Lynne's kindness by ignoring her letter?

No, that wasn't fair. She would return the envelope and wait for her call.

...

So it was that Mrs Beresford and Lynne Cooper sat uncomfortably opposite each other at a table in *Rosie's Cafe* just a few streets away from where Mrs B lived.

Lynne opened the conversation.

'Thanks for coming Mrs Beresford – is it alright if I call you Edna? I know we don't really know each other but it's much easier to say "Edna" than keep saying "Mrs Beresford!"'

'No, I don't mind. But what I want to say is I'm sorry you got the sack. It was my fault. If I tell them it was me will you get your job back?'

Lynne smiled.

'I don't want it back Edna. Didn't really like it anyway. It's lovely of you to worry about me but *you're* the one I'm concerned about.'

'I'm alright. Cleaning jobs is two a penny round 'ere. Don't you worry about me luv.'

'But I *am* worried about you. This pig thing – it's in all the papers. Have you seen it?'

'Yes. But that's good ain't it? Stop those devils doing even more harm to animals.'

'At this moment I'm more worried about the harm that could come to you.'

Mrs B looked puzzled.

'How d'you mean?'

'What I mean is it's only a matter of time 'till they cotton on to the fact it was you who blew the whistle – gave the game away by discovering those bottles. That means that you're going to have reporters coming round and asking questions, Edna.'

Mrs B gave it some thought.

'Well. I did nothin' wrong did I?'

It was a statement not a question .

'No Edna you did nothing wrong but you just can't trust newspaper reporters. They twist things around and make it look as if you've said and done things that you haven't.'

'Gawd.'

'It won't make any difference to them that you're just a sweet lady who loves animals. Before you know it they'll have you labelled as an animal rights activist ready to lynch anyone who dares even to pull a pussy cat's tail.'

Edna fell silent and lowered her eyes to the table top.

'Edna! Don't tell me…'.

'I wouldn't lynch no one. 'Corse not, but… well, I do do stuff for Mrs Ruth. Ruth Kelly that is. Marches, leaflets – that sort of thing. Known her for donkey's years.'

Edna dived into her bag and eventually produced a dog-eared business card: *Dr Ruth Kelly, Vice-President of Justice for Animals UK*.

'So. You're not quite the kind, sweet lady I thought you were Edna.'

'Don't get me wrong, I would never harm no one or break anything – but...'

'But it's possible that...' (looking at the business card) '... Justice for Animals might do that sort of thing, right?'

Mrs B nodded her head, still looking down at the table.

'Can't stand the way some people treat animals. Cats and dogs. They torture them you know that? I'm always telling it to Mr Davis and he sometimes puts it in the paper.'

Lynne felt that she was beginning to sound like a teacher questioning one of her pupils, but Mrs B was too confused to notice.

'Who exactly is Mr Davis, Edna?'

'He works in our local paper. *East London News* it's called.'

Lynne was dreading the answer to her next question.

'And ... Dr Kelly. Does she know it was you who discovered the jars?'

'No. Dunno really. But I promised to go to a meeting with her.'

'When?'

Pause.

'Tomorrow.'

Lynne gave this some thought, then gave out a deep sigh.

'Mrs Edna Beresford. I really think that I have to come to this meeting with you.'

Mrs B was too confused and worried to refuse.

...

Doctor Ruth Kelly, tall, late forties with long, slightly straggly light brown hair and a lived-in face was welcoming her two guests - one of them unexpected – who were presently squeezed side by side on a two-seater couch. There were also four members of her accompanying group present. These were looking on from their seated positions on uncomfortable chairs or cross-legged on the carpeted floor.

'Thank you so much for coming ladies – Edna, of course and ... Miss Cooper, isn't it?'

Lynne smiled and nodded, trying to keep her feelings under control.

'Well, I'm Dr Ruth and this is Gavin,' (sallow youth sitting on the floor), 'Tracy,' (nervous-looking girl wearing trousers and hugging herself on a chair), 'Bill,' (tubby, mid-fifties, round face, cropped hair and rimless glasses) 'and Peter.' (Balding, mid-forties with large mouth, prominent nose but a welcoming grin and a hand wave).

'I call these my fighting group, but we all belong to *JUFA – Justice for Animals.* Have you heard of us?'

'Sorry,' lied Lynne, looking at Mrs B for back-up.

'OK. But what about you Miss Cooper?' asked Dr Ruth helpfully. 'I have a feeling that animal rights might also be close to *your* heart?'

'I used to get pamphlets from *Farming Without Tears*... Always taken an interest.'

'I know a bit about FWT,' cried Gavin, uncrossing his legs in excitement.

'Yes,' agreed Peter. 'Doing a great job, I believe. Against factory farming – pigs, poultry – that sort of thing.'

Dr Ruth was less enthused.

'Well, I guess that qualifies you as a caring person, Miss Cooper,' she said, unconvincingly. 'It's truly dreadful the condition that some of those animals are kept in.' Her face grew even more lived-in at the thought.

Lynne felt she needed to add something to fortify her position of concern for farm animals.

'It was seeing little baby pigs not being able to get to their mothers that upset me,' she offered.

'Yes, and having their teeth and tails cut and all being squashed together indoors in those damned hell pens.' Gavin was warming to the discussion. The silent Tracy was fighting tears welling up in her eyes. This was the signal for Bob to get out of his chair and put a comforting arm around her shoulder.

'Takes it all to heart does our Tracy,' he announced unnecessarily. 'Too caring to be an animal activist in some ways. Inexhaustible supply of tears. Inexhaustible supply of compassion. Extraordinary. Extraordinary young lady.'

Seemingly unaware of the fuss Bob was making, Tracy delved into a large bag in which she obviously had a plentiful supply of tissues, thus graphically confirming her colleague's opinion. An inexhaustible supply of tissues to service an inexhaustible supply of tears.

It was now Peter's turn. He exploded with blazing eyes to complement his harsh features and cropped ginger hair. But his high pitched, squeaky voice was totally incompatible with his violent demeanour. This gave rise to a somewhat comical effect, but there was no doubting his sincerity.

'Bastards!' He squeaked. 'I'd hang 'em up and cut their balls off!' Everyone assumed he was referring to the farmers, not the pigs.

Lynne was beginning to wish she had not come. She was fond of pets, but she certainly didn't share the depth of feeling that was being unveiled before her. Although Peter's squeaky outburst was less than terrifying, she nevertheless found the intensity of his reaction and the obvious agreement of the rest of the gathering somewhat alarming. She was beginning to feel, for safety's sake, a need to justify her presence and was now racking her brain for an appropriate remark.

'What about chickens?' she enquired desperately.

The reaction to this was satisfyingly positive.

'I must confess the treatment of poultry in those horrific factory farms makes my blood boil,' offered Dr Ruth to general noises of agreement. 'Did you know that those butchers actually cut off most of the beaks of hens laying eggs with a hot knife without any kind of anaesthetic? Some of the birds are in such severe pain that they are unable to eat afterwards and starve to death.'

'Why do they do that?' asked Lynne, now even more alarmed at the direction the conversation was taking.

'To stop them pecking each other in frustration at being pushed so close together in those dreadful cages. Have you ever seen a picture of one of those factories?'

The temperature in the living room was rising.

'Bastards!' agreed Peter.

'Extraordinary! Extraordinary!' offered Bob, shaking with furious disbelief as the still silent Tracy reached into her bag for another tissue.

'You couldn't come up with a better reason for being vegetarian,' shouted Gavin, now standing, 'or even vegan for that matter,' he added with mysterious logic.

In the midst of this outcry, vigorously and sincerely enjoined by the whole of Dr Ruth's Fighting Group (with the exception of Tracy, who was undoubtedly as fully committed as the others in her silent way), Mrs Beresford had sat silent and curiously pensive. Seemingly she had been forgotten in the heat of all the passionate protestations. But now Dr Ruth, pausing to regain her breath, but still plainly agitated, turned her attention onto her invited guests.

'And what about you Edna and you too Lynne (can I call you that?). Are either of you vegetarian or vegan?'

It was an unfair question given the circumstances. Should Lynne lie and say yes? She didn't want to be branded a bastard by the slightly weird Peter should he ever find out that chicken tikka masala was her favourite meal and that she had eggs and bacon for breakfast that morning. However, Mrs B came to the rescue.

'Don't have any truck with that nonsense. My old man used to love 'is Sunday roast and pork chops on a Wednesday.' In truth, she was finding it hard to understand what she was doing here. It was certainly true that she worked for JUFA but that was to promote the idea of fluffy sheep with their lambs frolicking free in lush green fields and pigs rolling contentedly in mud or lying patiently to feed half a dozen cute little piglets from swollen teats. This talk of pain and suffering, whilst it might be reality, was not something she wanted to think about. It was too upsetting.

'But it was Mrs Beresford who found the jars with bits of pig in them!' cried Lynne anxiously attempting to redirect the subject of conversation onto safer grounds.

After a brief reflective pause, Dr Ruth gave a sigh, releasing the tension that the impassioned conversation had built in her like air escaping from a deflating balloon. She smiled.

'Of course. Forgive me, both of you. We tend to get a bit - carried away sometimes. We call it enthusiasm.'

*More like fanaticism* thought Lynne. Still, she could see their point. People obviously did vicious things to animals and that was very bad. But it didn't seem to have much to do with what Mrs B had uncovered.

'I think the idea of putting animal parts on the skin is a bit unnatural too don't you Mrs B?'

'Yes, please tell us what happened to you Edna,' invited Bob, temporarily relieving himself from his obligation to support the increasingly damp Tracy. 'Extraordinary!'

'You were working for this cosmetics company weren't you Lynne?' ventured Gavin having returned to the floor.

'Yes, but so was Mrs Beresford. That is – well, she'd only just started hadn't you, Edna? Practically her first day.'

'I can talk for meself, thank you,' advised that slightly irritated lady. 'It was me as discovered the pots.'

'Yes. Tell us about the pots,' suggested Dr Ruth. 'Did someone say they were in the laboratory?'

'Did you work in the laboratory?' asked Gavin, incredulously.

'No. I was just cleaning it. I'm a cleaner. Anyway, I found these pots full of red stuff and it said on the labels that they was full of bits of pig.'

'No!' squealed Peter.

'Yes!' insisted Mrs B. 'Practically full to the brim they was.'

'Did you take the lids off to look inside?' asked Dr Ruth.

Mrs B pulled a disgusted face. 'You must be joking.'

'Extraordinary! So what did you do then?' asked Bob.

'Well, I told the newspaper, didn't I? Showed 'im copies of the labels an' all.'

'I taught her how to do that,' interjected Lynne, modestly and with a smile. 'On the photocopier.'

'Well done!' applauded the now co-smiling Dr Ruth.

'Only when it got put in the paper, poor Lynne got the sack for it. Not fair. She 'ad nothing to do with it.'

'No but I'm on your side. Putting bits of pig into cosmetics – disgusting.'

'I found out that they put fish scales in my lipstick once.' offered Tracy, finally finding a tiny voice. 'I've never used make-up since.'

*Pity. You could certainly do with it*, thought Lynne, hating herself for thinking it.

Bob returned a comforting arm to Tracy's shoulder to help her over the shock of her traumatic recollection.

'Fish scales in a lipstick? Extraordinary. Did you complain?'

Gavin dashed to the rescue.

'No Bob. It's what those shiny sparkly bits in cosmetics are made of. Can you imagine?'

Tracy's renewed interest in the contents of her bag clearly indicated that she could.

'But surely fish are not factory-farmed to produce scales for cosmetics!'

Dr Ruth was determined to return to the subject that mattered to her above all others.

'I think Tracy's point was that animal bits are already being used in cosmetics,' advised Bob.

'Yes, disgusting,' interjected Mrs B, finding someone to agree with at last. 'Chemicals is bad enough, gawd help us, but putting animal bits on yer face is even worse in my opinion. Animals is animals and should be left alone, not rubbed onto people's faces.'

'Well,' said Dr Ruth after a slightly embarrassed pause, 'we can all certainly agree with that sentiment.'

She stood up to amplify an important message.

'It's our opinion that these people should be made to understand that what they are doing is wrong and furthermore, should be discouraged from doing it again. I think, Mrs Beresford, that your excellent contribution will enable us to re-enforce the idea that mistreating animals for cosmetic purposes will not be tolerated. Thank you. Thank you both for coming and thank you for your valuable contribution to our cause.'

In the tube on the way home, Lynne put her hand on Mrs B's podgy arm.

'Mrs B. Do you still talk to that newspaper reporter of yours?'

When she got home, Lynne received a message on her answerphone that made that question irrelevant. Mike Davis, a reporter from the *East London News* wanted to meet with her urgently. Would a 2 pm meeting tomorrow at their offices be convenient and would she be kind enough to bring Mrs Edna Beresford with her? Mrs Beresford was familiar with the location of the office.

# 10

The presentation and the post presentation celebration had concluded, and Simon found himself being shoehorned into a taxi between the twins. The twenty minute journey from Bath to Bristol airport was bizarre and uncomfortable, with Sophie and Marc looking speechless in opposite directions out of the smoked glass windows and Simon sitting in the middle in a state of shock and wondering what on earth was going on. At the airport, the taxi drew into the private parking area. Simon was helped out by a smiling Sophie, grabbing his arm and guiding him gently through a set of double glass doors into a private lounge. This was empty apart from a waitress looking anxiously at the trio. As if by magic, Sir David appeared behind them and without speaking, indicated by pointing that they should move to a quiet corner equipped with comfortable chairs and a table being populated with glasses of champagne by the waitress. Sitting down, as wordlessly instructed, Simon found himself surrounded by people who, two days ago, he could never have imagined in his wildest dreams of ever meeting. Seated cross legged on his left was his beautiful, hitherto fantasised dream girl. On his right, her smiling brother. In the centre, their father, one of the richest and most powerful men in the world who was waiting for his private jet to be readied. Unsurprisingly, the Great Man was the first to speak, turning towards Sophie and Simon as he did so.

'So, Sophie, we shouldn't ignore our young guest, should we? You're probably a bit confused by all this young man?'

*True. Very true.*

'Are you feeling alright?'

*Good question. Well, actually, no. What am I doing here and come to that, where am I?* Having nothing else to say, he gave the answer that was expected.

'Yes.'

Sir David sat back in his chair.

'As you've probably gathered, my family and I meet up whenever we can – which is not, unfortunately, all that often. So, it's nice to meet one of their friends. It's Simon, isn't it?'

'Yes.'

Sir David took a thoughtful sip of champagne.

'If I'm honest Simon, there *was* another reason I was quite keen to meet you. And this is an ideal opportunity to do so.'

*Now this really makes no sense. Head of a powerful business empire wants to meet me. This can't be real. What have I done?*

'Why? What have I done?'

'You've done nothing wrong. I just wanted to ask you a few questions - about your father.'

*My FATHER?*

Simon closed his eyes and shook his head. This didn't make any sense at all. Something was wrong - why the hell should this super rich industrialist who probably employs thousands of people be interested in his father? He was feeling increasingly uncomfortable.

'Look sir, I'm sorry. This is so – unreal. I honestly don't think I can help you, whatever it is you want.'

Sir David sat forward again in his chair. 'Just one question, then: do you know where your father is?'

*What!?*

'Yes of course I do. He's at home, where we live.'

The Great Man sighed.

'No Simon, he isn't I'm afraid.'

Anger was now beginning to overcome anxiety and deference. *This is unbelievable. This man wants to know where my father is. And why is he telling me he's not at home when I know damn well that he is?*

Simon screwed up his face up in puzzled disbelief.

'My mother and father are at home, sir. Why do you think they aren't?'

Sir David smiled.

'Simon, either you are lying, or you haven't been keeping in touch with current news. Sorry, but they are both missing.'

'My parents?'

'Yes.'

Sir David picked up a thin tabloid newspaper from the table next to him and placed it in front of Simon. It was folded open at an inside page and one of the articles printed on it was ringed in red ink.

'This is a local newspaper, the *East London News*. My company happens to own it. Read the marked article entitled *A Pig of a Problem*.'

Simon scanned it. Then he read it again with more care. *It's actually true. They're actually missing. Good god! What has mother finally done to him? It's my father and my mother. I should be telling him, not him telling me. How come he's taking such an interest anyway? It still doesn't make any sense.*

'This is not making any sense. My mother and father are at home. Is this a genuine newspaper?'

He felt movement as Sophie's brother leaned forward and spoke in a calm, quiet voice.

'I would listen to my father if I were you, Simon. It could be a great mistake not to. I'm sorry, but in all honesty, this *is* a genuine newspaper - and your mother and father really *are* missing. It's obviously very much in your interest to find them and we'd like to help you do so.'

Simon stood up, anger beginning to rise within him. 'Look, if all this is bloody true, then what's happened to them? What have you done with them? And why are you doing this to me?'

Sir David gave him one, long, last searching stare, then sighed and folded the newspaper.

'Take him home. He's no damn use – hasn't a clue where his father is.'

The seat moved again as Mark stood up to comply with his father's order. This was too much for Simon. An explosion of rage large enough to drown any remaining awe for the newspaper magnet took over. Visibly shaking, he leaned forward aggressively to confront the older man across the table. Finally. Too much. His suppressed emotions broke the dam and an impassioned avalanche of anger and indignation burst out. Although he was not aware of any coherent thought, he heard himself delivering a shouted tirade of protest.

'Now just a bloody minute! I'm not having this. This was all pre-arranged, wasn't it? You and your family? You've virtually kidnapped me, dragged me into this … place, you tell me my mother and father are both missing. And then you tell me that it's in my interest to find them? You bet it bloody is. Who do you people think you are? Just because you have power and money, you think it's OK to manipulate poor sods like me for your own greedy use and then discard us like rubbish when you've finished with us. *'Take him home?'* - on a lead from your bloody son? Well, fuck you. Congratulations, your little plan has worked wonders – better than you think. I would have been happy to be led anywhere by your daughter – but not now – the conniving bitch! I hope she and her spotty brother are proud of themselves. Well, let me tell you I'm not standing for it. Unless you tell me what's going on and what's happened to my parents, I'm going straight to the police to get this sorted out!'

Simon's fit of rage had propelled him close to and towering above his seated adversary – who simply smiled.

'Simon, you've no idea what you're getting into.' This from Marc, now standing at his side.

'Bloody right, but I'm going to find out one way or the other!'

'Father, I think he deserves some kind of explanation. We can't just treat him like a disinterested bystander.' Sophie's voice carried a clear note of real concern. 'Sit down again Simon. Please. You're quite right, you really *do* need to know what's going on. I understand that you don't trust me and with good reason, but I ask you to believe me this one last time. For your own sake, sit down.'

Still shaking, Simon was no longer fully in control of himself. His outburst had drained him of hostile energy – his tank was almost empty. Confused and undecided, he allowed Sophie to put her arm on his and ease him gently back down into his chair.

Sir David merely shrugged his shoulders.

'OK, sonny. I'm going to give you a priceless business lesson. You won't like it much – it's a wicked world we live in, but you will get your explanation. I sell newspapers for a living. My newspapers are successful because we print what most people are interested in. Sex, crime, sport, celebrity gossip, pop music, television soaps, natural and man-made disasters in graphic detail, bankers' bonuses, politicians caught with their trousers down – whatever the average punter is willing to part with his or her money to read about. And occasionally, just occasionally we publish real news and analysis so that we can satisfy the 'intellectual market' - but not too much because it makes their heads hurt. Do I have a mission to inform and instruct? Like hell I do. I have a mission to increase sales and stay ahead of my rival newspapers. Let me be absolutely clear, I really have not the slightest interest in your boring father and the fact that he has disappeared. At least, I wouldn't have if it wasn't for the fact that I anticipate a major story brewing here with the possibility of selling even more newspapers. When we spot a minor story capable of being exploited to become a major talking point and cause conflict, my organisation is ready and willing to provide the exclusive catalyst. And this is exactly what is going to happen with the story which I just showed you in the local newspaper. It will boost sales across a number of our publications. Just watch this space. As far as your parents are concerned, very soon a great many people are going to be looking for them. The country will be scoured for your father. Why? Because some weirdoes will want to string him up and others will want to offer him large sums of money in order to make even more. You can rest assured that as long as he and your mother are still alive, someone will find them. Very possibly it will be my organisation. You, on the other hand, will probably become a celebrity, God help you. My advice is to disappear into somewhere remote – but not without telling us where – and take whatever you can whilst the going is good. The very last thing you need to do is get the police involved to revenge yourself on me. You wouldn't stand a chance and you would very much live to regret it. I hope I've made myself clear. If you have any sense, you will go quietly back to college with Mark and Sophie and start packing your bags.'

The effect on Simon was dramatic and immediate. His brief burst of anger-fuelled energy had been drowned and extinguished. He still had things to say but no words left with which to say them. 'I've no idea what you're talking about' was the best he could manage with screwed up, tear filled eyes.

Mark put his hand to Simon's shoulder.

'You will, Simon. You will.'

There was a look of genuine sympathy on his face.

Sophie took over.

'You need to disappear, Simon. We found you too easily. Others will surely be on your back in no time. They will be looking for your family, and if they can't get that out of you, they will try to get his secret recipe from you. Some of these are nasty people. You just need to stay quiet for a bit. Stay out of the limelight but stay in touch with us. Of course, if you hear from your mum and dad, you will let us know.'

# 11

Miranda Stevens' editorial office at *the East London News* was by no means comparable to that of the impressive, luxurious version enjoyed by the editor-in-chief of the great *Daily Informer*. Nevertheless, the present incumbent of that prestigious post, Monty Meyer, did not appear to be in any discomfort as he flopped onto one of Miranda's modest chairs. He had thoughtfully brought with him two bottles of very good red wine and these were now resting invitingly on the table in front of them. This was treading new ground. Meetings of this kind between editorial staff at opposite ends of the hierarchal chain of command were extremely rare, and would normally have taken place at a *GLOCOM* head office rather than at one of its minor local outposts. Monty had decided, however, to keep the things discreet and away from the prying eagle-eyes of his own senior staff. He had also chosen to bring Mary Ellis with him rather than one of his own people. Mike Davis, also present, was spreading pages from the latest edition of the *Informer* on the table, having carefully displaced the wine bottles to make room for them.

'Sir David,' announced Monty ambiguously. 'Very interested.'

'I know, Mr Meyer,' countered Miranda. 'Your minions told me that when they informed me of your impending visit. Can you tell me why?'

'Mystery of the universe, Sir David.'

'I don't mean the story; I mean why have you graced us with your presence Mr Meyer? Not that I'm objecting of course,' she added hastily.

'On your patch, so I'm afraid you're lumbered. And it's 'Monty', old love. And I've given you one of our very best to help out.' He waved his hand in the general direction of Mary, who was rather more uncomfortable, perched as she was on a scratchy two-seater couch. But she raised a smile at the compliment.

'That's very flattering Monty. But you already have Mike on the case, I think. Miranda?' It somehow seemed appropriate to keep egos under wraps for the moment, even though Mary's opinion of local news reporters was less than positive. But to be fair this was based on experience rather than blind prejudice or elitism.

Mike reciprocated. 'We've never met before of course but I obviously know of Mary – and have admired her work.'

'How gallant,' smiled Mary, warming slightly. 'I'm sure Mike and I are going to get along famously.'

'Well, there you are, Miranda. Problem solved.'

'If only that was the only problem,' continued Mary, coming straight to the point. 'We've now been lumbered with a *third* missing person.'

'How so?' asked Mike.

Monty placed his hands behind his head and sat back in his chair. 'Apparently, the son of George Patterson, the missing Keynote chemist bloke, also disappeared.'

Mike looked puzzled. 'Simon Patterson?'

'The very same.'

'But he's at some art college or other, up in the midlands or somewhere.'

Monty released his hands to shrug his shoulders. 'Who knows where he is? People now looking for Simon as well as his dad. Dodgy.'

'We will all be taking part,' said Mary, 'but we if we find him, he will need protection and it will be difficult to keep it a secret. He's public property now, or soon will be.'

'That's true –people will be after the kid to force him to lead them to his old man. Somebody obviously thinks there's money in this invention with the piggy bits,' agreed Miranda, obviously concerned. 'It's getting quite scary, considering his mother is missing as well as his dad.'

'Tell us about the cleaning woman,' said Monty, changing the subject with typical abruptness. 'She an animal rights nutter?'

'Dear Old Edna Beresford, bless her?' responded Mike. 'She's got AR connections but she's harmless. Just a simple animal lover. It's not likely that she's involved in any kind of violence or kidnap plot. I did hear a rumour of some kind about a meeting she's been to recently, though. We'll find out soon enough, she's coming here later for a chat with me and Miranda.'

'What time?'

'I've asked her – and the receptionist girl from Keynote – to meet us here at three o'clock. Just for background, really. I'm not expecting to get much out of them – I don't think they know very much anyway. No, it's the local animal rights mob that I'm really interested in, and it's just that I think our two guests may have had a meeting with them. Actually, I don't think these local animal rights idiots are primarily interested in money. It's only animal welfare issues that get them worked up. In any case most of 'em don't have enough brains to hatch a kidnap plot even if they found Simon Patterson or his family.'

'I wouldn't underestimate their intelligence, Mike,' warned Mary. 'I've come across some pretty clever individuals – but I agree that kidnapping a teenager to get to money isn't their usual style. No, but there are other people in the hunt, and I think we need to find out who they are.'

Monty took the wrapping off one of the wine bottles.

'Got a corkscrew?'

'I'm a reporter,' grinned Mike, reaching into a pocket for his Swiss Army knife. 'Does the Pope have a balcony?'

'Got several threads to this story,' continued Monty, handing the bottle over. 'First, three little missing piggies: chemist and family. Very odd and spooky. Then more piggy bits in a bottle. All sorts upset about that. Animal activists, certainly, but consumer groups 'keep our cosmetics safe' – that sort of thing. Then there's the boffins. What do they think? Piggy bits good? Piggy bits bad? If so how and why?'

'Well, we've got hold of some weird dermatologist who is convinced the magic cream story might be true. Apparently, he is a key opinion leader in skin care industry,' said Mary.

'How much did you pay him?' asked Miranda, wishing that she hadn't.

Monty smiled.

'Naughty. Bad as Mary here. Quoted in our latest centre page however – have a look.'

Miranda, both relieved that she hadn't upset her big boss was happy to oblige and spread out the latest edition of the *Informer* on the table.

'You know,' she mused, 'I'm beginning to think that Sir David has a good point.'

### PROFIT IN PIGS?

There's a suspicion that the mysterious disappearance of a cosmetic chemist, George Patterson, may be connected to some experiments he had been conducting which involved putting bits of pig into creams for use in skin creams.

Allegedly, these creams have truly magical properties of skin rejuvenation. A spokesman for the company that Mr Patterson works for, Keynote Cosmetics, did not deny the rumour that their chemist had made an important discovery. 'We know that George was working on an exciting new cosmetic project –something big,' said Ms Beverly Curtis a company director. 'George is very secretive. It could have been anything – but he's a very clever guy.'

If Ms Curtis is correct then the discovery could be of immense value. Her theory is that Mr Patterson has decided to go into hiding to protect his invention, and this has started a race to find him. Professor Richard Bowen, a world leading expert from the *Centre of Skin Development* in London, commented 'Mr Patterson was not a very well-known cosmetic scientist – but that doesn't mean that he hasn't made some kind of breakthrough. As I understand it, he was using pig tissue in his experiments and this makes perfect sense, since pig skin and human skin are very closely related. If he truly has discovered a cure for aging, he has solved the greatest problem in skin science. I think that such an invention is entirely possible. It's a pity that he seems to have gone into hiding!'

However, Mr Patterson's apparent discovery has not pleased everyone. Questions are already being asked about the ethics of using animal parts to improve human cosmetic appearance.

'So, as you see,' said Mary Ellis, folding the paper up, 'there are going to be a lot of people looking for Mr Patterson – for one reason or another.'

'Poor sod.' said Mike.

'So. Boss wants us to up the ante. Going to need your undying loyalty.'

'What exactly does 'up the ante' actually mean, Monty?' enquired Miranda. She was beginning to worry that she could very quickly lose control of events with the intervention of these influential journalists, in spite of the story being 'on her patch', as Monty put it.

'You tell her?' requested Monty of Mary, adding weight to Miranda's growing concern.

Mary stood up, reached for the now open wine bottle and began to pour herself a glass. 'As I understand it, it means continuing space in the *Informer* and the red tops. Then there's the journals: *Farming Issues*, *Science Direct* – that sort of thing – and also (pause) TV and radio.'

'Good grief,' gasped Miranda. 'That's a bit out of our league here Monty. Way above my salary level. What radio programs are you looking to use?'

'Rumour has it,' said Monty, with a huge wink, 'that one of the major phone-ins is interested.'

'Can Sir David do that? I mean, does he actually have the…'

'Yes. You bet he does. He either owns the damn things or the people who make them. Power of the press over the oppressed if you get my meaning. Wicked, but live with it. Way of the world – not your cosy local one perhaps. Sorry. Have to expose you the sordid underbelly of international journalism and all that. No choice now the Boss is involved.'

There was a period of silence as each of the four began to absorb the magnitude of the proposals that Mary had just outlined. Monty, fearing that in spite of the resources that his employer was prepared to throw at it, the story could easily turn out to be a damp squib – which in newspaper terms, means a non-self-perpetuating saga that runs out of steam after a few days.

Miranda, seeing that her worst fears were about to come true, was left to wonder exactly why it was that she was being dragged in. Why had Meyer taken the unprecedented step of coming down to her provincial and previously practically invisible empire? The only answer that made any sense was that it was Monty's ploy to shift the blame onto her if things went wrong. One thing she could be certain of: she wouldn't get much of the praise if things went right. However, at this stage she really had no choice but to sit back and take whatever Meyer was about to throw at her.

Mary was intrigued and a bit excited about the prospect of playing a significant part in what seemed destined to become a major story. How major, however, remained to be seen. Of prime importance was to ensure that Mike got as little of the action as possible. Of course, her writing skills were going to be needed big time – but how was she going to fit into the television thing? Very interesting.

Mike was the first to break the silence. What had they overlooked? He needed a niche to raise his stake in the enterprise.

'I think I ought to get more local background on the Patterson family. Talk more with the local community. What sort of people are they? Do they go to the local pub, or community centre, or church? How do they get on with their neighbours? Do they have any special friends – people who may give us a clue to where the they may be hiding – favourite holiday resorts, that sort of thing. In fact, the kind of thing that the police should be doing but don't seem to be. Are they even conducting a missing person operation?'

'Agreed Mike, but you should already have done that.'

Mary was desperate to quash any sign of a useful intervention.

'No.' said Monty. 'Got a point Mary, Old love. Like it. Can you handle it?' Looking at Mike.

Mike smiled. 'My speciality,' and he stood up, pretending to stretch, just to let Mary know he was up for a fight.

'Vanishing chemist? Police involvement? Questions to be asked – nothing too strong, let the punters put their own two and twos together. We just provide the calculator. Your job, I think Mary.'

'That'll be in the *Informer*?' asked Miranda. 'Mike has made a good suggestion so what else do you want us to do – Mike and I?'

'Forward thinking Miranda. Need you two to get closer to the Keynote directors – weird lot I daresay. They usually are. See what they make of it all. What do they know about the piggy bits. Get some background on *their* take on the chemist and his family. Have they really lost him or are they hiding him? That sort of thing.'

'I think, as I've already indicated, that I'd like to have a further go with Edna Beresford and the Keynote receptionist. Hence our 3 o'clock meeting with them,' said Mike.

'Meanwhile, I'll stir up some interest around the use of pigs in cosmetics,' suggested Mary, not liking the way that the job distribution was going.

'Well, you've already started that, old thing, with the magic piece you gave me last week. Need more scientific angle. Piggy bits in creams or lipsticks? Any scientific justification? Or whatever? We need some more experts for the next phase.'

'Which is?' enquired Mary.

Monty stood up, a filled glass in hand – for greater effect.

'Stu Edwards. Phone-in king primed and ready to go! Keynote cosmetics will be the centre of the broadcast discussion!'

'Wow. That's quick. Your boss really has the bit between his teeth.'

'Beautifully put and accurate. That's why we love you so much Mary.'

'Love you too, Monty, especially if there's money in it. Can't say the same thing about Stu Edwards though. Yuk.'

It was Mike's turn with the wine.

'Might want to open the other bottle,' suggested Monty.

…

'I'm not sure what this has to do with me, Mrs Stevens,' said Lynne Cooper, stirring sugar into her cup of tea. 'Frankly, I don't believe a silly word of it anyway. So, sorry, but I really don't see the point of this meeting.'

Monty and Mary had long since gone, leaving Mike and his boss to tackle the somewhat confused Lynne and the very confused Mrs B.

'The point? The point is to warn you that you may be in serious trouble unless you keep out of the limelight.'

'You're not making much sense. What have I done? Why am I in trouble? What have I done wrong?'

Miranda sighed.

'Come on Lynne. You're a bright girl. Too bright to really believe that you can just walk away from the part you played in a major drama. Just look at the latest papers: your name is clearly mentioned. Like it or not, you are going into to be dragged into this, and it might not be pleasant.'

'Why?'

'In a word, Lynne – greed. They'll be after Patterson's invention, fictitious or not. And I'll add another word. Hatred. The animal rights mob can be pretty nasty.'

Lynne was shocked. She had been tempted to reveal her recent meeting with *Justice for Animals* but now she decided to keep her powder dry.

'You think they'll come after me?'

'Yep. You, any anyone else he was acquainted with at Keynote. Did Patterson tell you where he was going? Does he have a favourite holiday resort – you know, small village tucked away in Devon or somewhere? They'll threaten you until they're really sure you don't know.'

'Who are 'they'?'

Miranda hesitated, she was beginning to frighten Lynne, and although this was her intention, she needed not to overdo it. Feminine intuition and logic told her that the Patterson whereabouts were unknown to Lynne

'I have to tell you Lynne. If this article had just stayed in our local paper, it would have completely faded by now apart for a few pathetic letters from the tree-huggers. But for whatever reason, a major newspaper has not only taken this up but, as far as I can tell, intends to make a major issue out of it. And it may not just be the papers – radio and TV could get involved also. This puts an entirely different light on it and as the result, any one of a myriad of stupid, greedy misfits will try to chase the pot of gold. You could end up needing protection.'

'But it was *you* who wrote the first newspaper article…'

'Yes, and that's why I'm here, trying to protect you. I write the words – it's my living – but I don't always get to choose what is written *about*. That's editorial policy and it's sometimes way above my head.'

Lynne was now deep in thought, her tea forgotten and getting cold on the table as Miranda's dire warning started to sink in. The idea of being captured and made to talk was frightening – but also quite exciting. Being tied naked to a bed and surrounded by virile masked men was one of her favourite erotic fantasies. But the vision of having her fingernails pulled out was altogether less appealing and brought her back to reality with a shudder. She looked up at Miranda.

'Suggestions?'

'Keep your head down. Disappear if you can. Forgive me, but I've delved a bit into your background, and I know that you're not short of cash. Get away somewhere remote where you can be anonymous – or abroad even. The Canaries are very pleasant at this time of year.'

'But what about the others? The Keynote bosses. I don't care about the gruesome twosome, but Brett is OK. He's a really nice guy. And then there's George Patterson's son Simon. What about him?'

Miranda smiled.

'It does you great credit to think about the others Lynne. As a matter of fact, I heard that Brett Kander was considering going back to Australia. And as for Simon, well, he's a special case. He needs help and someone to look after him - when he's found.'

Lynne allowed herself a small grin. 'Brett going back to his wife? He must really be desperate!'

They both laughed briefly.

'Now let's talk about you, Edna,' said Mike.

Lynne agreed. 'We certainly have to look after you as well, Edna.'

Mrs B had been sitting silently in a corner of the office trying to understand.

'Wondered when you was going to get round to me,' she complained. 'Thought you forgot I was here.'

'Forget you?' smiled Miranda. 'Not likely. You're the heroine of our story. In fact, you are very special because you are the one important person who didn't actually know George Patterson or his family. So far, we've been able to keep your name out of it.'

'So nobody will expect you to know where he is,' continued Mike. 'But if they manage to find you, you will have reporters coming round asking questions about how you actually found the jars containing piggy bits – they'll want all the gruesome details.'

'We will do our very best to keep your name out of the papers etcetera, but it would be much better if you could get away somewhere, even for a few days. Would that be possible?'

Mrs B gave it some thought.

'I could stay with me sister for a bit I 'spose if she'll 'ave me.'

'Where does she live?'

'Birmingham.'

'Perfect. You get on OK with her?'

'She's alright. Don't like her old man but I could cope with 'im for a few days I 'spose.'

'Perfect,' repeated Miranda. 'Just a few days - to be safe. Don't tell anyone else where you're going to be.'

Lynne stood up.

'We'd better go. Thank you for arranging this meeting and for your warning and advice. I'll give it very careful consideration.'

'Do that, Lynne. And take my business card.' Handing it to her. 'Ring me any time if you need more info, or a chat or even help…'

As soon as Lynne and Edna had disappeared out of the door, Miranda dialled the number Monty had given her.

'All done Miranda?'

'As agreed, Mr Meyer.'

'Forearmed forewarned and all that crap.'

'Anyway, I've done my best. Nice girl, Lynne – I liked her.'

'Let's hope it's done the trick. We're going to the next stage. Stu Edwards.'

## 12

Beverly Curtis was feeling nervous and uneasy. This was understandable, since she and Stu Edwards were sitting opposite each other across a huge, semi-circular table with a large microphone in front of her and about to go live on air, possibly to a million or more listeners. Lest she should forget where she was, the huge "London Radio Online" logo shouted at her from the wall behind the program presenter. They were silent, looking at the producer in his hi-tech empire behind a glass wall, waiting for him to give them the 'go' signal.

As she bent to retrieve notepad and pen from her briefcase, Beverly noticed that her hand was trembling. She was about to embark on a battle and for her, losing was not an option. She was used to winning. She shifted her gaze to the ginger haired, somewhat podgy man wearing headphones. Beverly had done her homework. She had read about Sylvester Richardson Edwards - bullied at school because of his ginger locks and posh name but now king of the live phone-in. She had also listened to some of his broadcasts. Nobody bullied Stu Edwards anymore, quite the reverse. He was erudite, resourceful and with ill-disguised contempt for any callers or guests who he considered to be cranks or talked rubbish. She had already read the signs: the cold, formal handshake and the lack of direct eye contact at their introductory meeting did not bode well.

'One minute to air, Stu. Stand by everyone.'

The bespectacled, headphone-wearing figure behind the glass window was making a thumbs up sign.

Beverly had already been lectured on how to proceed.

'When I want you to speak, I will point to you. Until I do so, you will not make any sound or comment. Thank you.'

A light somewhere turned green and Edwards pushed a button on the computer keyboard in front of him.

'Good evening. This is Stu Edwards welcoming you to LRO where the big 'Issue of the Moment' is 'Animals and Cosmetics – Should they go together?' So, this evening's topic will be of interest to all you cosmetic-buying ladies who insist on spreading that gruesome waxy stuff on your faces in the hope that, by some miracle, it will convert you into a fairy princess. Up to now, I wouldn't have rated your chances of success much above zero, but now it seems you may be offered fresh hope in the form of a chemist working in an obscure cosmetic company who, apparently, *may* have found the elixir of life in some bits of mashed up pig. However, the story doesn't end there. In the process he has managed to upset the animal rights people. Sounds crazy to me, but here to explain it is Miss Beverly Curtis, a director of the said company. You can phone in on the usual number

03700 200 333 lines are open now. But first you, Beverly.'

The finger pointing aggressively at Beverly was a command, not an invitation.

'Tell us about this chemist. He's disappeared, hasn't he? When did you notice he was gone?'

'Well first of all I think you're being a bit unfair in describing Keynote Cosmetics as an obscure company! We manufacture make up and creams for all the major…'

'I'm sorry but we're not here to listen to an advertisement for your company, Beverly.' The phone-in host didn't even bother to look up as he intervened. '*I've* certainly never heard of it before and neither, I suspect, have most of my listeners. Let me know if you have. The important thing is that this man – your employee – claims to have made a major scientific breakthrough of some kind and now you seem to have lost him. Explain please.'

Beverly was now shaking with rage rather than nervousness.

'That's not right either. Mr Patterson hasn't claimed anything. Someone discovered some - extracts - in his laboratory after he disappeared. But we have every reason to believe that he'd been working on a revolutionary new type of skin cream.'

'You have reason to believe? You mean you don't know what he was doing in his laboratory? And now he's vanished, and you don't know where he is? What sort of company are you running?'

Beverly knew what the presenter's objective was. She had studied his methodology. If a guest or caller could be intimidated to the point of extreme anger, reason was lost, things were said or revealed which, under other circumstances the victim would not have admitted. Beverly was not going to fall for that one, although she was having trouble keeping the anger out of her voice.

'Of course we know what he's doing. But until we can ask him, we just don't know exactly how *far* he got.'

'So, what was he employed to do – chop up bits of animal to put into cosmetics?'

'Of course not! He's usually making skin creams, eye shadows, lipsticks and so on and checking them for the correct colour and consistency and so on, just like any other cosmetic chemist. But, with our permission, he sometimes finds time to work on other things – new ideas he wants to try out. That's how progress is made.'

'So, progress is made by mixing animal parts in with cosmetics? What do you think about that, listeners? Please phone in – usual number 03700 200 333.'

Beverly was beginning to wish that she was out shopping, rather than facing Stu Edwards. However, he had a clear message that he was determined to get across on the radio.

'First caller, Ann from .. Trowbridge. Welcome Ann what's your take?'

'Well, I think that putting bits of animals in cosmetics is a bit disgusting. But apart from that, what about the animals being used – perhaps slaughtered so they can be smashed up to be put into creams.'

'OK – but let me ask you this interesting question, Ann: do you eat animals?'

'You mean, am I vegetarian?'

'That would be fairly logical. I can't think of any other reasons why you wouldn't eat animals.'

'OK. Well OK. No. I'm not. But I only buy meat only from farms that treat their animals properly – free range chickens and pigs not factory farmed.'

'So, you eat animals but don't want them on your skin. Does that include products for treating skin diseases? Eczema for example?'

'I don't know about those sorts of cream – I'm talking about cosmetics. But even if eczema creams do contain animal parts it's not right if animals are badly treated to make them. Anyway, from what I understand, the stuff this chemist was making was not to cure diseases.'

'Is that right Beverly?'

'He didn't leave any notes. It might well have medical uses. Whatever it is, it's big.'

'Or it could all be bunkum. The bottom line is - we don't know what he was trying to do, and we can't ask him.'

Beverly couldn't let this ride. It was essential that she talked up the value of Patterson's invention up as much as possible. Her voice raised in pitch and tempo as she responded.

'Look, we're absolutely sure that it was something very important. Something remarkable. Why else would he disappear and take all his notes with him? No. I'm certain he was working on something revolutionary. Time will tell - you'll see.'

Stu's smile signified triumph. At last, he was looking directly at his guest. 'Well, there are all sorts of reasons why he might have disappeared. He might have poisoned himself with the stuff he was making, mightn't he? Don't forget his wife and his son have also both disappeared. Perhaps they were all part of the same experiment. We must hope not, of course but it's feasible don't you think? Perhaps he should have tried it out on animals first, Ann?'

'No. Whatever he's doing, it can't be so important that animals need to suffer like they do in other laboratory experiments.'

'Never,' said Beverly firmly. 'He would never test on animals. Didn't believe in it. In any case...'

The raised hand, palm first which Stu now pushed in front of her face made it very clear that Stu wanted no further discussion on this point. Stu's sudden, urgent adjustment of earphones and a hand gesture to the producer in his control booth seemed to indicate that the presenter was getting instructions. There were callers waiting to join in.

'OK. Thank you, Ann. Let's take our next telephone call. Don't forget, 03700 200 333 is your direct line to Stu Edwards, and we are discussing the use of animal parts in cosmetics. Joyce is calling from Sutton. Hello Joyce, what do you want to say?'

Joyce sounded middle aged and middle class.

'Well, I want to tell you that there are already a lot of animal ingredients in cosmetics, and they are all bad for your skin and dangerous.'

'What, *all* cosmetics Joyce?'

'No, only the ones with animal ingredients in them. But most cosmetics do, you see? Not all of them, but most of them.'

'Including the well-known brands? Don't mention any names here Joyce, but you know the ones I mean.'

'Yes. Some of them are the worst.'

'How do you know, Joyce? Are you a chemist, or a doctor?'

'No. I'm a beauty consultant – and I see the results every day for myself.'

'Really? So how do the cosmetic companies get away with it, Joyce, if all their products are bad for the skin? You'd think someone would notice.'

'The general public are not informed and the Government lets the big companies get away with it – it's big business.'

'So let me see if I understand you. Large – did you say Major? - cosmetic companies are putting dangerous animal ingredients in their products. And the government knows about this but lets them get away with it. Why?'

'Not all brands have animal ingredients. Some are animal free.'

'Ah. I'm beginning to see where you're coming from Joyce. But you haven't answered my question. Why do they use dangerous animal ingredients and why does the government let it happen if they know about it?'

'It's big business, that's why. And the small companies who make ethical, animal free products can't get a look in.'

'What sort of beauty consultant are you? Do you work for yourself, or do you advise companies, or what?'

'I do both, Stu. I try to point people away from cosmetics that are actually harming them and advising them which alternative brands to choose for safety. Brands like…'

'What sort of harm are we talking about Joyce, blackheads, pimples – that sort of thing?'

'Oh no! Much more serious than that. Some cosmetics can damage the skin permanently and even cause cancer.'

'Joyce, are you telling us that cosmetics containing animal ingredients can actually cause cancer?'

'Yes. Certainly.'

'And you have proof of this? I mean, proper, scientific proof?'

'Well, I see it all the time, Stu.'

'In your clinic?'

'Yes.'

'I was hoping for something a little more convincing Joyce. A paper from a scientific journal? A properly controlled investigation?'

'I don't need that Stu. I see it for myself.'

'Joyce, I think you are either dangerously misguided or are trying to flog some niche cosmetic brands on the program. Listen, if anyone has evidence - proper scientific evidence - that what Joyce is saying is true, that major cosmetic companies are producing cancer causing cosmetics, then I'd love to hear from you. 03700 200 333 is the number. I can promise you that if you can, there will be not just an outcry, but an explosion of protest and litigation. Until that happens, I'm sorry Joyce but I really can't take you seriously. Goodbye. Howard is on the phone from Nottingham. What's the weather like in Nottingham, Howard?'

Elderly Howard was not expecting this kind of question. 'Huh? It's raining. Listen, testing cosmetics and things on animals is wrong and I don't agree with it.'

'Is that it, Howard? Have you been listening? Nobody is talking about testing on animals, we're discussing putting animal parts into cosmetics. Do you have anything to say about that?'

Howard had already been thrown off course. This caused a discernible pause whilst he collected his thoughts.

'Well, I don't agree with it. Not if they've been tested on animals.'

'Thank you, Howard. Must move on. Beverly Curtis, since Howard mentioned it, what about this testing cosmetics on animals business? Does it still go on?'

Beverly was anxious to get back to the subject of the value of Patterson's invention.

'No. It's been banned. But we've never tested on animals and George Patterson, I know, has not tried his invention out on any animals. The effect on humans is probably quite sufficient proof.'

Stu did not take up the challenge.

'Banned in just in this country or all over the world?'

Beverly was unsure. 'Not everywhere, just in some counties I believe.'

'Perhaps Charles from Ealing can help us. Good evening, Charles.'

'The banning of experiments on animals for cosmetics is obviously a good thing – although it's still done for drugs. But it's not the experiments. Some animals – mice, rabbits, guinea pigs – even monkeys – are being specially bred to do experiments on. Just think about it. Suppose some more intelligent alien race came and conquered the world and set up breeding pens for human to do experiments on. How would we feel about that?'

'Well Charles, I get your point, but they'd better get here quickly otherwise the cosmetics companies would already have destroyed the human race. Thank you, Charles.'

In the distance, the producer was getting agitated. Stu needed to take another call.

'So, Janet is calling from Bishops Stortford. Posh part of the world. Good evening.'

'Good evening. How are you?'

The caller's voice indicates that she was past middle aged.

'I'm fine thank you, Janet. What's your point?'

'Well, two things really. Firstly, animal ingredients have been used in cosmetics for many years without any problem at all. I disagree with that lady beautician, or whatever she was.'

'I agree, Janet. I don't think many people will take her seriously.'

'Well unfortunately, that's not altogether true. They have these meetings you know; these anti-animal product people and they can be quite convincing for people who are not experts.'

'Interesting. And your second point?'

'The second point is about cosmetics testing on animals. The reason why cosmetic companies no longer test ingredients on animals - they usually test ingredients rather than the final product, by the way- is that they've all been tested before. If they hadn't been shown to be safe, they wouldn't be allowed to use them under European Regulations. So, any company can claim that they don't test but they are using ingredients that have previously been tested on animals.'

'You sound quite knowledgeable Janet – do you work in the cosmetics industry?'

'Not any more Stu!'

'OK Janet, so you've got nothing to lose, I guess. So, tell us the dirty truth. I accept that we no longer do cosmetics testing on animals. But I'm interested in the idea of putting animal bits into cosmetics – especially from pigs. Here's the point: suppose you wanted to put, say, pig extract into a cosmetic. Without animal testing, how could you prove it's safe to the cosmetics regulators, whoever they are? Do you have any thoughts on that?'

Janet didn't. 'Difficult, isn't it?'

'It looks like it, Janet. Thank you. I believe Ester may have a point to make about that. Are you there, Ester from Glasgow?'

'Yes, hello Stu. I'm no a big user of cosmetics m'sel, but I think some of the things people say about animal ingredients are ridiculous.'

'How so Ester?'

'Well, I have to have a wee laugh at people who are happy to eat beef, pork and lamb or whatever, but are appalled at the idea of animal products in their cosmetics. Get real for goodness' sake.'

'So, you'd be in favour of this cosmetic boffin putting bits of pig into, say, a face cream, and giving it to you to use?'

'Yes – provided it's safe, of course.'

Stu had spotted the flaw in this answer. 'But Ester, my darling, this is the whole point. How can we sure that it is safe? We had one beautician telling us that all animal containing cosmetics are harmful and can give us cancer, and another person telling us that cosmetics are no longer tested on animals to show whether they are safe or not.'

'Well, I agree it's a wee problem but the point I'm trying to make is that it's ridiculous to complain about putting animal products on your skin if you already eat them. Anyway, I'm not against putting animal ingredients in creams if they are safe and effective.'

'Thank you, Ester. Beverly, just how are cosmetics tested to ensure that they're safe to use if animal testing is no longer used?'

Beverly had included this in her homework.

'We have a European Cosmetics Directive which lists things that you can't put into cosmetics or can only use at certain concentrations…'

'What about your chemist putting bits of pig into his creams. Are bits of pig in the cosmetics directive?'

'No of course not. What Mr Patterson is doing is creating a new kind of cosmetic – a prototype which will have to be shown to be both effective and, of course safe before it could go on sale.'

'And how's he going to do that?'

Now Beverly was stumped. 'I, er, will have to ask him. I'm not a scientist.'

'I'd certainly like to ask him – if we can find him. There are apparently a lot of people who are desperately trying to find Mr Patterson, so that they can cash in his invention. If, dear listener, this applies to you, you won't be getting any clue from anyone here. Even his boss doesn't know where he is. Of course, if any of you have any useful information, I'm sure Beverly will be most anxious to hear it. Tell us a bit more about him, Beverly. What's Mr Patterson's first name?'

Beverly was so tight-lipped that she is almost talking through a closed mouth. 'George. George Patterson.'

'And he has a wife and a son – both of whom are also missing. Has he ever done this sort of thing before?'

'No. It just shows you the potential importance of his discovery that he's had to go into hiding. As you say, half the country is looking for him. That's an indication of how valuable they think it is.'

'Well George, if you're listening, you'd better get in touch with your Board of Directors. They seem pretty lost without you.'

Before Beverly could respond, Stu sailed on to the next caller. 'Keith is on the line – are you there Keith.'

'Yes I am and I'm really fed up with all this crap about 'anti-animal people' as though we are a bunch of idiots. Look, some of us are passionate about animals. I am disgusted by the way people treat animals as objects rather than sentient, living creatures and I *am* vegetarian – in fact vegan - because I am concerned about the ethical issues about how we use and mistreat animals for our own purposes. If you're vegetarian or vegan you can't win. If we don't ask whether the product has got animal materials in it, we are labelled as hypocrites, but when we do, we are seen as crazy obsessives. I am personally horrified that this guy is putting bits of pig in his cosmetics. Are pigs being especially bred for this?'

'Good question, Keith. I don't suppose you know the answer, Beverly?'

'No, animals are not specifically bred for use in cosmetics. Apart from anything else, it would be far too expensive. I can't see that you would breed pigs especially for cosmetic use.'

Keith was not convinced. 'You can't automatically assume that. People do such terrible things to animals.'

'OK Keith. Thanks for the call. Melanie, you are on the line to Stu Edwards. What would you like to say?'

'Hi Stu. Love your program. I'd just like to ask: what do these people think should happen to the inedible parts of animals that come from food production. Should they just be put into landfill and allowed to rot, or put to some use like making cosmetic and pharmaceutical creams? I don't see the problem. I'm sure that they can find cosmetics that don't contain animal bits if they look hard enough.'

'An interesting point, Melanie. Thanks for your call. Let's have a look at some of the other calls people have been making. Here's one from Bill. 'My granddad used to rub pig fat into his hair every day and he had a full head of hair when he died at the age of 89. It never did him any harm.' Well it might have improved his hair but probably not his social life. Can you imagine what stale pig's fat smells like? Here's a thought from Stephen. I believe you are an animal activist Stephen?

'Look. I get sick and tired of people assuming that all of us who care about animal rights go around damaging buildings and threatening people. We're not terrorists – we just care about the way animals are treated and want to change it for the better. What's so terrible about that?'

'You mean animal activists don't threaten lab workers and their families and damage laboratories so that they have to have barbed wire fences built around them?'

'I don't deny that there is a lunatic fringe, but these people are not the vast majority. Most of us work by publicity and argument – bringing facts out into the open so that the public can see what's going on and what the government and big companies try to hide. Argument and discussion, not violence. That's why I phoned into this program.'

'And thank you for doing it. Argument and discussion, Beverly Curtis. I imagine you might have a comment on that?'

'What I'm talking about is a small-scale experiment in a laboratory, not a full-scale product launch. Talking as though we have set up a pig farm to do it is ridiculous. I'm happy to defend what we are doing – or what our chemist has done in the name of scientific discovery but I'm not here to defend the whole cosmetics industry. Simple as that. I believe that Mr Patterson may have discovered something very important – not just for cosmetics, perhaps for pharmaceutical creams to heal skin problems as well'.

'So this is Stu Edwards on 020 0402 334455. The subject: is should cosmetic companies be allowed to put bits of pig into cosmetics? What are the health, ethical and legal implications of that? And not just bits of pig. We've learned that other animal parts are also used in cosmetics and, according to one of our listeners, this is dangerous enough to possibly cause cancer? Do you agree or is this just scare mongering to entice us to use 'animal free' cosmetics? (Not me personally, you understand, I admit here and now that I don't use cosmetics myself, much to my wife's relief). My guest in the studio is Beverly Curtis, a director of Keynote Cosmetics whose missing chemist has been putting piggy bits into some new type of cosmetic. Paul is on the line. Paul?'

'Oh good evening. I just wanted to say that it's your animal rights guy who is talking a load of crap. We have the best record of humane farming anywhere in the world in the UK and our animals do not suffer. And as to whether his crowd set light to the factory, I wouldn't be the least bit surprised. These people should be locked up the amount of trouble and anguish they cause. I've had some so I can tell you they are a bunch of ... well, I shouldn't use the word on live radio.'

'Are you a farmer, Paul?'

'Yes I am. I breed pigs and cattle and if anyone wants to come and see how we treat our animals they are welcome. We've got absolutely nothing to hide!'

'There's an invitation to you animal rights activists, you are welcome at Paul's farm – just leave your box of matches and semtex at home for fear of misinterpretation. Thanks Paul, leave your address with our producer.

The producer was making cutthroat signs in his window.

'Benjamin from Croydon – want do you want to say?'

'Yeah, I got something to say, man. Animal bits in cosmetics is the work of the devil. Cosmetics is sinful – it says in the Bible. If you use it, you are gonna end up in hell – but even worse if you let the devil drag you down even further by using animal bits. Then you in *serious* trouble.'

'Forgive me Benjamin, I admit it's been a while since I read the Bible, but I don't remember seeing a single mention of face powder or eyeshadow or lipstick. Where does it say that using cosmetics is a sin?'

'You a fool man. I got it in front of me: Jeremiah 4:30 *'what do you mean that you dress in scarlet, that you adorn yourself with ornaments of gold, that you enlarge your eyes with paint? In vain you beautify yourself'*. You know I'm right. You got to see yourself the way God sees you when He made you, fearfully and wonderfully. How does your cosmetics glorify the Lord? You never heard of Jezebel?'

'You ever heard of common sense and sanity Benjamin? You'll probably find that in the Bible if you look for it. Goodbye.'

As the censorial finger cut the caller off, Stu's opposite hand was pressing his headphones closer to his ear. An extravagant nod to the producer indicated an important message had been received.

'Talking about the Bible, we now have an expert on the line. Professor Sean Sitwell is Professor of Comparative Religion at Scarborough University. What did you make of Eric's contribution, Professor?'

'Good evening. Well, I only caught the end of it – but it's a view that a good many people hold, especially in parts of the USA. But what I wanted to mention is that any cosmetic containing any part of a pig would not be used by followers of Judaism, Hinduism or, again, Islam, since all of these consider pork to be unhealthy or worse. So, your guest's new product could not be used in quite a large area of the world.'

'Thank you, professor. Bit of a bummer, Beverly?'

The response to this was a steely stare and a scribbled note pushed under Stu's nose. 'Bastard!' The presenter's smile and the tick he drew in the air registered his triumph.

'Beverly, I was reading in the paper that Mr Patterson was not very well known among the cosmetic scientist community – yet he has supposed to have come up with this landmark, breakthrough product. Can you explain that? I mean, if he's so damned good, why isn't he better-known among the cosmetic fraternity. He's been around for a few years, hasn't he? It's not like he's a fresh-faced youngster.'

'George is a quiet, family man. He doesn't put himself about like some people. He just gets on with his job quietly and efficiently and when he gets time, he works at his own inventions without shouting about them or making a fool of himself.' Beverly made no attempt to hide her irritation. She knew she now that the battle was very uneven, Stu had all the odds stacked in his favour. Control and power rested exclusively in his hands. But she hadn't yet lost her fighting spirit.

'Let's have a look at some of the in-comings. Pig parts used for transplants ... pigs make perfect pets, how could you use them on your face? ... What about mad cow disease, could pigs give us something similar? ... oh, here's a little poem: *'Mary had a little pig Which sadly fell quite sick. Now Mary wears a ruby smile, Her piggy friend is lipstick.'* Nice try Nigel – doesn't quite scan but nice try.'

Stuart ignored Beverly's look of thunder and waved at the producer in his glass box.

'Anyway, it's time for the news. After the break, we will turn to another subject: the shortage of doctors and the inordinate amount of time it takes to get to see your GP. Over to you at the news desk Chris...'

# 13

It was Sunday and the factory was closed. Gus at was home and angry. The world was conspiring against him. His anger had been mounting for days as surveyed his fast-emptying factory. His business was falling to pieces before his eyes. More newspaper articles were appearing every day to make sure that everyone knew that Patterson was missing, and that Keynote was on the blink. Kander had not been in the office for days supposedly looking for new business but probably looking for a new job. Beverly had responded to death threats or worse after her performance on the London News Online phone-in by going into hiding where she was presumably buzzing as furiously and fruitlessly as a trapped wasp. He, Gus, was flying solo. Whisky no longer eased the pain and sleep was very hard to come by. Like many of his generation, Gus's thoughts were confined and entrapped in his own bubble of misery and was consequently protected by ignorance from the firestorm of abuse that had so badly affected the other two. As he paced his modest flat, trying to diffuse some of the pent-up energy that anger produces, his mind directed itself to the focus of his pain.

All that money, all that he had had to do to get it, and now it was slipping uselessly and irretrievably away.

By coincidence, just as he was passing the telephone, it rang. He let it go to answerphone. *'I'm not available at the moment. Please leave a message after the tone…'*

'Giovani, you old fraud, it's me. We last met at the seaside if you remember. A few years ago – but I haven't forgotten you or our little business venture. How are you doing? Speak to me, my old friend, we have a lot of catching up to do.'

Did he remember? Gus certainly remembered. And as he did so, his heart quickened and sank even further. *Minchia! My life is in ruins and now this! What else can the Devil throw at me?*

'Come on Gus. Pick up the 'phone. Don't be a party pooper. You know who I am and I'm not going away. We need to talk.'

Reluctantly, Gus took the phone off of its stand, and held it at arm's length as though it was contaminated with a deadly virus. Even from that distance the caller's change of tone could be heard quite clearly.

'Stop buggering me about Giovani or whatever your fucking name is now. Speak, or there will be consequences.'

'Ok. Ok. I hear you. What?'

'That's better – Gus. Isn't that what they call you? You've become quite famous. I keep seeing stuff in the newspaper about you.'

'*Basta con le stronzate,* Guffrie. You tell me. I listen. So again. What?'

'Whoa – don't be in such a hurry. I just wanted to commiserate with you over your missing chemist. What a blow to your lovely business. Any sign of him?'

'Why the fuck you care?'

'I bet you got him hidden away somewhere, knowing you, you old toe rag. Cosy little cottage in Cornwall is it? Or somewhere on a remote Scottish island? Next to a nice distillery perhaps. Come on, you can tell me. We're old friends.'

'You crazy? You think I let my business go to zit if I know where he is?'

'Good point, Gus – at least, it *would* be if he wasn't sitting on mega fortune, which is what he *is* doing according to the papers. So who cares about the business when there are much bigger fish to fry, eh? Plenty of helpings to go round I imagine.'

'Papers got it wrong, Guffrie. No fortune. No fucking invention. All crap.'

'Well… I'm sorry to have to tell you that I'm having trouble believing that, my old mate. The papers seem to be very sure. You wouldn't want to ruin our friendship by telling me porkies, would you? Because I would get very cross if you were to do that.'

'You want the truf? I tell you fucking truf. Patterson is dead for all I know. No sign. No fucking sign. And I got out of my mind.'

'You're touching my heart strings Gus. But you *would* say that wouldn't you? Have you been looking for him?'

'Have I been looking? Are you crazy? What's it to you, anyway?'

'What's it to me? I'm surprised you ask, Gus. Surely you haven't forgotten our business arrangement. Sharing of profit was key if you remember. Why, I was only looking at your file the other day. You know, just familiarising myself with the details. What I agreed to do for you and what you would do for me in return. It's all there in black and white for anyone to see. Of course, it's all locked safely away and out of sight. We wouldn't want to get you into serious trouble should it get to the wrong people.'

'So, blackmail?'

The caller chuckled. 'That's an ugly word Gus. Blackmail? I like to think of it just as good business practice. You know, making sure that your business partner keeps to the agreement.'

'*Brutto figlio di puttana Bastardo* Guffrie. I tell you to rot in hell. If I knew where the fucking hell he was, I wouldn't tell you.'

The caller paused and made an audible sigh.

'Goodness. I don't speak *Italiano*, but that didn't sound very nice to me. Nonetheless, I'm going to give you some free advice and I recommend that you listen very carefully. If you are telling the truth, and your business is going tits up, I can understand why you are pissed off. But don't be too hard on yourself – after all, you're a survivor. People less lucky than you would be dead by now. But if you are lying to me, then maybe you haven't got long to live anyway. Either way, before you plan to unveil Patterson or as soon as you manage to find him - whichever it is - tell me first. Before the police. Before the papers. Before the Pope. Before your own dead mother. I'm first in line with my wallet open ready to receive. If not, if you shit on me, you can be sure that you won't be needing any money where you're going. Remember, I look after my valuables much more carefully that you do yours and I'll be watching your every move. Get it?'

'You a bastard Guffrie. Remember, you tell on me, I tell on you *capisci il tuo bastardo*?'

'Yes, I know. But the odds are in my favour. Me? Lost career. Tragic, but I'll survive. You? Prison and probably much worse. Your Italian friends would love to meet up with you again once they know where you are.'

Gus hesitated as he tried to find a way of making a non-submissive response.

'Patterson may be dead.'

'In which case you don't have a problem. Just make sure that if and when he does turn up, you tell me pronto and before anyone else. Don't underestimate me, Gus. I can be *really* nasty when I want to be, as you are very soon going to find out... Be warned and write this telephone number down. Keep it safe.'

Gus reluctantly complied and then slammed the receiver down to abruptly end the call.

The 'phone immediately rang again but before Gus had a chance to answer it, there was a loud and frantic knocking at the door. Phone in hand, he crossed to fling it violently open, expecting to see his tormenter there in person. But instead, there was Brett, looking shaken and holding onto the stair banister for support.

'Christ, Gus. The bloody factory's on fire!' Brett's hoarse voice matched his distraught and unsteady appearance.

Gus's first reaction was to drop the still ringing phone, causing the back to detach itself.

'I think you'd better answer that, Gus. It's probably the police. They've been trying to call you but you've been engaged.'

...

They arrived at the factory as the fire brigade were beginning to roll up their hosepipes and pack their equipment back into two fire tenders. On the way, they were passed by an ambulance going in the opposite direction at speed, blue light flashing.

The fire chief was standing on a small waterfall, cascading down the front steps of the factory and into a large and expanding puddle on the pavement below.

'Is it out?' demanded Brett.

'And you are?'

Gus was unable to answer this simple question.

'This is Mr Volante, the owner of the company, and I'm a director.'

'In that case, yes. It's out. Didn't take us long. Better speak to the policeman chap inside, however. Seems quite agitated.'

The choking smell of burned wood, paper and plastic hit them as they entered the building. Then they saw the blackened remains of what had once been the reception area and became aware of the dark, sodden mess they were standing on that used to be a blue carpet.

The 'policeman chap' was just about to descend the stairs from Gus's office when he spotted them.

'Mr Volante? Excellent! We need to talk to you – outside. Be careful.'

The fire chief intervened. 'Sorry, we have to get you out to secure the premises. Outside please gentlemen. Sorry about the mess. Unavoidable.' And he stood aside to let them out of the front door.

Brett took a last look before he was ushered out.

'Jesus, look at this place! What kind of stupid bastard would do this? They must be out of their fucking minds.'

'Bit of a state, isn't it?' asked the policeman sympathetically. 'Did you spot anything unusual, gentlemen? Anything out of place – not where it should be. Anything here that shouldn't be?'

Gus was standing by the outside on the steps, with one hand on the rail to steady himself. His eyes were closed as his overloaded brain struggled to comprehend and make sense of this, the latest catastrophe. Brett answered for both of them, wandering around and looking back through the door.

'Difficult to say – so much mess, but I don't think so…'

'What about downstairs? Would you take another look? Just look from the top of the steps – don't go back inside.'

Brett took another look to inspect what was left of the reception area.

'No. Nothing unusual that I can see, officer.'

'Well, if you're certain, that's about all we can do here for the moment. The fire investigation boys will be here any minute, so we'd better get you over to the station. There's a car waiting outside.'

'Are you arresting us?' gasped Brett.

'No, not at all. But we need to do some background research and that means we need to ask you some preliminary questions. Our initial discussion with you – hopefully it won't take too long.'

Then as they turned to go down to the police car, they both spotted the graffiti scrawled in white chalk on the wall.

*'A present for animal torturers. Stop now or there will be more.'*

…

'Mr Volante, as I said, I need to ask you some questions.'

They were in an interview room. Tea, coffee and biscuits had been supplied and were available on the table in front of them – but it was still an interview room, dark, green and featureless apart from the obvious one-way mirror on the smallest wall.

The speaker was a uniformed policeman inspector seated on the other side of the table.

'What can I tell you. *Questa è una catastrofe.* Dis is a..a catastrophe. Who would do such a thing?'

'That's interesting, Mr Volante. So, you don't think this was an accident. Can I ask why?'

'This fire was started by mindless vandals,' interjected Brett. 'It's bloody obvious. There's nothing more to it than that. Did you see the graffiti on the wall outside the front entrance? Who else would it be?'

The police inspector sat back in his chair and put his hands behind his head.

'Well – just as an example, we could start with someone with a failing company who wanted to clean up on the insurance.'

Gus slowly raised his head and looked the inspector straight in the eye.

'Mr Policeman. I regret, but I have no fire insurance.'

The inspector frowned, nodded and made a note on the A4 pad in front of him.

'Well, yes. It's obviously possible that vandalism *is* the cause of the fire. However, it's going to be a little more serious than just pure arson.'

'What do you mean, more serious?' asked Brett.

The policeman paused for a moment.

'What I mean, gentlemen, is if there is clear evidence that it was started deliberately, then it could amount to attempted murder. I haven't told you yet, but your colleague, Miss Beverley Curtis was in the building when the fire started.'

'You're joking!'

'*Mama mia*!'

Brett had turned white.

'My God. Beverley, how... where... is she alright? Can we see her? What happened?'

'According to the fire officer I spoke to, she was showing signs of smoke inhalation and was carted off to hospital. I'll get my sergeant to...'

Before he could finish his sentence, another uniformed figure knocked on the door and entered the room. News from the other side of the one-way glass window.

'Just heard from the hospital sir. Miss Curtis is OK. Nothing life threatening, but she's on oxygen they're going to keep her in for observation.'

Brett stood up, preparing to leave.

'Well, if that's all inspector, we'd like to get over to the hospital. Which one is she in? Can we have the telephone number?'

The inspector held up his hands in front of him, palms first.

'Sorry gentlemen. But we've a way to go here before you leave. This may be an attempted murder enquiry and you are, or may be, material witnesses. Please sit down – you too sergeant.'

'Neither of us had anything to do with it. Why in God's name would we try to burn down our own company and murder our close colleague and friend? We've lost everything. You saw that infantile scribble on the wall – this is down to animal rights nutters. Instead of imprisoning us here, you should be out there looking for the bastards who did it.'

The inspector sighed and turned to the sergeant.

'Did you hear me accuse them of anything? No? I thought not.'

He leaned forward, confronting the irate Brett at close range.

'Mr Kander, far as I am aware, you haven't been accused of starting the fire – yet - and you certainly *haven't* been imprisoned. You have been invited down to the station to give us help us with our enquiries. I would have thought that it would be in your interest to give us all the help you can. So, sit back down, please.'

'It's OK Brett,' mumbled Gus, having regained some composure. 'Do like he say. We sort this shit but stay cool, eh?'

'OK,' said Brett, sitting. 'But look, can we get this over with as soon as possible. I'm very worried about Beverley, you understand?'

The inspector straightened the A4 pad in front of him.

'Before we continue with any form of questioning, I think it would be useful to fill you in with a few facts. Firstly, as yet we have no reason to believe that either of you were close enough to have started the fire. That is why you are not under arrest. However, it *is* possible that someone connected to your company may have had something to do with it. And it *could* still turn out to be you two – or one of you.'

Brett's mouth had formed into a 'W' but he never managed to ask the inevitable question because Gus got in first.

'Why in hell you say dat? You say we want to kill Beverly? Sure, many times - but not for real. I had no idea where she was. Hiding in the office? Clever – because you policemen can't protect her, so she scared stiff. But I didn't know. I was at home. What about you Brett?'

'We will come back to whether she was hiding later, Mr Volante. Meantime, where *were* you at the time the fire was reported. Mr Kander?'

'I was at home until you guys called me on my telephone, inspector – what kind of people do you think we are?'

The inspector spread his arms again.

'Hold on. Like I said, nobody is accusing you of anything at the moment. But the fact of the matter is that when the fire brigade arrived, there was a blaze in the reception area and the door was firmly locked, with no key on the inside to open it with. We need to account for that, so, the next question is, who has the keys to your factory?'

'I don't,' said Brett. 'Only Mr Volante has a set. Right Gus?'

All eyes turned to Gus Volante.

'That true, Mr Volante? Only you with the keys?'

Gus gave a hesitant 'Yes.'

'So, after work, every evening, you're the last person out – to lock up?'

Hesitation morphed into a painful pause. Then, eventually, 'The door, she closes on her own. Pull shut and it clicks. No key.'

The inspector gave this some thought and clasped his hands together before responding.

'You're telling me that when the last person leaves your premises after the working day, the door is simply pulled shut and it clicks? Presumably that automatically locks it?'

It was an unanswered question. Gus looked at Brett and Brett looked down at the floor.

'So,' continued the inspector. 'If I understand you correctly, the keys are in your possession, but you don't need them to lock up because the door locks itself - correct?'

Gus gave a brief, unconvincing nod of assent. 'Only I don't keep the keys in my pocket.'

The inspector nodded, produced a transparent plastic bag from his briefcase and laid it on the table. It clearly contained a set of three keys.

'We found these in a desk draw in the upstairs office, Mr Volante. Would these be the keys we are talking about? The key or keys to the front door of the building?'

Gus nodded assent without looking at them.

'Well, Harris,' said the inspector, turning to his sergeant. 'That begs a fairly obvious question, wouldn't you say?'

'Yes, sir! How the hell do you get *into* the factory the next morning without a key?'

'Mr Volante? Mr Kander?'

Silence. Brett continued his intense study of the floor and the waves on the forehead of Gus Volante intensified into a violent storm.

The inspector waited for a full thirty seconds before speaking.

'Gentlemen. The sergeant and I are patient men and we can wait here for an answer for the rest of the day if you like. But I should warn you that a significant silence or refusal to answer a question satisfactorily might give rise to an inference under the Criminal Justice and Public Order Act 1994 16. Now, at present you are not under caution, but unless I get some reasonable co-operation from you, I will be obliged to consider cautioning you on the grounds that you may be deliberately attempting to obstruct a police investigation – and that would change everything. So, gents, let me ask you this simple question again. How do you get into the Keynote building first thing, without a key, having locked the door the previous evening when the keys are in a desk drawer inside the building?'

It was honest Brett who supplied the answer.

'The door doesn't lock when it's pulled shut. You can open it by pushing the handle up in a certain way, it's a trick. It's more convenient than messing with keys and you need to know exactly how to do it to make it work, anyway.'

The two policemen looked at each other in disbelief.

'Does your alarm company know about this?'

Brett shook his head, no.

'Don't tell me – you don't have an alarm system?'

Silence.

The police inspector stood up and began pacing thoughtfully back and forth, hand on hips whilst the sergeant grabbed the A4 pad and began writing furiously on it.

'Well, gentlemen,' said the inspector, still pacing. 'We have very strict rules about how to treat the public when, at our request, they come into the station to answer a few questions. We have to make them comfortable, treat them with respect and definitely not be rude to them or harass them, whatever our private opinions might be. Bearing that in mind, I have to politely tell you that I think, in future, you should reconsider your policy over the security of your premises, since I believe it could be improved. In particular – and just to be helpful – my suggestions are as follows. Use keys to lock up. Employ an alarm company and get the premises insured. On the latter point, you are almost certainly breaking the law in not proving suitable insurance for your employees – not my speciality, so I won't pursue that one, but I advise you to do something about it urgently. As policemen, the sergeant and I do our best, every working day, to protect the public from harm and criminal activity. We do ask, in return, that the general population help by taking reasonable precautions to protect themselves and their property so as not to overload us with avoidable enquiries and investigations.'

'Can I make a point, sir?' piped up the sergeant 'This means that the lady – er - (looking down at the notes) - Miss Curtis – may not actually have been *locked in* as we thought. I mean she could have just pushed the door open…'

'Excellent point sergeant. We must assume that she was unable to get downstairs because of the flames and smoke after she had made the emergency call on the company phone. Had she been able to get to the door, she could have escaped before the fire brigade got to her.'

Gus spoke at last.

'*Oh mio Dio!* Beverley! She must have been so scared! Can we go now, please? You get a taxi Brett.'

'Please be patient gentlemen – I understand your concern,' said the inspector. 'Sergeant, see if there is a car available to get them to the hospital, will you?'

As Harris left the room, the inspector sat back down and leaned forward across the table again for emphasis.

'This remains a serious, ongoing inquiry involving arson and a potential resultant death. In the circumstances I am not going to detain you a moment longer than I have to. But at present I require to question you further and you should therefore remain here until I'm satisfied. Is that clear?'

'If we haven't done anything, why are you treating us like criminal?'

'Sorry Mr Kander,' replied the inspector. 'I can assure you that we don't supply tea and biscuits to people we think are criminals. Put it down to our woeful lack of luxury facilities here. I thank you for agreeing to come to the station and once again, we promise that we'll try not to keep you too long.'

'Not that we had any bloody choice,' complained Brett.

The inspector stood up and stretched.

'You see, that's the kind of reluctant co-operation which makes us suspicious Mr Kander. Seems to me that you and your colleague are still not being as helpful as you could. This is a bad sign. We don't appreciate being pissed about. Not normally, let alone when there may have been an attempted murder. Let us turn to some of your employees. I see that you used to have a warehouse /factory manager, Mr (looking down to check the name) Mr Patel.'

'Yes, but haven't had a factory manager for six months. And even if we did, he would never have a key. Didn't need it. He always left the premises before us.'

The inspector inclined his head to one side and looked at them both, one at a time.

'This is a very peculiar factory you've been running,' he concluded. 'No factory manager, no fire insurance, no alarm. Doesn't sound like good management practice to me. What do you think, sergeant?'

'Got to agree sir,' said the sergeant, returning from his mission. 'Car can be made available as soon as you are ready.'

'Okay,' interjected the rapidly recovering Gus Volante. 'We run the place by what you say? Shoestring. You know? Difficult times, gotta keep cost down. We managed okay until –.' He waved his arms around the room, 'until all this happen.' He took out a handkerchief to mop his brow.

'So, you have an address for Mr Patel, please?'

'Won't do any good, officer. He and his mother went back to Mumbai a couple of weeks ago. That's in India.'

The inspector took in a deep breath.

'Thank you for the geography lesson, Mr Kander. Seems like we can eliminate those two then, unless they slipped back into the country. Miss Lynne Cooper?'

*'Mio Dio! Quella fottuta troia!'* shouted Gus.

'That didn't sound too complimentary. Do you have a problem with her?'

'Problem? No. I just kill her if I see one more time. Cooper get stabbed – you come arrest me, *presto.*'

'She – caused us a few problems recently,' explained Brett. 'She's not in our good books.'

'As the result of which you presumably sacked her?'

'Yes.'

'Without notice?'

'Yes.'

'Without pay?'

'What are you getting at?'

'I assume you can give me Miss Cooper's last known address?'

Brett nodded. 'Of course. You think *she* might have done it?'

'Employee crime is surprisingly common. Fired or disgruntled employees may sabotage or vandalize their company as a form of 'pay back' – not for personal gain, just for revenge. That includes committing arson and even attempted murder so it's an obvious area for us to investigate.'

'I can't believe that Lynne Cooper is capable of that.'

'Nevertheless, she stays on our list until we speak to her. You'd be surprised.'

Gus could restrain himself no longer.

'Sure. It make sense, no? First, she shit on us, then set fire! *Problema risolto*. Arrest her!'

The inspector raised his hand.

'Whoa Mr Volante. We going to need a bit more evidence before we arrest anyone.'

Brett felt the need to intervene.

'Calm down Gus. You'll have to excuse him officer – apart from the fire – which I can't believe she started - we are convinced that Lynne Cooper is responsible for giving away valuable and highly confidential information to the newspapers. You've no idea…'

The inspector sat down directly opposite the two Keynote directors, leaned back and took another deep breath.

'Gentlemen. I'm pleased to able to tell you that great strides have been made recently in the recruitment of police officers. Nowadays we can be practically certain that most, if not all of us can do basic reading. In the present context, this is a skill which has come in handy since we have been able to follow the copious amount of newsprint in the local and national press concerning your company. Let me see if I've got it right. You have lost a chemist – at least, he has disappeared, and you don't know where he is. Correct? Now, I can vouch for the fact that many people, when they have lost something valuable, a car, or a wife, say, they tend to call the police for help. However, we can find no evidence of your reporting a missing chemist to us, and that worries me.

Why not? Don't you care? Were you happy to see him go? Even worse, did you think it was waste of time because you don't think we are competent enough to find him anyway? Which is it?'

Brett answered after an awkward pause.

'We think he might be hiding. On purpose.'

'Ah yes. It's coming back to me. Secret formula, life-changing properties, extremely valuable. Safety first – keep out of the limelight – that it?'

'Yes.'

'So where does Lynne Cooper come in. Why do you think she gave you away?'

'The photocopier.'

'Pardon?'

'She used the photocopier to steal company secrets which she then passed on to the local newspaper.'

'How do you know it was her and not some other employee?'

'She's the only one that knows how to use the photocopier.'

'Come on! Even my kids know how to use a photocopier,' said Harris. 'You just have to push a button.'

'Not ours – it is – or was – password protected to prevent it from being misused.'

'So who, apart from Miss Cooper, knows the password?'

'Well, I do, but I'm probably the only one.'

The inspector and sergeant looked at each other in disbelief.

'What?' cried Gus 'You believe I, boss man, manging director do the photocopy? Why do I need *cazzo* password? And you speak to me, not just him.' (Pointing at Brett.) 'It's my company. Give me some attention.'

The inspector smiled.

'Don't worry Mr Volante - you can be sure that I will be giving you a *lot* of attention. Now, as I understand it, there was a cleaner involved.' (Looking at his notes). 'A Mrs Beresford? Cleaners sometimes work after hours. Did she, and if so, how did *she* get out of the building?'

'The cleaner comes in as soon as the production staff leave, but not before we do,' advised Brett. 'In any case, the latest cleaner was only working for us for a day – we sacked her when we discovered she had also stolen some valuable information…'

'Ah yes. Bits of pig in your cosmetics, wasn't it? Now that *is* interesting because she's a bit of an animal-lover, according to the paper. She might have joined your company with the specific intention of burning it down. Inside job. Where is she now? We're looking for her, or at least we should be.'

'No idea,' said Brett. 'Never even met her.'

'OK. But we will need to find her fairly quickly. So, now let's talk about Miss Curtis – haven't been able to interview her yet – bit too soon after her traumatic experience – but what was she doing in your office on her own a Sunday? Working perhaps?'

'No,' snapped Gus. 'She scared shitless. Hiding so bastards can't get her.'

'She was on a radio program,' explained Brett. 'As the result she got all kinds of threats. Notes through the door, anonymous letters, insulted in the street ... you name it.'

'Now *that* I can fully understand. Poor lady. But she could have come to us for help.'

'Hmpff,' was Gus's response.

'See if the car's ready sergeant. I think we have enough for now – let's get these gentlemen over to the hospital. I sincerely hope that Miss Curtis is not too badly injured.'

'Car available sir!'

Gus was the first down the stairs to get to it.

...

'*Madonna*!' cried Gus looking down at Beverly in her hospital bed. Her oxygen mask had been removed but it was hanging limply at her side attached to a cylinder.

Her eyes met his. No word was spoken.

'Who the fuck…?' She croaked. 'You?'

'Come on Bev,' said Brett. 'You can't really think that Gus set it alight. Are you in pain?'

Her eyes shifted to him.

'Fuck off.'

'Where were you?' asked Gus. 'When it happen?'

Bev closed her eyes. 'Your office.'

'You didn't see?'

'Just a fucking noise. Window broken. Smoke. Flames on the stairs.'

'They probably use petrol,' said Gus 'Make it spread more quickly.'

'How you feeling, Bev?' asked Brett.

'Fucking think?' Was the reply.

'Wadda we do now?' asked Gus. 'Jeez.'

'You fucking stupid?' croaked Beverly. 'Get a fucking cab!'

'To get you home?'

'No, idiot.'

Beverley paused for a fit of coughing and accepted Brett's offered glass of water from the bedside cabinet.

'I'm not sure what you are getting at, Beverley. Are you sure you're thinking straight? Perhaps you should get some more rest.'

'Get a cab,' she said hoarsely, 'back to the factory. With me so fucking far?'

'Go on,' said Brett.

'Then you get in through the back door... You have the other set of keys Gus?'

By 'other', Beverly was referring to a second set of factory keys which Gus kept in his flat, and which they hadn't bothered to inform the police about.

'Yes, but why? What you up to Beverly?'

'Because, you fucking idiots, we need to get our hands on those fucking bottles of red pig shit from the lab before those bastard coppers take them.'

'What will we do with them?'

Beverly looked at Brett in exasperation. 'Hide them of course, for fuck's sake.'

Her frustration caused another long coughing fit, which brought in a nurse.

'Sorry gents, I think that's enough for now. I'm going to have to throw you out. The doctor is on his round anyway.'

In the street outside, Brett, still not understanding, waved his hand at a passing taxi for the trip to Gus's flat.

...

Having consumed a couple of large whiskies to give them courage, Brett and Gus drove off in Gus's car, parking a couple of streets away from the factory entrance. As they strolled as nonchalantly as possible by the front doors, they noticed that these were now closed with police "keep out – restricted area" tape across them. A lone policeman was standing on the steps, studying his finger nails. It was easy for them to slip around the corner and through the locked gates into the factory yard using one of Gus's keys.

The small rear entrance factory door was secured only with a Yale lock. The door was situated in a wall of the production area, separating it from the yard, and was only used was by production staff popping out for a quick fag at break or lunch time. It took some time to find the correct key from his collection, but eventually and with a frighteningly loud squeal, it opened. George Patterson's small lab was next to the main filling area and the door was never locked. After a brief search, they found the two offending bottles on a top shelf. They secreted both into Brett's M&S shopping bag and made their escape, locking the door behind them.

## 14

Mary Ellis had finally found some time to relax. What better way than to ponder a chess puzzle on her computer with a glass of white wine on her desk in front of her. The sound of a blackbird in the garden and her husband Ralph's gently snoring in the lounge downstairs added to her enjoyment. Then the telephone rang. Who rings the telephone on Sundays?

'Hello?'

'In need of very posh lunch, sweetheart. Table booked for one thirty tomorrow. Jean-Georges restaurant at the Connaught. Bring that hubby of yours – don't want him thinking we're up to naughties.'

'Monty, I …' but he had put the phone down.

…

Ralph had had to close the shop early – something he hated to do because some of his customers came in late for their reserved papers and magazines. Consequently, he was not very happy, although the prospect of an expensive lunch and a meeting with Monty – whom he liked – helped to assuage his annoyance. Mary was also annoyed at being bullied once again by the *Informer*'s Editor-in-Chief. Still, needs must.

They swept by the top-hatted doorman and into the restaurant to find Monty already seated and accompanied by the wine waiter who was pouring out three glasses of red.

'What-ho folks!' he said cheerily – too cheerily for the suspicious Mary. Ralph, on the other hand was happy to shake Monty's hand with a certain amount of enthusiasm.

'Good to see you, Monty. Nice office you have here,' he said, waving his arms expansively around the restaurant.

'Just relax, Ralph. Put your feet on the table.'

'Don't even think about it!' warned Mary, aware that with her husband's bizarre idea of humour, he was quite capable of bypassing common sense.

'If you intend to put your feet on the table sir,' said a waiter, suddenly appearing at Ralph's elbow, 'we would be happy to supply you a suitably sized towel and a complimentary pair of slippers.' He was smiling. 'My name is Jan and it's my pleasure to be serving you today. Always a special pleasure to welcome you again Mr Meyer.'

'So, this *is* your office Monty,' said Ralph. 'Quite a menu for your lunchtime snack. What do you recommend?'

Jan having been instructed and dispatched, Mary turned her chair to enable her to face Monty directly.

'Mr Meyer – much as we love and adore you, it has to be noted that splashing out on an expensive lunch is not something that I would normally associate with you. Looking back, quite the reverse. If memory serves, burger and chips at a McDonalds is the only other time you've treated me to a company nosh, and that was over a year ago. You will forgive me, therefore, for suspecting that you are buttering us up for something – something you want us to do. Correct?'

'Mary. You've pained me. Cut to the quick. Show you my generous side, cheque book and wallet at the ready and what do I get? Low blow!'

Mary sighed.

'Come on Monty, they're not even *your* cheque book and wallet. I doubt whether you even have either. If the *Informer* is dipping into its vast funds to treat a couple of minor nonentities like us, then logic tells me there has to be a very good reason. So come on. Open up.'

'Incidentally, and for the avoidance of doubt,' said Ralph, 'I differ slightly from my wife. I'm always at the ready to accept whatever measure of generosity you happen to throw my way. I'm not proud.' And he clinked his glass with Monty's.

Monty grinned and took a long sip of wine and put the glass back down on the table slowly and with great apparent precision.

'Well. Matter of fact. Small favour required as it happens. This chap Patterson that all the fuss about?'

'Go on.'

'Everyone looking for his son. Simon.'

'They certainly are. The whole world is. Why, have you found him?'

'In a word, Old Sport, yes. Not only found but playing Mother Teresa to him.'

There was a slight pause while Mary and Ralph took this in.

'Bloody hell,' offered Ralph. 'How did you do that?'

'Best not to ask.'

'But I don't understand, Monty. If you've got him, why isn't it splashed all over the papers?' asked Mary. 'And what do you mean by playing Mother Teresa to him?'

'That's where you both come in.'

This time, the pause was longer.

'Go on, Monty.'

'Weird development. The Boss has discovered a conscience! Miracles do happen. Apparently. Can't be sure but... possibly something to do with his kids. Anyway, the order is 'hide the Patterson boy away until all this blows over.' I've been lumbered. God knows why *me*, but there it is.'

'Now wait a minute,' said Mary. 'If you are expecting us to take Simon Patterson into our home, even for a short time, you can forget it.'

'Yeah, can't be done,' agreed Ralph. 'Don't have the room for a start.'

'Children, children! No need to *adopt* him. Trust your uncle Monty. Have I ever let you down? Don't answer that.'

'What then?'

Monty took another sip.

'Found the blighter a bijou pad. Rent paid for six months. Quiet part of Brighton – street away from *your* palatial residence. Getting my drift?'

'Unfortunately, yes. Still don't like it,' said Mary.

'What do you want us to do – his shopping? Feed him? Keep him company?' asked Ralph.

'We've supplied more than enough loot for his own shopping. Just keep a weather eye, O.K.? He knows where you live – an occasional visit needed. Port in the storm if he gets into trouble – and then you let me know. Simple.'

'And what in it for me?'

'*Us*,' corrected Ralph.

'What I love about you two. Straight to the point. Did I tell you that I'm looking for a number of in-depth articles for the *Informer*, next few weeks? Any ideas you'd like to suggest?'

## 15

Lynne Cooper lived alone – she liked it that way, it gave her freedom to entertain friends, male and female, without having to worry about housemates. She had inherited a small, terraced house from an aunt together with a modest amount of cash, so she had no urgent need to find another job. She had been shaken by the warning from Miranda Stevens and Mike Davis and had consequently booked a two-week holiday in *Mykonos*, one of Greece's party islands. Far enough away, she thought, to be safe while the Keynote turmoil was going on. She had become nervous and fretful and had taken to looking out of the front window for suspicious characters in the street outside and not answering the door to strangers. Not surprisingly then, a loud knocking and a ringing of the bell on her front door in the middle of her holiday packing was enough to set her heart racing. The late afternoon was dark and her front room lights were on so her visitor knew she must be at home - and the knocking sounded urgent. What should she do? Heart racing, she approached the front door and called out without opening it.

'Yes? Who is it, please?'

The reply through the door was clear.

'I'm hoping to speak with Miss Lynne Cooper. Is she in, please?'

'Who are you and what do you want with her?'

'I'm a police officer. Here is my identification.'

A small black leather wallet was pushed through the letter box and fell onto the welcome mat, displaying POLICE in large silver letters on the front.

'You'll find my photograph and number inside. You can phone 911 to confirm it's genuinely me if you wish. I'm happy to wait.'

Lynne opened the flap. *'Detective Chief Inspector C.M Pedersen'* with a full-faced picture of a good-looking blond man.

Lynne felt herself relax slightly, but what on earth did the police want to speak to her about? Oh God! Bloody Keynote. She'd just been reading about the fire. Must be. But what had *she* done? A chief inspector as well…

After a moment's further hesitation while she gathered herself together, she unlocked and opened the door to reveal the inspector and a uniformed female officer.

'Sorry…'

'No need to apologise. Miss Cooper, is it? I fully understand your hesitation. You are taking sensible precautions.'

Lynne's brain was still racing.

'Er… I'm a bit confused. Have I done something?'

Pedersen smiled.

'No. It's just that I'm conducting a police enquiry and I'm hoping you may be able to help me with it. I've a few routine questions for you – shouldn't take long. We're not here to charge you or anything. This is police constable Sally Payne. She won't mind you calling her Sally. You didn't bring any handcuffs with you, did you constable?'

'No sir. Sorry. Left them in my locker.'

'There you are Miss Cooper - we promise not to lock you up.'

'How can I help you?'

In spite of her nervous state of mind, Lynne found herself attracted to the tall, handsome police inspector.

'Just a few routine questions. We're happy to chat here in the comfort of your own home, but if that's not convenient, we can always go down to the station.'

'No. Come in. Excuse the mess, I'm packing at the moment. Please find a chair - if you can. Remove any junk on it.'

'These are really nice', said the PC, carefully moving a pile of folded tee shirts form a chair onto a nearby table. 'I certainly wouldn't call them junk.'

'Are you holidaying or just visiting friends or family?' asked Pedersen.

'Holidaying. Greece.'

'Very nice. When are you going and how long for?'

'Why are you asking? Have I done anything wrong?'

'Just curious. Done a bit of holidaying in Greece myself.'

'Me too. Don't think much of their wine though,' grinned the PC.

'OK if I sit here?' Pedersen descended onto a kitchen chair. 'Miss Cooper – is it alright if I call you Lynne?'

Lynne nodded.

'Lynne, I'm sure you can hazard a guess as to what this is all about. A company you recently worked for has been subjected to an arson attack which has injured another employee and might have killed her. No need to tell you this is serious, and my job is to find the person or persons responsible. Now, let's be clear. Nobody is accusing you anything, but as an ex-employee we have to eliminate you from a list of what we call 'persons of interest'. You might have some bits of information that could help us fill in some of the gaps in our understanding. Are you OK with that?'

'I'm not sure I can help much, but I will if I can.'

'That's exactly what we wanted to hear. I am sure you will answer as truthfully and completely as possible.'

In spite of herself, Lynne was trembling slightly.

'It's alright Lynne,' said the PC. 'There is absolutely nothing for you to worry about. As the inspector said, it's just a process of elimination.'

'Nothing to worry about? You really think I'm capable of setting fire to a factory? Look at me!'

Pedersen shock his blond head.

'No Lynne. No. I don't. But, as I say, you just might have some information that will help us find the true culprits. It's often the case that seemingly unimportant bits of memory can unexpectedly supply missing bits of the jigsaw puzzle. I'm sorry if we've startled you, but I thought it would be best to set things out clearly in order for you to understand what is going on. Perhaps a cup of tea? Can you oblige, Sally?'

'No. I don't want a cup of tea. Let's just get this over with.'

'Quite right. Sorry sir, but you may have been watching too many cliché-ridden TV cops programs,' said Sally, smiling. 'But try and calm down a bit, Lynne – believe me it'll make things go quicker.'

Pedersen sighed.

'OK. Let's start with your employment at Keynote Cosmetics. You were a receptionist?'

'Yes.'

'The only receptionist. There were no others?'

'No. Just me.'

'What exactly did you do?'

'How do you mean, what did I do?'

'What did the job entail? Describe a day's work.'

'Answer the telephone, look after visitors. What else would you expect?'

'What does 'look after' mean?'

'I would have thought that was obvious. Check if they have an appointment. Who with? Put them in touch – it's not rocket science.'

'What sort of visitors – customers?'

'Sometimes, but mainly sales reps looking to sell chemicals or packaging.'

Pedersen made a note.

'Tell me about the chemical reps – who did they call to see?'

'The chemist of course. There was nobody else who knew about chemicals.'

'The chemist – George Patterson.'

'Yes.'

'Did any of the chemical reps ever get angry – if they were unable to get a sale, for example.'

'Yes of course, that's human nature, isn't it?' Lynne was beginning to see where the questioning was heading. 'But none of them angry enough to burn the factory down for Chrissake! Wouldn't be much use for future business would it, destroying your customers premises?'

Pedersen let that pass.

'What about other Keynote employees, Lynne. Any of them have a particular grudge against the company?'

'Can't speak for all of them, but nobody I know are likely to have done it. They all had grumbles – didn't like the managers and the way they sometimes got treated, that sort of thing – but that's the same in any company, isn't it?'

'What about you, Lynne. How were you treated? Not very well I suspect since they sacked you without pay.'

Lynne was about to admit her intense dislike of Beverly Curtis, but remembering that Curtis was the person that was nearly killed in the fire, she decided to reach for a half open pack of Polo mints on the table instead. Care was needed.

'I felt pretty much the same way about them as everyone else. The senior person that most of us got on with was George Patterson, to be honest. The only director most people came into contact with was Mr Kander when he was showing customers around.'

'OK. Let's get back to your day job, Lynne. Answering telephone, greeting visitors, anything else?'

'Such as?'

'Any paperwork? Typing – that sort of thing? According to my information, the company didn't employ any secretarial staff.'

'An occasional bit of typing, yes. Most people did their own.'

'So, you had a typewriter?'

'Yes.'

'Photocopier?'

'Yes. I was put in charge of that.'

'Just the one?'

'Come on inspector, why would we need more than one?'

'Agreed. So, one photocopier and you were in charge of it. Nobody else was allowed to use it?'

'No just me.'

'Because?'

Lynne really didn't want to go into details of her adventures with the photocopier. Not that she would get embarrassed, but for present purposes, she felt the need to paint a picture of herself as a sensible, reliable hard-working employee.

'Too many people were just making… inappropriate or unnecessary use of it. Photocopying personal documents, that sort of thing. The management was complaining about the wastage, so they put me in sole charge.'

'Nobody else was allowed to operate it? Ever?'

'Correct.'

'What about when you were away from reception – lunch time or going to the ladies?'

'No, they installed some security device - software. You needed a password, otherwise you couldn't turn it on.'

'And only you knew the password?'

'As far as I know – I set the original password anyway. There might have been some way to override it – I don't know. I can't imagine Beverly Curtis being happy about me being the only password holder.'

'Sounds like Beverly Curtis didn't trust you?'

'She didn't trust anyone...' Lynne just stopped herself from adding 'the bitch!'

Pedersen paused as he wrote more into his notebook.

'We will come back to your relationship with Miss Curtis a bit later. But for the moment, back to the photocopier. You say you put the original code in the security device?'

'Yes.'

'So it was vital you remembered it, if only you knew what it was. Do you have a good memory, or did you write it down somewhere?'

'No. I kept it very simple. I thought the whole password idea was stupid and unnecessary anyway.'

'Can you still remember it?'

'Yes. I can tell you what it was – no use now is it? It was just 1234.'

'Thank you, Lynne. That was very interesting.'

Another pause for note writing. Then the inspector sat back in his chair.

'Well. TV cops or not, quite frankly, I could now do with a cup of tea!'

Lynne made to stand up, but Sally was quicker.

'I'll do it – tea, cups and sugar Lynne? Milk in the fridge I expect.'

'In the cupboard over the microwave,' said Lynne resuming her pose with her hands folded in her lap.

'Lynne, Mrs Edna Beresford...'

'Yes.'

'How did you meet her?'

Lynne was now getting annoyed.

'You *know* how I met her. She came for a job as a cleaner. Look, can we stop wasting time with all these questions that you probably already know the answer to?'

Pedersen spread his arms and inclined his head slightly to one side.

'I met Mrs Beresford when she came to replace our cleaning lady, Mrs Patel. I was given the job of showing her the ropes – where everything was and what she had to do.'

'Why you?'

'Why me? I guess there was nobody else available and I've always been the dogsbody.'

'You had never met her before?'

'I told you, no.'

'So how did she know your previous cleaner – Mrs Patel wasn't it?'

'I don't really see the point of that question. As far as I know, they used to go to bingo together.'

'Mrs Beresford is quite an animal lover, isn't she?'

'I don't know.'

'And Mrs Patel – was she an animal lover too?'

'I have absolutely no idea. I don't have much in common with the cleaners and I'm not usually in the main building when they are cleaning anyway.'

'Right. And Mrs Patel left the company – because?'

'As far as I know, she went back to India with her son.'

Pedersen looked down at his notes.

'Ah yes, Raj Patel. Didn't he used to be the warehouse manager?'

'Yes. Look, what has that got to do with the fire? He couldn't have started it from India, could he?'

'Not if he's *genuinely* in India, no. So, Mrs Beresford got the job and she started when?'

'The day after.'

'The day after you – showed her the ropes, you mean? And you say that you're not normally in the building when the cleaner is working?'

'Correct. I had gone home. Apart from one or other of the directors, the cleaner is last to leave the building in the evening.'

'A new cleaner, left alone in the building on her first evening?'

'That's the way it always worked with Mrs Patel. All the important doors – access to the factory and management offices etcetera is – was - not possible. Everything got locked up before people left.'

'Not the laboratory, obviously.'

'No. Mr Patterson was a bit messy and often spilt stuff on to the floor. He nearly slipped over more than once so it was decided to get the cleanser to give the floor a quick once-over before she finished.'

'Right, and when she finished, the cleaner would just close the front door behind her when she left?'

'Yes. It locked automatically – or was supposed to.'

The two policemen looked at each other with raised eyebrows.

'*Supposed* to- that's about right, Lynne. What I'm hearing is that it is remarkably easy to get in and out of the building without a key.'

'I know what you're interested in – the jars of pig stuff. That's got nothing, repeat, absolutely *nothing* to do with me. My job was, as I've said, just to get her started. I didn't even see her come in the next evening when she started work. End of.'

'Well, since you mentioned them, let's go back to those containers which you describe as containing pig stuff. Did you know about them before the cleaner found them?'

'No. Mr Patterson kept himself to himself. I don't think I ever went into the lab – except just to show the new cleaner the state of the floor. As far as I recall, there were no such jars on the lab bench, and I never looked up at any of the shelves.'

'Nor did Mrs Beresford?'

'No – she just commented that the floor was going to be a job to get clean.'

The uniformed PC re-appeared from the kitchen with a tray of teacups, which she plonked down noisily on the table.

'Help yourselves,' she suggested unnecessarily.

'Let's be clear,' said Pedersen, cup in hand. 'When Mrs Beresford found those containers, you say you were not in the building?'

'I went home as soon as she arrived on her first day. By the time she'd started on the lab floor – her last job, I was at home.'

Pedersen nodded.

'Well, you may not know this, Lynne, but those piggy containers have now gone missing.'

'You mean she stole them after she'd photocopied the labels?'

'No. They were removed afterwards by someone who knew about a back door to the factory and had a key to unlock it.'

'You don't mean you think... I've never had any keys...'

'Once again Lynne, I don't think it was you, and to be honest, the theft of a couple of jars from the laboratory is not my main concern. But graffiti daubed on the factory wall just before or after the fire, presumably written by the arsonists, refers to 'A present for animal torturers.' So, a possible connection between those jars and the whoever started the fire is an obvious possibility.'

'Mrs Beresford was known to be an animal lover with a tendency to support local animal rights groups,' said Sally. 'And she photocopied those labels on the jars from the laboratory. But she didn't steal the jars – that happened later.'

'So, you tell me that you are in sole charge of Keynote's only photocopier, but unless Mrs Beresford had one of her own, a fair conclusion is that those labels were copied on *your* machine. Right?' continued Pedersen.

'Yes…I suppose so.' Hesitantly.

'So did you copy the labels for her?'

'No. I told you. I wasn't even in the building.'

'In that case,' said PC Sally, 'since you are the only person with a password to use the machine, how did she manage to do the photocopying?'

'To be fair to Mrs Beresford,' said Pedersen, 'she is not of the generation or disposition likely to be able to hack into the machine's software, is she?'

Lynne had returned to looking down at her hands clasped tightly together in her lap.

'No.'

'So – if it wasn't you, as you say, how did she do it?'

Silence.

Pedersen sighed, put his cup down and leaned forward across the table.

'Lynne, I don't want to frighten you and you should clearly understand that you don't have to answer any of my questions or submit to any more questioning. Tell us to leave and we will. But if I get the impression that you may be withholding valuable information, that would place doubts on the whole of your testimony and that risks our coming back with a charge sheet, and *that* would change everything. We would have to caution you, and you would probably need to have the support of a solicitor. If you lie then or withhold information which you know to be of importance you may be further charged with the offence of perverting the course of justice, which is punishable by a prison sentence. Just remember that the perpetrators of this arson attack may be charged with attempted murder. Now, I'm not deliberately trying to intimidate you – just telling you what could or what's likely to happen. But none of us want that, Lynne. So please, Lynne, for all our sakes, how did Mrs Beresford or someone else photocopy those labels on the containers?'

'I… I may have shown her. Not on purpose. By accident. I didn't know what she was going to do, did I?'

'Go on.'

'She was interested in a picture I had on the wall. It was a print of a dog with a gerbil and a chinchilla She spotted it – apparently, she used to have a copy herself, but she had lost it. So I… made a photocopy of it for her.'

'And she watched you do the copy?'

'Yes… several times actually, I had to make some adjustments to the intensity to get it to come out right.'

'And every time, you needed to put the password in?'

'Yes.'

'Just 1234?'

'Yes.'

'What do you think PC Payne?'

'I think we've got the answer to our problem, sir.'

Pedersen stood up and started to gather up his notes replacing his teacup on the tray.

'You know Lynne, I've never met Mrs Beresford. She's disappeared temporarily but she'll easily be found. All the information I have about her comes from a local newspaper reporter. As Sally has already said, it seems she was quite active in the animal rights movement – used to complain to the paper about animal mistreatment on a frequent basis and she used to distribute leaflets for the *Justice for Animals* organisation. Heard of them?'

Lynne felt as though she had just been kicked in the stomach. She had been desperate to keep her visit to *Justice for Animals* a secret so as not to be seen as an animal's rights campaigner. Now what did she do? If she continued to keep quiet and the police found out, she could be guilty of just what the Inspector had just been talking about. What was it? Perverting the course of justice with a prison sentence?

'Did you say that she had disappeared?'

'Mrs Beresford? Yes. One of the growing list. George Patterson and his wife for starters. Nobody seems to know where their son is either. You don't happen to have a clue, do you?'

'No. I never even met him.'

'Thought not.'

'Mrs Beresford is probably going to be less of a problem. Our local newspaper reporter thinks she may be visiting some of her relatives.'

'So… are you out looking for them?'

'Me personally? No. We've got something called the NCA who are experts in finding people. They are out looking as we speak. Why do you ask? Are you worried about Mrs B?'

'Well… you know you asked her about her connection with *Justice for Animals*?'

'Go on.'

Then, hesitantly 'I happen to know that she went to a meeting with them.'

'Interesting. So not just leaflets then – active contact. That changes things.'

'How did you know about the meeting, Lynne?' asked Sally.

Lynne hesitated again. She now had no choice if she was not going to risk an outright lie.

'Because I went with her. Please believe me, I'm not a member of the organisation and I don't even agree with everything they say or do. I only went to… to look after Mrs. Beresford. Edna.'

Detective Chief Inspector C.M. Pedersen sat down again and re-opened his notebook.

'Go on Lynne.'

'The honest truth is that I felt sorry for her, and I sort of felt responsible for the mess I thought she might be getting into – you know, with the containers and everything.'

'So?'

'I sent her a letter. After I'd left the company, just really to find out how she was. She agreed to meet me. I think she felt it was her fault that I got the sack. That shows you she's got a heart.'

'Where?'

'Pardon?'

'Where did you meet with Mrs Beresford?'

'Oh, just at a local café – *Rosie's*, I think it's called.'

'I know it,' revealed Sally. 'They do great blueberry muffins.'

'So Lynne, there you were, face to face with Mrs Beresford in Rosie's café where they sell great blueberry muffins. And what did you talk about?'

'My concern was that they might find out that she was the one who found the containers, and that she would be hassled as the result, and frankly, I don't think she would be up to coping with that on her own.'

'Who might find out and who might hassle her?'

'I don't know – the newspapers probably. The story was all over them.'

'Yes. I see. Go on.'

'Well, it seems like the animal rights people had already found out, and they were asking for a meeting with her.'

'This would be the *Justice for Animals* organisation?'

'Yes. The local branch of it I think, anyway.'

'And how do you think they found out about Mrs Beresford's link to the containers before the press?'

'I think she must have told them. She told me she used to speak to a lady at *Justice for Animals* quite regularly. A Doctor Kelly – I met her.'

Sally was thumbing through the pages of her notebook at speed.

'I've already looked her up, sir. 'Ruth W. Ellis, co-founder and Vice President of *Justice for Animals,* UK. She has a PhD in *Animal Biology and Ethology*, from *Oxford University*.'

'Thanks constable. And what do we know about *Justice for Animals?*'

'As you see, sir, they're already on our radar. There will be lot more information back at the ranch. However, I quote from their leaflet: *'JFA is a non-profit making charity whose aim is to educate the public about cruel practices involving animals and promote the right of all animals to be treated with respect. We believe in non-violent protest'*.'

'Non-violent? What did that graffiti say? *A present for animal torturers. Stop now or there will be more*? That's if they were the actual arsonists of course. What did you make of them, Lynne? Non-violent? How many of them were at the meeting?'

'As far as I can remember there were five of them, including Dr Kelly. But the only one I found a bit frightening was a guy with a squeaky voice – he sounded quite potentially violent.'

'I'm going to need a list of their names.'

'They didn't use surnames – but I think I can remember their first names.'

'When are you leaving for Greece, Lynne?' asked Sally.

'Tomorrow. Flight leaves Gatwick at about 2 pm.'

'Before you go,' said Pedersen, 'I want as detailed account as possible of that meeting. What was discussed, more information about who they were, whether they had any plans that were discussed etc. PC Payne will come around tomorrow morning to collect it.'

'OK. I'll do as best I can.'

'I believe you will. And that is the reason why I'm allowing you to go on an overseas holiday. Your frank admission about your meeting and your clear account of your relationship with Mrs Beresford has led me to believe your full account. I hope I'm not wrong. In any case, I will need your home phone number and one where I can reach you on holiday, if you have one. I also need the address of the place or places where you will be staying in Greece. Please tell me you understand and will comply.'

'Yes, of course. Do you want them now?'

'No, the PC will collect that information with your report tomorrow. Meantime, I want you to make a note of my police identification number from my warrant card. If you think of anything else that might be useful or for any other reason you want to contact me, all you have to do is dial 101 and give the operator my number – they'll put you straight through to me. OK?'

Lynne nodded.

'Well, it only remains for us to wish you happy holiday and to thank you for your voluntary co-operation. If you feel that we have not treated you properly, you can contact the Police Complaints organisation, the IPOC. Just fill in a complaints form.'

'That won't be necessary Inspector. I really don't feel that you have bullied me or anything.'

'Excellent. Well, goodbye for now. You will meet with PC Payne tomorrow morning.'

'Not too early I hope.'

The PC smiled.

'Ten o'clock suit you?'

# 16

*Bath Centrum University* was not situated in *Bath* and was certainly not central to anything. It wouldn't even have become a university had it not unjustly benefited from the Further and Higher Education Act of 1992 which carelessly converted it from a minor polytechnic, its true status, into an independent university, a wholly doubtful one. The entire University was actually contained in one large mansion estate some three miles from Bath City centre. This provided one of the few advantages of studying at *BCU* because it was able to provide agreeable accommodation for all its students within its campus. In Simon Patterson's case, this amounted to a small but comfortable single bedsitter which opened directly onto a large kitchen which he shared with three other students.

Since learning about his parents' disappearance and the commotion that resulted from it, Simon, in a confused state of mind, had taken to his bed, where he curled himself up into a ball like a threatened hedgehog. Sleep, which had always been a problem, had now become almost absent from his life. He was consequently wide awake in bed at six thirty in the morning when he heard a soft knocking on his door. He sat up, heart pounding. Who the hell could that be? It was holiday time and all of his housemates were away. In view of the fuss created by his parents' disappearance and the warning he had received about possible consequences, his first thought was to ignore the knocking and pretend not to be in. But the knocking was very gentle, as if his visitor was being careful not to wake him should he still be asleep. Maybe he'd better answer it in case it was something important – a letter perhaps. So thinking, he grabbed his scruffy dressing gown and donned it as he stumbled to the door and opened it.

'Hello Simon,' said Sophie with a smile. 'I hope this is not too much of a shock.'

She was wearing a lilac, very short mini-dress and her eyes and long blond hair were sparkling in the morning sunlight.

Simon's gasp was audible as he stepped back in disbelief.

'Could you spare me a few moments?' she asked. 'We could talk out here in the kitchen if you would prefer.'

'Sophie – what the hell do *you* want? Give me a minute to gather my thoughts and get dressed.'

'Sure. I'll make us some coffee if I can figure out how to do it.'

Just when it seemed impossible for Simon to become more confused than he already was, Sophie, the physical embodiment of his imaginary lover, *Lisa* was on his doorstep and waiting for him. But *that* Sophie, the Lisa/Sophie whom he'd adored and fallen instantly in love with had gone. This new Sophie was the one who had manipulated him, filling him with false hopes and promises.

The aroma of the freshly made coffee hit him as he re-opened his bedroom door. She was sitting at the large circular table in the centre of the kitchen and smiling at him. But Simon's anger had pulled a shutter down. This woman was too perfect. Impervious and impregnable. Beautiful but as cold and hard as a china doll.

His thoughts had now been well and truly gathered, and what he was feeling was anger.

'Not again Sophie,' he said, standing aggressively over her. '*Never* again. What is it you want now?'

'I don't blame you for being mad at me, Simon. I expected it.'

She pushed a full cup towards him - an invitation for him to sit down.

'I've nothing to say to you. Haven't you tormented me enough?'

Sophie paused, and then gently, 'Yes Simon. More than enough – and that's partly why I'm here. To apologise sincerely for what we did. It was cruel, and if I'd known beforehand what sort of person you are, I would have refused to do it.'

'That's no compensation, Sophie.'

'No. I guess not. But I want you to believe that my apology, and that of my brother are both sincere.'

'And what about you father?'

Sophie sighed.

'My father, Simon, who I love dearly, nevertheless operates and lives in another dimension entirely. He will not apologise. I don't think he's capable of it.'

'Well, thank you for *your* apology. If that's it, I'd like you to leave now.'

'Give me some space, Simon. That's *not* it. That's *far* from it. I want to tell you about my father.'

Simon gasped in exasperation.

'I already know about your bloody father. I read about him and to be brutally honest, I was never much interested in him in the first place. Having met him, my honest opinion is that he is a shit. Why would I want to hear more about him?'

'I understand why you would feel that way Simon, I really do. But you see, that's exactly why I wanted to talk to you about him. I think you deserve to know why he's done what he's done.'

'How can I make you understand that I don't give a fuck about him – or you, for that matter. Not anymore. There was a time when I... well, it doesn't matter now. That's all changed.'

'Just give me five minutes Simon. Just five minutes. Then if you still want me to go, I will.'

He slumped down on a kitchen chair and folded his arms.

'Five minutes. I'm listening.'

'As I've said, he won't apologies for what he's put you through and I can't pretend to apologise for him. For people like him, empathy is in short supply – from his point of view, you are just collateral damage. His world is dominated by one thing – beating his rivals. The overriding objective is simply to outstrip everyone else. Personal considerations, family and children very much take the back seat simply because he hasn't got time for them. Business is his first love – family is lower down the list. That's why my mother and his previous wives divorced him.'

'And this is a man you dearly love? A father who puts family second to business? Money before love? How much money does he need for God's sake? Hasn't he got enough to retire on and spend some time with you?'

Sophie shifted her position revealing even more of her perfect legs as she did so.

'It's not about money, Simon. That would be too easy. It's about passion and desire for the winning, the beating of competitors and the joy of creating the means of doing it. I know. I've spoken with him about it many times. Please believe me, it's not his conscious fault. He can't help it – it's embedded in his DNA. It doesn't mean that he doesn't love me in return, it's just that love often - usually - gets in the way.'

'Boy! And I thought *I* had problems with my parents.'

'You *have* got problems with your parents, Simon. I've checked up on your background. Your problems are different from mine, but in a way, they are the same. Marc and I have played second fiddle to business interests; in your case, it's second fiddle to alcohol. But in many ways it's the same issue, the same pain and the same effect on your personal life. And in your case, the fact that both of your parents have disappeared only adds a degree of complexity to that. No wonder you are angry. Of the two of us, I think you have by far the worse deal.'

She picked up her cup and walked over to the kitchen worktop to re-fill it. Simon had not touched his.

'This is all very interesting, but you still haven't told me why you're really here. I can't believe it's just to swop family problem stories.'

Sophie remained standing.

'Actually, in a way, it is. Let's go back to the beginning. The chemist from a small cosmetic company has disappeared and someone has discovered some dodgy-looking jars filled with red goo and labelled 'Pigs in Castor Oil'. Shock and horror but only on a local scale. One article in the local paper, a few letters of disgust, and a week later, all has been forgotten and attention has turned to… potholes in the high street, or a hundred other local stories. Right?'

'If you say so.'

'But this particular local story was destined, by pure chance, to come to the attention of my father. I think someone wrote an amusing letter about it, and probably passed it on, thinking Dad might find it amusing.'

'So?'

'So simply put, Dad decided that he was going to blow the story up into a major national, if not international story using many of the enormous resources available to him. And the obvious question is…?'

'Why?'

'Correct. And the answer is, I don't know. I studied psychology at Uni, and I can tell you that *nobody* understands the way that the brains of people like my dad work. He saw a list of ingredients. Missing persons, bits of animals in cosmetics, protests – animal rights, consumer outrage, game changing cosmetic wonder cream. Raw materials with which to construct something he felt would be new, original, exciting in its own way. And he has the power to do it.'

'Did he ever think about how it would affect all the people involved?'

'No. Absolutely not. As he told you, he is not the slightest bit interested in you or your family except in so far as you are part of the collection of ingredients. You, Simon, may have been damaged – your life may have been ruined but as I say, you are just collateral damage. Inevitable in a time of war. And that is where I come in, and why I've come here today.'

'I can't believe this – have you come here to gloat?'

Sophie walked slowly over and put her hand on Simon's shoulder. He could feel the warmth of her body and sense her fragrance.

'Quite the reverse, Simon, I assure you.'

She sat down next to him.

'After you'd gone from our meeting, I had a chat with dad – mainly about you and what we had done to you. I told him that I felt dreadful, and we ought to do something to help.'

'So, this is about easing your conscience, is it?'

Sophie sighed.

'Yes, I can't deny it. He agreed, and that was a double whammy for me. As you say, I'm trying to massage my conscience, but it also proved to me that my father actually *does* possess some kind of empathy - something that, over the years, I've reason to doubt. It might only be some intellectual sort of empathy, but he saw my point and agreed with me that we should help you.'

'What makes you think I want or need help from you and your bloody father?'

Her long blonde hair swayed as she shook her head.

'Look, it's an offer – and I sincerely hope that you will accept it. I think you are in a dangerous and vulnerable situation at the moment and I – or rather we, my brother, father and I – fear for your safety. There are a great many people looking for you and some of them will stop at nothing to get at what they think you have.'

It was Simon's turn to stand up. He went over to the window and stared out at the lawn below.

'You bastards have got me exactly where you want me, haven't you?'

'When you hear what I've come to offer you Simon, I hope you will see that there are no strings attached. Look on it as *my* offer – not my father's. He sanctioned it, but that was the only part he played. Honestly.'

'I suppose you *still* think I know where my father with his stupid magic formula is hiding, right? Well, sorry to disappoint you. I don't know where he is and if I'm honest, I don't really care.'

'Sorry, but you are wrong Simon. Frankly I don't believe a word of the magic cream story. All I am interested in is getting you safe somewhere. My father also agreed to keep your whereabouts – and your storyline – out of the papers.'

Simon turned away from the window to face her.

'You really think I'm in danger? This is not another kind of trick of yours?'

'The time for tricks is over. I'm serious – please listen to what's on offer.'

Simon retuned to the table and sat down on the opposite side as far away as possible.

'OK.'

Sophie reached into her bag, removed a large brown envelope and opened it.

'Firstly, a debit card,' she said, laying it on the table. 'It's in the name of Patrick Scott and gives you access to a NatWest bank account containing seven hundred pounds sterling. The pin number is the first four figures of your birth date. We have rented a safe, anonymous apartment for you in a quiet area near Brighton – it's an *Airbnb* rental, and the owner is away for six months, so no rent to pay. A car will pick you up later this morning at 10 o'clock to take you there. That should give you time to pack - and the driver will help you load if needed. When you get there, someone will greet you and make sure you have everything you need. He or she will also be able to help should you run out of money, but you must only use the account for essentials. The address is on this piece of paper, which you should destroy once you have remembered it. OK so far?'

Simon was speechless. He was not expecting this.

'Next is the difficult part, Simon. You need to abandon your name. This can obviously be used to trace you. From now on, you are Patrick Scott. When you get to Brighton, your helper will supply you with a telephone registered in your 'new' name. You will have to use only this for a while - until it all blows over. For your own safety, don't use it to call friends or family, but it *will* give you access to local help. Be careful how you use it. Any questions?'

'Christ Sophie, what do you expect me to say? It seems like you've got everything mapped out and me by the balls. What if I refuse?'

'That's entirely down to you Simon. You can just tell the driver no and walk away. But if you do that, it's the end of any help I or my family can offer you. You'd be entirely on your own.'

Sophie collected her bag, stood up and walked to the door. And spoke over her shoulder.

'I hope you accept our offer, for all our sakes, Simon.'

Then, almost as an afterthought, she turned, walked back to Simon, leaned over and gave him a soft but firm kiss on his forehead.

'Good luck, Si. Hold on, it'll soon be over.'

And with that, she left.

...

The journey from Bath to Brighton took just under three hours, and Simon slept most of the way. As promised, the apartment was on the middle floor of a substantial, end-terraced house in a quiet street, well away from any main road. He followed the driver up two flights of stairs and between them, they deposited his meagre collection of belongings on the landing. Then, with a brief wave of his hand, the driver disappeared.

Simon took a deep breath and tried the door handle, which turned easily, causing the door to open slightly. Expecting an empty room, he pushed the door fully open, picked up his backpack and walked into the room.

'Hi Simon,' said a voice.

Looking up he saw the owner, a slightly tubby, middle-aged, bespectacled man wearing a warm smile and a casual jacket and offering a hand in greeting.

'Welcome to Brighton. I think you were told to expect me. I'm Ralph, and I run a little newsagent round the corner. Pleased to meet you. Do come in – I'll help you with your luggage.'

# 17

At midday during the working week, the lounge bar of the *King George Hotel* in East London's *Bow Road* is usually deserted. Should you be looking for somewhere to have a clandestine meeting, this large room with its fading wallpaper, elderly, polished wooden tables and uncomfortable chairs would be the ideal place to have it. This is precisely why the three directors of the similarly disintegrating Keynote Cosmetics Company had gathered here to have such a meeting. No policemen, no newspaper reporters.

Gus Volante, attired in an old open neck shirt with his vest showing beneath it had temporarily abandoned his usual penchant for sartorial elegance. Brett Kander, unable to shake off his in-built sardonic smile, sat to his left at the round table. On his right sat Beverly Curtis, recently released from hospital. She looked dreadful and when she spoke it was in an unrecognisably hoarse voice interspersed with occasional coughing.

'You sure you should be here, Bev?' asked Brett.

'What else am I going to fucking do?' was her response. 'Leave you two to fuck everything up?'

'Your voice, she still sounds no good,' said Gus, unnecessarily. 'Maybe you should be at home.'

Beverly made use of an aerosol inhaler before answering.

'That better?' she enquired, sounding a little less hoarse.

'That smoke must have damaged your throat,' said Brett. 'Do they think you will recover – get your old voice back?'

Beverly drew her shoulders back and the other two waited for another outburst of abuse.

'OK. Thanks, OK? I hear your concern. I'm a bit tired and sore,' she said gently, 'but I'm going to feel a lot better once we've made some fucking decisions here. I'm not sure you idiots understand what a bloody mess we're in.'

Brett and Gus looked at each other.

'Look, if you've got something useful to say, spill it out Beverly,' said the Australian, rapidly losing his sympathy. 'We need to get our thinking straight. You got any more brilliant ideas?'

Beverly ignored the question.

'What's happening at the factory?' she asked.

'Full of policemen,' growled Gus. 'We were there this morning. You tell, Brett.'

Brett paused to calm himself down.

'Not much going on, Bev. Manufacture wise, there's a small amount of cream-making going on, but very much winding down. We are not going to get any more business in the near future I'm afraid. Parts of the building are still cordoned off – the reception area of course, where they are still investigating the fire. The main manufacturing area and the warehouse are still accessible, but frankly, even if we had George back, I can't see how we can survive with the amount of business we have.'

'Are all the rest of the staff still in?' asked Beverley.

'Not all of them. There's a little bit of work for the filling line, but that will finish by the end of the week. Some of them have stayed away after being questioned by the police – they're very upset and worried by that.'

'Questioned? About what?'

Gus put his head in his hands.

'So, I lose everything. Maybe we sell off the equipment?'

'Peanuts, Gus. Second hand market is overflowing with good quality stuff. The only idea I can come up with is that we close down the filling lines and just become a bulk manufacturer. Just creams and alcohol-based stuff.'

'Hmm. What you think Bev?'

'You honestly think we can make a living on bulk fucking manufacturing, Kander? You're out of your fucking mind as usual,' was the hoarse response.

'So. Nothing eh? I just go down the pan – all my money gone. You two walk away, yes? Get another job. Me? I kill myself. Thank you very much.'

'Gus, that's not fair,' said Brett. 'I've been racking my brains… But the situation is desperate. If we're not careful, we could all end up in prison with that crazy magic cream story of Beverly's. That's probably business fraud or corruption, and as directors, we are all liable. So it's *not* just you Gus. We're all in this shit together.'

'Brett. I ask you again. What were the staff questioned about by the bloody police?' insisted Beverley.

'Er... about where they were when the fire started - that sort of thing. That's what got them upset. Some of them thought they were under suspicion of starting it. And apparently, they were also questioned about the disappearance of the containers.'

'They also asked about that?'

'Yes. Quite aggressively apparently. I think the police are quite embarrassed about not collecting the jars until it was too late – bit of police incompetence. Someone probably got a bollocking for that.'

'They think someone took them, what... for fun? Or do they think they might be valuable?'

'How do I know? Anyway, just to remind you, *we've* got them. And I want to know what the hell we are going to do with them.'

'Listen,' said Gus, 'we have to make sure nobody find those damn containers. If damn police get them, we finished. *Finito.* What are English jails like?'

'OK... but I'm not sure I fully understand, though...,' said Brett. 'If they *do* contain pig bits, then that just backs up our story, doesn't it?'

'Yes. But if they don't? You crazy if you think Patterson was playing with animal bits. And he puts them on a damn shelf – not even in a fridge *per amor di Dio*!'

'Gus is right,' croaked Beverly. 'That's why I had to tell you idiots to grab them before the police did.'

'So, you never believed the story then?'

'Are all Australians as thick as you?'

Gus banged the table.

'Enough! We work together, OK? So, Brett, you take the containers. You still 'ave them, yes?'

'Oh my God! You gave them to Brett to look after? What have you done with them, put them in your fucking window as ornaments?'

Brett sighed.

'No Bev, I've hidden them.'

'At home?'

'Yes. They are under a pile of stinging nettles in my garden waste bin.'

'Great, there'll be bugs crawling all over them.'

'Once again Bev, no. They are inside a plastic bag. Give me a break, will you?'

'So, the bin she get emptied, and we lose the damn lot?'

'You as well Gus? You guys really think I'm stupid, don't you? No, the bin I've got them in is *not* the one that gets emptied. They are safe – for the moment.'

Beverley was the first to beak silence after a long pause.

'Have you two been questioned about it? About the 'missing' containers?'

Gus shook his head and frowned.

'No.'

'Me neither,' said Brett.

'Don't you think that's bloody strange? I would have thought we should be the prime fucking suspects.'

'Maybe they're saving us 'till last for some reason.'

There was another pause, ended by Gus.

'Simple, my friends.'

Another pause – this time for effect.

'Are you going to enlighten us, or just sit there with a stupid smile on your face?'

'Care Beverley. You swear at Brett – OK. Maybe he takes it because he a nice guy. Me? Not a nice guy and also your boss. So, now I will tell you why they've not yet question us about the containers. It's because they *know* we got them!'

'But that doesn't make sense,' complained Brett. 'If that's true then surely, we should have been the first to be put through the ringer. And why haven't they searched our premises?'

'They *know,* yes, but prove – *no*. I know how the damn police think, Brett. Believe me, I know!'

'Gus is right,' said Beverley. 'They are going to watch us. They are waiting for us to reveal our hiding place. They can't search our premises because they need a warrant and they don't have enough evidence to get one, so they're waiting for us to give them some.'

'That's crazy. Are you saying they've got policemen watching us? Surely not, not just over a couple of stupid containers. You've been reading too many spy stories.'

'I think they know we have them,' repeated Gus. 'For now, they watch to see what we do with them. They know that sooner or later we have to move them. Too dangerous to keep at home.'

'Yes. They're probably working out how to get a fucking search warrant as we speak, and Brett's bin will be one of the first places they will look.'

'Whoa. I don't understand. All this just to prove we lied about the magic cream?'

'Exactly. Just because we lied about the fucking cream. Is it that important? Yes, it *is*, because it's all over the national press, TV and radio. It's making the police look stupid. They've lost the main evidence because some stupid fucking copper forget to collect it and now it's been stolen, and they can't find out who did it. What a load of wankers.'

'So, Brett, my friend. They have to solve very fast, eh? *Rapidamente!*'

'And that means we are in deep bloody trouble. Once they get their hands on the containers, we're not only up for business corruption but also for deliberately misleading the police investigation. That would bring the factory fire into it as well, I expect.'

'You reckon? You really think we're being watched? It's like Big Brother.'

'You'd better believe it.'

'Strewth! In that case we'd better move the damn things, hadn't we?'

'What a good idea,' said Beverly, with heated sarcasm. 'We just need to ask them to stop watching us while we do it, so they don't spot where we're moving them to. Right Gus?'

'Moving the containers is what police want, Brett. We move, they follow.'

'I still don't get it. How will they see me taking the bottles out of the bin in my back garden? Are they watching us with spy cameras or something?'

'Brett, you not think straight my friend. Stop. Now you have the bottles in your hands, so what you do next, huh? Easy. You put them in bag, get in your car and drive to storage company, yes? You put them in - what you call it? In a... locker and take the key back to your car.'

'And a fucking copper is there waiting for you,' continued Beverley. 'Thank you very much, sir. Hand me the key. You're bloody nicked.'

'They've followed my car?'

'CCTV Brett. Every step of the way. There's a whole police department – nothing else but monitoring live footage videos with number-plate recognition.'

'How do you know all this Beverley?'

She smiled. 'Because, old fucking fruit, I *was* that soldier in days gone by.'

'How do you mean? Don't tell me you were a policeman?'

'Not quite. I was a watcher. It was my job to do the watching.'

'You never told me, Beverly,' said Gus, quietly but gravely. 'You never told me you were police.'

'That's because I never was, Gus. I was a data controller, that's all. Just watching screens, day after bloody day.'

'And now you have no connection with police? No friends, maybe?'

Beverly paused and shook her head before answering.

'Gus, I don't know why you have a problem with the police. It's not my business, but it's a bit fucking weird. But if it's any help – no. I don't have any connection with the police force any more. I just left and that's that.'

'Can I ask why you left?' asked Brett.

Pause again and this time with a sigh.

'It's where I learned to swear, Brett. The bloody boredom and frustration. That, and the fact I'm female…'

Gus broke the silence.

'OK. So, we up the bloody creek, yes? We can't move them. We can't leave them. You have any suggestion?'

'Well, if we can't use our cars to shift them, why can't I just take a bus or train? Put 'em in a plastic bag as though I'm going shopping. Wouldn't that work Bev?'

'Number one, where are you taking them? Number two, they will follow you all the way. They can track your location and hack your phone calls. Then it's back to CCTV coverage. There is no way to escape fucking CCTV cameras nowadays, Brett, you wouldn't stand a chance.'

Gus stood up violently, pushing his chair over backwards.

'*Cazzo Madre di Dio.* What the hell we do for chrissake!? Maybe we just give ourselves up, yes? Sorry mister policeman it was me. Which way to the cells?'

'Look, calm down Gus. You're losing it. That's not going to help. Bev, you're the one with all the knowledge, is there any way out of this?'

'I'm fucking thinking, if only you two would stop shouting at each other.'

Gus walked to the window and stared mindlessly through it at nothing.

'Tell me about these containers, I've never seen them. There are two of them, right? How big are they?'

'They're just the standard little flat-sided plastic containers with a handle. You must have seen them - we use them everywhere in manufacturing for storage of samples and the like. They're about a couple of litres in size, I think. Let me check.'

So saying, Brett opened a notebook and searched through some files.

'Yes, here we are. They are two litres in capacity – so quite small. "*Translucent HDPE jerry cans 2000 ml.*"'

'You've got it all there in your fucking notebook? You got the whole of the warehouse contents on it?'

'No. Of course not. It's just that we recently ordered half a pallet load of them, and I've got the invoice copy. Here, look for yourself.'

Beverly looked. And then, Beverley smiled.

'It says here ten cartons.'

'Yes. It was the minimum order, two hundred units.'

'So, twenty units per box?'

'Yes.'

'How many cartons have we opened Brett? You say it was a recent order, so hopefully, not many?'

'I don't know off-hand Bev. Perhaps just one or two.'

Beverley's smile widened.

'Well, fuck me. In that case, I may have a solution to our little problem. Sit down Gus.'

She took another shot from her inhaler.

'You think?' said Gus, standing his chair back up.

'Well, someone has to do the fucking thinking round here. Yes, Gus I *think* there might be a way out.'

'Awesome,' said Brett. 'Thank Christ for that.'

'Christ had nothing to do with it. Thank me. It's really quite simple. Just ask yourself this question: where in the whole fucking universe could we three go without causing the police to be suspicious?'

Gus was the first to answer after another brief pause for thought.

'I get it!'

Brett was a bit slower.

'I'm not sure…'

'Where were you this morning?' asked Bev.

'I was... *at the factory*! Yes, of course.'

'So what is to stop you going back to the factory. Into the warehouse to check the stock, with your fat briefcase containing all the stock lists plus two small containers... There are no cameras in the warehouse Brett. And and at the moment, there are no fucking policemen either.'

'But where do I hide them in the warehouse Bev where they can't be found?'

'I get it!' repeated Gus. 'You open a new carton...'

'Remove two empty containers and replace them with our full ones,' continued Brett, finally understanding. 'That's a ripsnorter Bev. Genius.'

'Then we just re-seal the carton and …'

'…put it back on the pallet under all the others. With the factory closing down, the pallet won't be touched for ever. Brilliant – except…'

'*Si* Brett?'

'If it looks the same as all the others, how will we know which is the carton with the samples when we want to remove them eventually?'

Beverly sighed.

'Don't you think, you fucking Australian half-wit, that our carton might just be a tad heavier than the rest?

# 18

The Situation Room is buried deep in the bosom of *GLOCOM's* immaculate headquarters and is only marginally less hi-tech than the original in the USA's White House after which it was named. This is where a daily religious service takes place. Here the editorial staff pray, passionately, for the next blockbuster story. And if none arrives, this is where they diligently set about manufacturing one from anything that trickles in from reporters and telephones. The insatiable god, *Deadline*, has to be appeased and fed on time: failure to do so could result in consequences too terrible to contemplate.

The long executive table is no stranger to the tuneful clink of long glasses being filled with *Bollinger* during the celebration of yet another successful campaign, as measured; success being measured by an increase in *GLOCOM's* share of the country's newspaper readership. More often, however, it is replete with the dull thud of coffee cups and hiss of gas from violated Coke cans. This latter this is the case today, but the meeting is tinged with an element of hope.

The walls of the SR are adorned with framed copies of past front pages commemorating previous triumphs. This is done in the hope that they will provide inspiration and encouragement for the current staff to go and do likewise.

They also mark the progression of *GLOCOM's* journey from comparative obscurity to its present status as a possessor of enormous power and influence under the guidance of its revered founder and owner. Coronations, assassinations, impeachments, sexual scandals, tales of daring do, global catastrophes, wars, financial collapses are writ large on the pale green walls – a veritable history of main events, but with plenty more space available to add to it. Today, the hope is that a story involving a small cosmetic company with a missing employee, a company with questionable ethical standards, may soon take its place among them. And today, the Editor-in-Chief, Monty Meyer has the awkward job of trying to convince his sceptical colleagues of the viability of the project. Seated around the table are a group of talented professionals and their immediate task is to plan the front-page coverage of the next edition of the country's best-selling red top newspaper, *Sunrise.*

The editorial and supporting staff are arranged around the table in strict, hierarchical order. Monty sits at the head, nearest to the door with an empty, conspicuously luxurious chair to his immediate right. This is reserved for the chairman and owner of the Company, should he wish to attend. Today the chair remains empty. The rest of the staff are arranged in order of seniority and importance, the highest-ranking staff sitting closest to Monty. Visitors and other individuals of minor importance for whom no table space is available are relegated to a line of less comfortable chairs arranged along the end wall at the junior end of the room. Today, however, a special table space next to Monty has been found for Mary Ellis. Strictly speaking, Mary is not a member of staff but has been invited so as to provide a more detailed background to the main item of discussion.

Monty speaks.

'Welcome, ladies and gents, to the Monday Heads and Eds madhouse. Some of you know Mary Ellis. Writes a lot of stuff for us. Some of it even good. Reason for her being here will be clear when Wally has done his stuff. So over to you Wal.'

Wally is a senior sub-editor. He is a short, bald-headed man and peers around the assembled company through thick-rimmed glasses. He is smiling, which is not something that sub-editors do very often. Today he is smiling because he was told to. Wally has been pre-programmed by Monty to be incredibly excited about the cosmetic company story, whatever his real feelings might be.

'Yes. We've got a cracker, people. A major front-pager in prospect I think you will agree.'

A puzzled murmur has arisen like a sudden breeze, signalling the coming of a storm. Monty has sniffed the air.

'Mary,' he cries, changing tack and waving a hand at that name's startled owner. 'People here need filling in.

Look at the puzzled faces. Your story, Old Sport. Give it to us.'

Mary has also been primed, but the suddenness with which she has been pitched into battle has taken her by surprise. She clears her throat to give herself time to think.

'Er, yes Monty. Well, it's all about this cosmetics factory. As you know, we've already run an item on it...'

Wally feels the need to push back in.

'Putting bits of pig into cosmetics. AAGH. That's bad enough. But then some bugger sets fire to the place with someone inside it, for god's sake.'

Mary would be happy to slip back into Wally's shadow but Monty is determined to make her shine.

'And that's not all, is it Mary old fruit?'

But before she can answer, a small hand is raised at the other end of the table – the most junior end. It belongs to Amy, who has just joined the company from college and is attending her very first Monday editorial meeting. Having read the article that Mary had just referred to, she has clearly not been fired with the same enthusiasm as those at the opposite end of the table. It may have to do with an understandable lack of appreciation about what makes a really important newsworthy story. She is perplexed and being armed with the fearlessness of youth, she is not afraid to ask questions. This actually suits Monty's present purpose, so he puts a restraining hand on Mary's shoulder, much to her relief.

'Yes, er... Amy?' glancing down at a paper in front of him.

'Mr Meyer,' Amy begins brightly. 'I've been following this story, of course. And it's interesting for sure, but... I'm a bit surprised about the emphasis we're going to give it, considering what else is going on at the moment.'

Monty is smiling, but only on the outside. 'Live and learn Amy my love. Strong need to sharpen the old newshound antennae.'

'I certainly want to, Mr Meyer. That's why I am asking.'

A mid-table voice joins in. It is gruff, worn and tattered and belongs to the similarly endowed financial editor. He wants to know what other news items Amy thinks might take precedence for space on the front page of tomorrow's issue. What, in her opinion, might possibly vie for importance and therefore space with the Keynote Cosmetics factory and its attendant mysteries?

Amy is prepared for this question because she has done her homework.

'Well, civil war has broken out in Angola with the loss of hundreds – possibly thousands of lives. The Australian prime minister has resigned after being exposed as a homosexual who used rent boys, leaving the government with no clear majority. Then, of course, there's the threatened strike of NHS nursing staff in Wales over plans to cut their salaries...'

Monty, a man with a lifetime of journalistic experience immediately sees where the problem lies. Amy is clearly confusing news that their readers *should* be reading about with news that they *want* to be reading about. That is the road to financial disaster. Amy is pretty and bright, so Monty, reverting to his much-admired paternal mode, decides to put matters right.

'Amy, my sweet. LOVE your enthusiasm. And you're here to learn. Credit where its due. Wally will put you right. Wally?'

'You have to consider…' Wally is talking slowly, placing each word carefully in front of another like the feet of a tightrope walker, '…consider the… interested reader. Our readers are of the greatest importance to us. We need to get… I mean, *anticipate*… their interest and pay attention to it.'

Everyone except Tracy understands exactly what Wally is trying to say. Nothing. But Amy remains puzzled.

Mary feels the need to help. It's a woman-to-woman thing.

'Who would you say was the most influential reader we are likely to have Amy? The person you would least like to offend or disagree with? We all need to make a living, don't we?'

The penny drops.

'You mean…'

Monty resumes control of the lesson. 'We *will* make the right decision today. Then everyone smiles on us. Confirms that we have identified, the most important and pressing issue. See?'

Amy sits down. 'Thank you, Mr Meyer,' she says quietly. 'I see it all now.' But she doesn't. None of them do.

'Fine. Mary, please continue.'

'Thanks Monty. She glances at her notes for reassurance. 'As I see it, there are three main themes running through this complex story. Theme one is what I'm calling "Keynote". This covers the background to the cosmetics company, including the mysterious disappearance of the chemist and his family, the background to the board of directors (interesting stuff there, I'll cover them in a minute) and, of course, the finding of jars of piggy bits in the lab. The second stream I'm calling "Piggy". This deals with the *outcry* over piggy bits being put into cosmetics. This issue has, as expected, attracted a lot of attention and debate especially from the "pure and natural" brigade and the animal rights lobby. Some scientific input and controversy here too, but anyway, that's me. *I'm* dealing with that. Don't want to hurt your readers' heads. Then finally, we turn to greed and corruption. I'm calling this theme "Perversion".

A mid table occupant, balding but with a compensating moustache, wants to know if all this is going to fit onto the front page and if so, how?

Monty bursts back into life.

'Freddy! Ever a practical man, eh? Mary's background. Lead into inside pages by a honeypot for the front page, d'ya see? Mystery, suspense and sex – even the Pope would be tempted. Just what our readers are looking for. So, not all on the front. We continue inside.'

'I think most of the detail will be on the inside page?' She looks at Wally, who nods his head in agreement.

Amy has stopped scribbling on her writing pad and raises another, slightly hesitant finger.

'Excuse me. I don' see where the sex comes into it.'

'Good point Amy,' agrees Monty. 'Enlighten us if you would Mary.'

'I asked a reporter on our local newspaper, *East London News*, to look into the Keynote staff backgrounds to see if anything useful turned up. Interestingly, it seems that the Keynote receptionist is quite sexually active and used to pose for *Glamour Magazine*. I think this is her on the centrefold.' So saying, she holds up an opened copy, inducing necks to be strained forward to get a better view.

'Could we get copyright for publication, Charlie?' asks Wally. Charlie, the mid-table picture editor thinks it might be possible for a fee.

This time Amy doesn't even bother to raise her hand.

'You mean you're going to put that picture in the paper?'

Monty sighs, making a mental note to ask who had invited Amy to the meeting.

'Certainly Amy. Might do a bit of modesty coverage of the naughty bits.'

'Sorry, but I thought pictures of naked women was the province of our lesser rivals.'

Amy sinks back into her chair and begins another scribble.

'OK. So, let's leave the rest of "Perversion" until later,' suggests the ever-observant Monty, noticing the emergence of a quiet hum of unease. 'What about Keynote Mary? Give us a glimpse into the murky cosmetic world.'

'Our local scouts from the *East London* tell us that Keynote is – was - on the brink of total collapse. A board of very iffy directors, an absent chemist and a warehouseman, now gone back to India. The chemist, one George Patterson, and his alcoholic wife have disappeared into oblivion and no trace of them has so far been found in spite of the combination of our effort, plus the police Missing Person brigade and a few hundred greedy people who think he might have something very valuable on him. They have a son Simon, with whom we have made contact, but he clearly doesn't know where his parents are.'

'Did you say you've made contact with the son?' asks Amy, reckless now that she has decided she has probably lost her job. 'But according to the latest piece in the *Informer* we are still looking for him.'

'Bright girl, isn't she?' asks Monty. 'But still a bit wet behind the ears, methinks.'

'Finding the son would be a *good* news story,' explains Mary. 'Good news doesn't sell newspapers. Anyway, let's keep him off limits for the moment – he's a bit hush hush, so keep *shtum*, OK? As far as you at *Sunrise* are concerned, he is still missing. So, now back to the Keynote board…'

# 19

On the other side of London, in far less salubrious surroundings, another business meeting was taking place. Office room at the factory being far from useable, the Keynote Board had re-assembled in Gus Volante's living room. Gus himself was seated at the dining table and was mopping his brow with a handkerchief - not because he was hot but because he was Italian. Beverly sat opposite to him, leafing through papers, whilst Brett, beer can in hand, had opted for the wide-open spaces next to the large windows, which he was patrolling with some relish.

At last, they may have some good news. Beverly's plan seemed to be working, as evidenced by the pile of papers she is carrying.

'So, Beverley, is good?' asked Gus by way of opening gambit.

She placed the pile on the table before her.

'Mainly threats and foul-mouthed crap from animal rights weirdoes, nature conservationists, doom-predictors, religious nuts and so on.'

'Nothing else?' asked the distant Brett, not looking.

'Just one that's interesting,' countered Beverly. 'But it's a bit fucking odd – looks like some sort of agreement. We haven't agreed anything, have we?'

'Is an easy question, Beverly,' said Gus ambiguously and with an odd grin on his face. But nobody bothered to ask him what the answer was.

'Why didn't we think about putting the company on the stock market, Bev?' asked Brett, still not looking. 'With all the publicity we've been having, there would be a rush for shares, surely.'

Beverly rolled her eyes in disbelief.

'Why the fuck Gus ever made you a director is totally beyond me. You've about as much business sense as a concussed tortoise. What do you think would happen to the shares when it's realised that the invention is a myth? When they finally find or dig up Patterson and expose him for the clueless nerd he really is? And what about the need to provide detailed accounts and all kinds of information that would see us hung drawn and quartered by the bloody revenue and the law? Please get this into your thick Australian head – we sell the company or rights to the invention privately and then disappear with the cash and hope the buyer never finds us. End of story.'

Brett's admirable restraint in the face of Beverly's constant defamatory outbursts was beginning to crack.

'You're a real narky bitch Beverly, you know that? But let me just point out a tiny fault in your profound bloody logic. Who in their right mind is going to part with large amounts of cash without seeing the invention and proof that it works? Did you think of that, you vicious tart?'

'Hey,' said the rejuvenated Gus, waving an arm. 'Wasamatter with you two, huh? You behaving like *bambinos*. Cut it out. Listen, we gonna make good money, you gotta trust me. You want the brainy one who solves the problem? OK. You looking at him.'

'You?' said Beverly disbelievingly.

'Me,' confirmed Gus, picking up the single sheet of paper from the table and waving it. 'I already done the deal – almost.'

There was a pause of disbelief.

'Let me get this straight, Gus,' said Beverley. 'You're telling us that you've done – actually *done* – a deal to sell, what? The company? The invention? And you did this without consulting or even telling us?'

Gus smiled.

'Sure. She's my company.'

Brett had frozen in mid stride, beer half way to his lips. 'Jesus!'

Beverley took a deep breath. This was not entirely out of character for Gus Volante. Since she'd known him, he had surprised and alarmed her several times by his propensity to make quick and often ill-considered business decisions, depending on his mood swing at the time. During frequent bouts of depression, he became negative and almost helpless, depending on her for tackling even the most minor problems. When on a high however, as he clearly now was, he gave the impression of invincibility, needing no help whatsoever. In this mood he was apt to make instant judgements and act on them without consultation or warning. A combination, Beverley had concluded, of a bipolar disorder and an Italian ego. She turned to confront the Italian, leaning forward so as to close the distance between them.

'Gus. Now you are going to tell us, your partners, about this wonderful deal you have pulled off behind our backs. We are all fucking ears.'

'Sure. So, this guy he contacts me…'

'Which guy?'

'You wanna listen, or go stuff yourself? This guy he comes to my place, here, and knocks on the door. "I wanna buy your invention" he says, "You know, the piggy one everyone is talking about." So, I tell him to join the queue. "With my kind of money" he says, "I go right to the front of the queue. In fact, I don't queue at all." So I figure best to string him along a little – find out how serious he is.'

'And?'

'Boy! Was he serious! Five hundred thou for exclusive option and the rest when we deliver.'

Beverly and Brett looked at each other in despair.

'That was five hundred thou what?' asked Brett. 'Monopoly money?'

'It was euros, Brett. Euros. Why you looking at me like that?'

'Because Gus, this has all the hallmarks of a scam,' said Beverly. 'How much was the rest?'

'Three million,' said the smiling Gus. 'Three million euros. That's the deal I done for you guys!'

Beverly sighed and put her head in her hands.

'And what are we going to deliver for three million euros, exactly? Patterson's non-existent fucking invention? Patterson's head? And how, exactly are we going to do that since we don't have a fucking clue where he is, and even the police can't find him?'

Gus sat back and put his hands behind his head, still clutching the paper. 'You guys gonna love this. Did I sell the invention? No! Did I offer Patterson? No! I don't offer what we don't have, Beverly. You think I, Giovani, is stupid? You think wrong if you think that. We *got* want he wants for the money.'

Brett and Beverly looked at each other in despair.

'Go on, then,' demanded Brett. 'Tell us what we've got that he wants badly enough to pay millions for it.'

'See? I tell you, and you will be amazed. But you have to work it out for yourselves. You so clever Beverly, but not enough to see what I did.'

'OK Gus,' said Beverly, furiously. 'Stop playing games. Our futures are on the line here. If we don't get this right, we're all likely to end up with long prison terms. What exactly do you think you've sold to this fucker?'

Gus smiled.

'OK. Not the company, only the containers!'

Brett groaned in disbelief.

'You're telling us you sold - what? – the containers? With the pig bits in them?' he said incredulously. 'The ones we've just hidden? And you actually think that you've sold them for three million euros?'

'What?' said Gus angrily, clearly perplexed and frustrated.

'Did you sign anything – papers of any kind?' asked Beverly with eyes closed.

'Sure. I signed the exclusive option,' waving the paper again. 'Here! See? I read it carefully. I'm not that stupid.'

'Gus. Where's the upfront money?' asked Brett.

'Never mind about the fucking money,' said Beverly, 'What did you sign? Show me the copy.'

'Hey' protested Gus clasping the paper protectively to his bosom. 'I don like this. I bring you a good deal – a *fantastico* deal and to treat me like a baby. Why you doing this?'

Beverly opened her eyes. They were blazing.

'Because, you stupid Italian, the deal is too good to be true. Ask yourself this. Why would somebody part with that amount of money for three bottles containing some red goo that nobody knows what it consists of. All based on an invention that nobody has seen, nobody understands, nobody knows whether it works or even what it does and the only guy who can explain it is missing? Does that make sense in your stupid brain?'

'There won't be any money.' said Brett from the window.

'Will you stop talking about fucking money?' said Beverly. 'Of course there won't be any money. It's what this idiot has signed away, that I'm worried about.'

This was too much for Gus.

'Enough already,' he shouted standing up. 'This gonna stop. I tell you the deal is done. It's my company and I do what I like. OK Beverly, so I tell this guy "Why do you part with good money before you know what the piggy invention is – what it does?" He say it doesn't matter if invention doesn't work. He will sell the containers for profit. People he sell to will think the secret formula is *actually in the containers* – he says he knows people who will believe that and have the money for him to make a big profit.'

'Did he explain why *he* could do it but not us? Why wouldn't we sell them ourselves?'

'Sure. I asked him. He's going to sell, how you say… anonymous? Black market? He knows how to do this - it's his living. We can't do it without getting caught, but he can, see? Makes sense, yes? But he has to have both the jars of pig shit and he needs the whole story from us and then we get the money'.

'And this is what you signed – an agreement to give him the jars?' asked Beverly incredulously.

'Sure. Why not?'

'Why not, you stupid fucker, it that you have signed a bit of paper virtually saying that we *have* the jars. Now we are at double the risk we were before…'

But Beverly never got to finish her sentence. At that moment, the window next to Brett exploded, showering him with glass fragments and something flew across the room, hitting Gus in the ribs at exactly the height his head had been before moments before.

On inspection, the missile proved to be a large flat stone with a drawing on it. Crude, but clear enough. It was meant to be a women's body with a pig's head on it.

The board meeting was thus brought to a premature end and an ambulance was called to take both Brett and Gus to the local hospital, with Beverly following diligently behind in her car.

## 20

Down in Brighton, Mary Ellis was sitting uncomfortably in a comfortable chair in her living room, watching afternoon television. Her discomfort was due to the content of the program she was listening to – *Today in Parliament*. The program's radio presenter was playing a recording of bits of that day's prime minister's Question Time. The MP for the East London area where Keynote was situated, Mr Norman Lately, was asking a question.

> *"Mister Speaker, is the Prime Minister aware that a factory building in my constituency has been set alight by animal rights extremists resulting in serious injury to one of the company's directors and further, that senior employee of the company and his family are missing, in spite of an intensive search for them, and that these circumstances have been the cause of great concern and alarm to people living in the area?"*

The reply from the PM had been carefully pre-prepared and drafted.

> *"I can assure the honourable gentlemen that I understand his concern and that a full police*

*investigation is underway. The Home Secretary has asked for an interim report from the metropolitan police commander in charge of the operation, and he is confident that the perpetrators of this appalling crime will be found in the near future. I am also advised that a widespread search for the missing family is also underway and that their photographs will be widely published in the news and on television."*

'Christ,' said Mary to herself. 'This has got really big. And scary. What the hell have I got myself into?'

The telephone rang. It was Simon Patterson's phone - the one that *GLOCOM* had provided him with. She picked up the receiver.

'Hi Simon, how are you? As a matter of fact, Ralph is on his way to you to check that you're OK…'

'It's not Simon, Mary. It's me.'

'Oh, Ralph. What's up – is Simon alright?'

'I don't know Mary, because he's not here.'

'What do you mean – is he out shopping or something?'

'No Mary. I mean he has completely gone. Apart for the furniture the flat is empty. He's left the key and the debit card on the table.'

There was a pause while Mary took this in.

'Where's he gone?'

'How the bloody hell should I know?'

Pause.

'No… note or anything?'

'Nothing. The place is completely bare. You'd better get onto Monty Meyer, and good luck with that. We've lost him and we're probably going to get the blame for it.'

Mary sat down. He was right; no matter that it was not their fault, they would be blamed. And that could be disastrous both financially and for her future career.

'Put your thinking cap on, Ralph. We need to find him before I tell Meyer – if we can. Where in God's name is he likely to go?'

'Not a clue, Mary. The bugger could be heading for South America for all we know. Look, be realistic. The chance of us finding him on our own is practically zero. Wait until I get home, then I'll hold your hand while you speak to Meyer. What do you think he will say?'

Actually, Monty Meyer's response was surprisingly mild. Mary was not to worry. She and Ralph had done everything they'd been asked to do, and if the silly sod rejected the help he was being offered and he got into trouble as the result, then it was his own stupid fault. They had all done everything they could to protect him and now he was on his own. *GLOCOM* had never revealed that they had found him, so Monty could not see that Simon's disappearance caused any problems. In fact, since its readership had not, in practice, been misled, Monty was a bit relieved. The search for the missing teenager was simply ongoing and would now be increased. Simon could no longer be protected; the headline would now have to continue along the lines of

**THE SEARCH GOES ON! WHERE IS THE MISSING TEENAGER?**

Good luck, Simon.

...

Fifty miles away from Brighton, in East London, someone *did* know where Simon was – or at least, he had correctly guessed it.

## 21

Obviously, Gus Volante was unaware that Simon had been found and hidden in a Brighton flat, and Gus's need to find him was greatest of all. George Patterson had seemingly disappeared from the face of the earth, and enthusiasm for the search for him was consequently fading fast. But they hadn't yet given up on finding his son – far from it. Gus's need had fired up his thinking processes. His mission was simple, primitive and direct. He needed to know what was in those two containers before he sold them to the potential buyer. George Patterson was the only person who could reveal that, but George couldn't be found. The next best thing was to get to his damned son because Gus was absolutely convinced that Simon knew where his father was.

Gus had taken Beverly's dire warning to heart. The police were watching him so he had to be very careful. He didn't know what was going to happen to the jars once he had handed them over to the purchaser – and supposing the police spotted the transaction, or if the purchaser messed up and got caught? Then the contents would be analysed, and after that, who knows? If they really did contain bits of pig, then the story might become even bigger. It could even make the press in Italy. There would be photographs in the Italian newspapers, and that would put him in mortal danger…

Searchers with far more proficient brains had briefly considered going back to the Patterson family home to look for him. This idea had been roundly rejected however, on the basis that it was far too obvious a place for the teenager to hide. So why bother to look there? Gus's brain did not operate at this level. To him, it seemed the obvious place to go. He had found the address of the Patterson family home, and that was exactly where he was standing now, 23 Langmead Drive, a modest semi in a quiet road lined with a twin palisade of plane trees.

The house was in almost total darkness as he approached the front door – but there was a light in one of the upstairs windows. Not a direct light, but a dim spillage from another room.

He was not sure whether his knock on the door would be answered and not sure what he was going to do if it wasn't. He checked the house number again: this was definitely the house.

His knock was loud and urgent enough to get sleepers out of bed. Then, to be certain, he repeated it and listened. Good! Someone was moving inside - down the stairs – the sound of a light switch - fumbling at the door latch. At the first sign of opening, he pushed the door violently open to reveal a skinny youth looking understandably alarmed.

'Simon Patterson?'

'Excuse *me*, who the hell are you?'

'*Cazzo! Dobbiamo parlare al mio amico!* Inside please!'

Simon gave out an involuntary 'Ow!' as he felt himself being pushed violently backwards along the corridor and into the kitchen at the end.

'OK. Take it easy, eh? I no gonna hurt you, see? So now I ask again: you Simon Patterson? You know who I am, huh?'

Gus was in a hurry. He had a desperate need and the means of satisfying it now stood blinking before him. Even the pause to give Simon time to recognise him was difficult.

Considering the shock he had just experienced, Simon managed a commendable response; anger but with an understandable tremor.

'I know how to phone the police, *mister* Volante. Breaking and entering and threatening behaviour and possible common assault, isn't it?'

Gus closed the kitchen door and leaned back on it. He found the light switch on the wall beside him and turned it on in time to reveal Simon reaching for the kitchen telephone extension. *Madonna Mia!*

'Wait! Ok. Ok. Simon, I'm a-sorry. *Scusa* me please. I am in bad trouble and need help. You listen first then, if you think I'm crazy, *then* you call police. Yes?'

'You must be joking!' said Simon dialling a number. Gus launched himself across the room and put a restraining grip on his wrist before he could finish.

'Simon, listen! You and I be friends, yes? You help me and maybe I help you. Sit down please, huh?'

Simon felt the grip on his wrist tighten and he realized that the little Italian was far too strong to pick a fight with.

'Alright, alright. Just let go of my wrist, you're hurting me.'

The kitchen was a half-tiled green and yellow rectangle with inexpensive worktops and cupboards on three sides with a door and windows leading out into a rear garden in the fourth. A circular table stood in the kitchen centre accompanied by four chairs. Gus pulled Simon over to one of them pushed him down on it before letting go. The Italian was breathing heavily with effort but managed a grim smile.

'Like I say Simon. I wanna be friends. No sweat huh? Just talk.'

'I don't want to talk. Just go please.'

Gus, suddenly calmer and continuing with the smile he didn't feel, sat down facing him across the table.

'Simon, I want to talk about your papa. He work for me, you know?'

'Yes, I know. He hates you. He told me so. He really *really* hates you. He says you're rubbish and you're ruining the company. Did you know that?'

Gus did not appear to be offended.

'So, when he tell you this Simon? This morning maybe over nice cup of coffee?' Looking around. 'Maybe at this table, eh? Or last night you have beer together? And your mamma too? Happy family? You have beer in this kitchen, Simon? You wanna beer to make you relax maybe?'

He stood up and started opening cupboards.

'I haven't seen either of my parents for months. They're certainly not in the house.' Simon hesitated slightly before saying 'Look for yourself.'

Gus opened a drawer and stood examining its contents.

'Listen Simon. I had a papa too who I loved.' A pause, then turning back to Simon. 'I understand why you want to – protect him? From the bad guys? The greedy guys? Me, I understand, but believe me Simon. I not a bad guy. I not a crazy guy. I need his help for my business, see? No papa, no business. I'm in the deep trouble and your papa can help me. *Only* your papa. You see, simple? We do a deal. Smuggle him back then we afford to pay him well. You too perhaps. What you say?'

'Even if I knew where he was, why would I tell *you*? Do you know how many people are looking for him? How much money being offered? How I've been chased up and down the country trying to avoid people asking the same question? Listen carefully. I do *not* know where my father is. Full stop. I cannot tell you because I don't bloody *know*. Is that clear?'

Gus, still smiling closed his eyes and slowly turned his head disbelievingly from side to side. But Simon wasn't finished yet.

'Even if I did know, I don't believe you about the business. You want to get your hands on his secret formula like all the others.'

Gus broke into a sarcastic laugh and sighed.

'Secret formula? You kidding me, Simon? That story is shit. I know – we invented it! Secret formula? She doesn't exist. Believe me Simon, is shit!'

'Then why has he disappeared – and my mother too?'

'My God. The million-dollar question! Why the fuck? Why you ask me? Is simple Simon. Trust me. I swear to keep it secret. Where *is* he and your mamma? I'm a real friend Simon. Whatever the problem I can help.'

Simon was a picture of exasperation.

'For the last *bloody time*. I *do not* know where they are. Even if I did, I still think you would sell the information. Don't you think I want to know where they are? They're all the family I've got. I'm as desperate to find them as you seem to be. But I just don't know.'

Gus now icy cool, sat back onto his chair and studied Simon's face. The prospect of getting nothing was too much to bear. He still wasn't sure about the kid. He had to squeeze him – get something useful out of him at the very least. There was no other route to salvation, it was him or nothing. He changed tack.

'Simon, I think you know where they are - but maybe you don't *know* you know.'

Simon looked away and stared out of the window into the dimly blackness of the garden.

'I haven't the faintest idea what you're talking about.'

Gus spread his hands out on the table.

'Your mamma and papa, they hiding somewhere. Somewhere they feel is safe, eh? Somewhere perhaps you also know Simon. Where they go on holiday? Small holiday cottage? Maybe another place, Ireland or Wales maybe? Or France or Spain – maybe even Italia? Hell, even Australia for God's sake? Think Simon, think. They have friends in Australia?'

'Don't you think I've already racked my brains thinking and checking every possible place they might be? I've thought of nothing else for three weeks now and I've exhausted all the possibilities. I promise you; they have just completely vanished into thin air. You are wasting your time here: I do not know where they are or where else to look.'

Gus stood up, head down and with his hands clasped behind his back, he made a complete circuit of the little kitchen, deep in contemplation. He stopped, purposely, at the still-open kitchen draw and resumed his study of its contents. He was still not sure whether Simon was lying. Reaching into the draw he took out a large knife and held it in his hand, studying it closely. Was this the last throw of the dice?

'You know I come from Italy, Simon. Pretty rough where I lived. Crazy people, you know? Best not to make them mad! Best not to keep secrets if they want something. This is why I come to England. Crazy people here too? Sure. But not so violent. But in Italy, I learn their methods – not very nice. Shall I tell you Simon?'

'Are you threatening me?' said Simon, visibly shaken.

Gus turned to face him, still holding the knife.

'So young, Simon. Still so much ahead of you. You never had much already. Sure. Nothing much to lose, I guess. Me? I work very hard to make a living. Sure, I make good living but I work very hard for it. Now, someone try to take it away. All my life. All my hard work. Do you understand that, Simon? Can you guess? Can you understand - a man like me, tough Italian, would do anything not to lose his life work? Anything?'

The tremor had returned to Simon's voice.

'I don't know where he is. I honestly don't. For Christ's sake!'

'But can I believe you Simon? I need to be sure.'

Gus took a step closer to the seated Simon who cringed back in his chair.

'You...you wouldn't dare use that knife on me...'

'I wouldn't bet on it, son,' said a deep male voice from behind them. 'Very unpredictable, these Italians, especially when they're angry.'

Gus turned to face the speaker, but he had recognised the voice even before his eyes made contact.

'Guthrie! *Merda!Testa di cazzo*!'

'Yes, it's me, Gus. Aren't you pleased to see me?'

Guthrie, well-built, middle-aged with short cropped hair, an early-growth beard, wearing jeans and an unbuttoned bomber jacket was nonchalantly leaning against the open door-frame with folded arms and feet crossed, grinning.

The effect on Gus was that of being caught *in flagrante* by the wronged husband. *How the hell did he know where I was?*

The newcomer was clearly enjoying the effect he was having on the startled Italian.

'Not sure what you said, Gus, but I bet it wasn't complimentary.'

He turned his gaze on Simon.

'Mr Patterson. Nice to meet you, but you really shouldn't leave your front door open. As you see, all sorts of uninvited visitors are likely to waltz in. Fortunately, there are proficient and capable police officers, like me, to prevent them threatening or harming you. Allow me to introduce myself: detective sergeant Stan Guthrie. Here is my warrant card. I'm here to protect you, but I suggest that you don't hang around down here while I deal with this criminal. Your bedroom upstairs might be a safer place.'

He stood aside in the doorway. But Simon had sensed that something more than a simple arrest was going on. Something that Simon didn't want any part of. He was already on his feet, backing away from the two protagonists: safety had precedence over valour. Saying nothing, he squeezed past Guthrie, but as he did so, the detective put a hand on his shoulder.

'If I were you son, I would just curl up under the covers as if nothing was happening. No point in calling the police, I'm already here and that would only complicate matters. Calling for help would be a *big* mistake, believe me. Keep quiet and I will call you when you can come down.'

Simon nodded and made a hasty ascent of the stairs. Guthrie watched him enter a bedroom through a door at the top.

Gus had calmed himself and was thinking fast.

'What you want, *policeman?*' With venom.

In fact, Guthrie was far from sure what he wanted. He hadn't had time to work it out. The shout had only come 60 minutes ago – Alec Williams, the duty Sargent had been standing next to him at the urinals in the station toilet and happened to mention that something had just come up about that cosmetic company. What was it called? Missing chemist – Patterson? You must have read about it in the paper Stan? Well, the owner, Italian bloke, bit suspicious, is being watched and Emily just told me he's been spotted heading in the direction of the Patterson house and could be looking to break in. Probably nothing. Look. Just needs checking out – would you be interested in doing it, Stan? Save uniform the bother if you've nothing better to do. The stupid bloke thought he'd sold some bottles of gunge to one of our CHIS blokes. Gave us quite a laugh. Anyway, we're after these bottles, apparently, whatever they are, so keep an eye open. That's why the wog owner is being watched to see where they are hidden. Interested?

Guthrie's reaction was predictable and instant. *The bastard is trying to screw me.* They had a deal, fifty-fifty.

'Sure, I'll handle it, Alec. I know the little sod. Who's got the address?' *No problem at all. Just me and the little bastard in the same room. How did he get so badly injured? Well sir, it happened when he attempted to resist my arrest.*

Guthrie hardly had time to zip his flies up. And his luck was in – when he got to the house, the front door was open and there he was, the little fucker, standing with his back to him...

'What you want, Guthrie?' repeated Gus.

'That's such a good question, you slimy dego grease ball. You know, I haven't made my mind up completely as yet? I've only got as far as breaking every fucking bone in your gruesome little body.'

'And how you think you get away with that? How you explain that to your policeman *friends*?'

He had thought about it, of course on the way to the house. Even rehearsed the opening threat, but what are you supposed to do when faced with a man who has tried to screw you? He hadn't got that far in his mind. During his career Guthrie had dealt with many attempted murders. Motive? Opportunity? Ability? Witnesses? Pre-medicated or spontaneous? Just an arm's length exercise. Tick the boxes. But this. This was different. This was *personal*. The other end of the telescope. Bottom up. *This bastard actually trying to screw me.*

'Well, you know, it's amazing what sometimes happens to people who try to resist arrest Gus. You wouldn't believe the damage they sometimes suffer! Even get themselves killed.'

Guthrie was quite capable of violence, but not of murder. An amoral, money-grabbing, opportunistic sneak thief, yes. But not a murderer. He knew he didn't have the courage to kill Volante, but how far should he go? He needed more thinking time.

'Gus. That's what they call you nowadays I hear. A bit different from the first time we met, no?'

Gus was focussed, never more so; his mind was turbocharged with fear. He glanced around the kitchen again but this time he looking for a means of escape. The glass panelled door to the garden was closed and probably locked. It briefly occurred to him to throw himself through the glass, but it was bound to be double-glazed and impregnable even to his heavy frame. In any case, even if he made it to the garden, Guthrie would easily outrun him. The door to the hall was still open, and so was the front door beyond it, and he could see the rear of his car in the roadway outside. If he could get past

Guthrie and dash down the hall pulling the doors shut behind him...

They stood facing each other across the central kitchen table, Guthrie standing between Gus and his escape route. How could he get the policeman out of the way? He looked down at the pointed tip and the long sloping blade of the chef's knife he still held in his shaking hand. How many years do you get for stabbing a policemen? The problem was that this particular policeman had probably been trained how to deal with knife threats.

'You come near me, *fottuto bastardo*, and I kill you. You worth nothing. I kill you and do the world a favour.' Gus gestured with the knife. 'We know how to kill in Italy.'

He tried a threatening step closer, making a stabbing gesture with the knife. Guthrie's broad grin stayed stuck to his craggy face but he backed off slightly and moved to his left as Gus took a further threatening step towards him.

The dance continued. Another knife-waving step, this time to the left, edging closer to the door. Guthrie was co-operating, following Gus's lead so as to keep maximum distance between them. Just a few more feet... Then, as he was edging towards the door, Gus slipped and fell on his knees. It must have been an oily residue left over from Simon's recent cooking. Guthrie laughed and turned away, turning his back to the sprawling Italian. Now Gus seizing his chance, was quick on his feet. Without even standing completely up, he made a dash to the door and actually got part of his body into the hallway. But this is what Guthrie had been waiting for. He had laid a trap and Gus had fallen into it. With lightning speed, Guthrie traversed the distance between them and grabbed Gus's trailing arm, swinging him violently around, smashing him against the kitchen wall. Gus collapsed to the floor, bloody-nosed. Guthrie turned him over onto his back, putting a foot on his chest.

'Well, well my old friend, this is a very sharp and dangerous knife,' said the policeman, picking it up from the floor where it had fallen from Gus's hand. 'You could have a really nasty accident with a knife like this. You ought to be more careful.' Then kneeling down with a knee on one of the helpless Italian's arms, he placed the blade on his freshly bloodied neck.

'Now, you slimy bastard, we need to get things straight. I want answers and if I don't get them, I'm going to cut your fucking ears off, you understand?'

'Go to hell!' Gus managed to gargle.

'If I go to hell my friend, then you are coming with me. We had an agreement, didn't we? If you made a profit. from your business, then it's fifty-fifty. I'm sure you remember. For years you fucked everything up, but I've been watching you, closely. And guess what? Just when I decided to give you up as a dead loss, you accidently found a way to make some real money by selling something valuable. So of course, the first thing you do is to contact me with the good news? Do you buggery! What you do is try to screw me, you useless, slimy cunt. But I've found you out. And you are going the learn what happens when people try to screw me. What shall I do to you eh? Maybe I'll just cut your throat, eh?' and as he said it, he pushed the knife even closer into to Gus's throat but without cutting him.

'Just one little cut and I can watch you bleed to death…'

The now terrified Gus could feel tip of the blade pressing on his throat, next to his jugular. He closed his eyes, but managed to spit out 'Fuck you!' before brilliant lights came on; white lights and blue lights.

There was the sound of breaking glass as three uniformed policemen burst through the smashed glass garden door, door grabbing Guthrie's arms, pulling him up onto his feet and forcing his hands behind his back. The knife, cluttered to the floor.

'Shall I cuff 'im, sir?' asked one of the uniforms, addressing a tall, plain-clothed officer who had entered the kitchen, rather less dramatically, through the front door and hallway.

'Hold on,' yelled Guthrie. 'You've got this all wrong. I'm a policeman.'

'More's the pity,' said the officer. 'Yes, cuff him, constable and arrest him. Read him his bloody rights and charge him with… with threatening with an offensive weapon. That'll do for the time being.'

'But I was only doing my duty, trying to make an arrest. I wasn't going to hurt him…'

The tall man smiled. 'Tell that to the judge, Guthrie. You are well and truly nicked and you are in a shit-full of serious trouble. Take him away and put him in the van. I'll think of some more things to charge him with later.'

Then looking down at Gus…

'Get up, Volante, or whatever your bloody name is. I'm also arresting you, for illegal entry into the United Kingdom.'

'Cuff him as well, sir?' asked uniform.

'Nah. Waste of good metal. Put him in the car and read him his rights. Better get someone to look at his nose and face. Have we got a medic on-board?'

'Yessir. Ambulance just turned up.'

'Anyone upstairs?'

'Yes, sir.' A second uniformed policeman, entered the kitchen accompanied by Simon.

'Ah! Mr Simon Patterson? Good to meet you at last. We've been looking for you for some time. I'm a detective chief inspector (showing a warrant card). Look, You must be pretty shaken after what you've just been through. I'm sorry about that. Couldn't be avoided if we were to catch the criminal in the act. If you need help, we can take you to the local hospital, although I've just been told an ambulance has arrived.'

'I don't want an ambulance,' said Simon unsteadily 'What I want is to know what the hell is going on.'

'Sure. I completely understand. So I'm going to put you in some very capable hands. Someone who will tell you everything you need to know.'

Looking round, he gestured to a female uniformed officer to join them.

'Simon, this is PC Payne and I'm going to assign her to you for as long as it takes. PC?'

'Hi Simon,' she said, smiling. 'Please call me Sally. I suggest we find somewhere a bit quieter, and then I hope I'll be able to answer all your questions and … well, just fill you in. Would you like a cup of tea? I make really good cups of tea…'

## 22

The scene is the splendour of the oak-panelled 'family room' in Monty Meyer's, large, Hampstead red brick, pile. It's a frosty Sunday afternoon but Monty is relaxed in shirt sleeves and seated in his favourite green armchair. He has just poured a glass of whisky from the decanter on the low table in front of him. More glasses are scattered on the table because Monty has visitors. He is entertaining them not only with his whisky but also with his famous Monty Meyer Grin, which he is directing at the three occupants of the long, red couch opposite him on the other side of the coffee table. At one end sits Mary Ellis, white-jacketed, red lipped, jet black haired, looking gorgeous and knowing it. She is returning Monty's grin with a confident, generous smile. Sitting uncomfortably next to her is Mike Davis, also jacketed but, having been pushed once again into the disconcerting ambit of newspaper royalty, his expression is of a more nervous variety. The third occupant of the couch is the careful Miranda Stevens. She is wearing a dark, anonymous business suit together with her habitual and impenetrable smile, which involves the generous use of her mouth without too much disturbance of her eyes.

'Pleasure to have you guys here,' says Monty in the manner with which he addresses his daily news meetings. 'Welcome and all that. Don't shun the booze – wine available if you prefer it.' There's a thoughtful and awkward pause while he takes a whisky sip before he continues. 'Suppose you're all wondering what's going on?'

Mary accepts the responsibility. She knows Monty better than the others. She is used to his off-putting staccato speech delivery but continues to wonder at the contrast between this and the beautiful, seamlessly flowing prose which pours from his pen. She feels obliged to open the batting and she does this with minimal attention to deference on the assumption that it's not going be a sticky wicket.

'Can hardly contain ourselves Monty. Summoned to the splendiferous, intimate lair of a Global Newspaper King at a weekend, and not a sign of a barbecue to be seen anywhere.'

'Newspaper king, eh? Slight exaggeration, old thing,' says Monty. 'But only slight.' He broadens his grin. 'You like the pad then?' producing an all-encompassing wave of his arm, nearly spilling his drink. 'Amazing what fiddling your expenses can do. Make a note, Mike.'

Mike is not a quick responder by nature. At the sound of his name, he looks up in alarm from cleaning his glasses with his handkerchief. Miranda helps him out.

'No chance of that, Mr Meyer. I keep him on a very tight lead.'

'Right! It's *Monty*, don't forget. Permission to speak freely as they say on Star Trek.'

'I have to admit,' says Mike eventually, 'that I *am* a bit perplexed. I wasn't sure whether to come in a lounge suit or a suit of armour.'

'Or with an exercise book tucked down the back of your trousers, eh?' laughs Monty. 'Don't worry, you and your boss here - high on the approval list. All will be revealed. Just waiting for one more to arrive.' Looking at his watch. 'Late. Trust a policeman.'

The mood changes. The word *policeman* triggers individual searches for circumstances of possible interest to the law. Monty, however, is quite impervious to the effect of his revelation. Draining his whisky glass, he calls through the door to his gentle, dark, diminutive wife Molly.

'Any sign of a police van, sweetheart? Crowds of coppers? Flashing blue lights?'

'Just a bloke getting out of a taxi, dear,' comes the clear but disembodied reply. 'Tall, young and *very* good looking. Just my type. Can I grab him and take him into the kitchen?'

Monty grunts and rises, ready to extend a welcome to the tall, blond, young, good-looking bloke as he appears at the door clutching a large, manila envelope. He is smiling broadly.

'Chris *Velkommen!*' cries Monty, shaking him vigorously by his free hand. Turning to the perplexed assembly on the couch, 'Ladies and gent, meet Inspector Christopher Pedersen. Ex youngest ever captain of the Royal Military Police and now damned near youngest chief inspector of our revered Metropolitan Police Service, Special Branch. Correct Chris?'

'Now you've embarrassed me, Monty. Hello everyone.'

'No need for further introductions. Afraid Chris knows a lot about every one of you!'

Nevertheless, Pedersen strolls over to the couch, still smiling broadly, and shakes everyone by the hand.

'Really pleased to meet you all in the flesh. Monty has filled me in on all your backgrounds.'

Pedersen's appearance and demeanour speaks clearly of his origins. Casually combed blond hair above a high forehead and blue eyes derived from his Danish father, square, confident jaw from the good luck fairy and a sharp sense of humour from his Irish mother. This combines admirably with his light blue quality jacket and open neck shirt.

'What have we done to earn the interest of such a senior officer, Chris?' asks Mary. 'Have we been aiding a terrorist group?' She is still smiling sweetly.

'No, something *much* more serious,' replies Chris as he lowers himself into the remaining, overstuffed armchair and crosses his long legs. 'What you've done is to attract the interest and attention of the infamous Monty Meyer. I just hope you don't live to regret it!'

General restrained, slightly false laughter.

'OK,' says Monty, still standing and pouring a drink for his latest guest. 'Now we are all met. Time to open up. I admit it! All down to my self-indulgence. Invited you all so we can get to the bottom of the PICO Project.'

Another, puzzled pause.

'And that is?' – Mary again.

Monty keeps them waiting. He hands the glass to Pedersen and returning to his armchair. Sitting back, he addresses the air above the occupants of the red couch.

'That, gentlefolk, is the name given by my newspaper to the whole Keynote Cosmetics fiasco.' He spells it out slowly. 'P- I- C- O. PICO. Pigs in Caster Oil. Catchy, eh? Thought of it myself.'

This time, Mike manages the first response. 'I thought *that* was all over with. Put to bed. Keynote no longer exists and the owner banged up in prison. Am I right?'

'*Put to bed*. Excellent. Mike, you just illustrated why you're a good local reporter. Put to bed. Key to good local news, don't you think?'

'Local news has to stay current?' suggests Miranda, look sideways at Mike.

'You know it, Miranda. Straight news is what your local readers want. Long post-mortems and detailed backgrounds? Forget it. Leave that to columnists in the heavies. The likes of Mary here. She caters for the intellectuals! Oops, sorry Miranda. Not suggesting your readers are thick. Point I'm making, in my view, the Keynote fiasco – PICO, the whole damn local thing, *should* have faded into obscurity. Quite right too, from your point of view. As you say, put to bed. On with the next current news item.'

'But that didn't happen, did it? You made it into a national issue. Splashed it all over the *Informer* and put it on the radio. Even knowing the outcome, I've never been able to understand why you did that.'

'To be honest, Mike, it wouldn't have been my decision. Couldn't see it myself.'

'*I* can understand it,' boasts Mary. 'The extravagance of a powerful man. It tickled the fancy of Monty's boss.'

'Spot on,' grins Monty. But Mike is incredulous.

'You mean it was all done on the whim of David Corbet? The whole thing. All that money spent? All those people involved?'

'That's *Sir* David Corbet, by the way,' Monty reminds him. 'Money? Yes, you bet. Nine percent increase in sales while we were running it. Pays for my extravagant lifestyle.'

'So, you blew the whole thing up into a national issue just to make money?'

'Only word I wouldn't agree with is *just*. Use of animal bits in cosmetics? Animal rights? Cruelty and misuse of our dumb friends? People get *very* hot under the collar. Cause for concern. Wouldn't have worked without *that*. A real issue, wouldn't you say? Newspaper sales increased nine percent. *That's* money. Chance to highlight and complain about misuse of animals? *That's* priceless for some people. Where's the problem?'

'OK. But where's this leading Monty?'

'Who knows Mary?' Then more intensely. 'Who knows? Let's see. That's the beauty of it. Much more to this story than you might think - and all the story tellers are gathered here! Top up your glasses and let's huddle round the campfire. Where shall we start? Had to do with a cleaning lady, I think? Miranda? Mike?'

Mike is uncomfortable. For a start, he is squashed in the centre of a not-quite-wide-enough couch like the centre seat in the back of a car. He has been making a concerted physical effort to avoid thigh contact with the women on either side of him less this be misinterpreted. At the same time, he is having trouble understanding the whole point of the gathering and the need to regurgitate the details of a dead news story. And now he is being expected to participate in it, without notice and without notes or any form of preparation. His tone becomes unavoidably reticent. The whole story? OK. If he can remember correctly, he'd just returned from lunch – coffee and crab sandwich as a matter of fact. And there was Mrs Beresford sitting in reception holding a shopping bag to her bosom as though it were a baby that someone had just tried to snatch. His heart had sunk.

He'd a very heavy workload on that afternoon and could have done without her.

'You knew her already, then?' asks Mary.

'You could say that,' says Miranda. 'If you were being polite, she is what you might call a frequent contributor –in other words a pain in the bum. We call them Complainers.'

'We get our share of those,' says Pedersen sympathetically.

'Trouble is,' says Miranda, 'you can't just ignore them. They sometimes come up with something useful. Case in point I suppose.'

'My usual policy,' says Mike, warming slightly to the topic, 'is to listen as politely as I can bear, then concede the point and tell them I'll look into it. That leaves them nowhere to go.'

'At least Mrs Beresford was a single subject complainer,' said Miranda. 'It was usually about some animal that had been lost, stranded or mistreated.'

'Normally I could deal with her fairly quickly,' continued Mike. 'Just leave it with me Mrs B, I'll see if we can use it. But this time it was different. Our receptionist said she had been waiting for me for nearly an hour and refused point blank to budge. Needed to see me urgently. It's those wicked people at the cosmetics factory, Mr Davis. You won't believe it, but they're putting bits of pig into their cosmetics! What factory? Keynote, of course. How did she know? She'd seen it with her own eyes while she was cleaning the laboratory. She had proof. Look! And she dived into her bag to produce the two photocopies of the labelled jars with red goo in them.'

'Labelled "Pigs in Castor oil?"'

'Exactly. And that's when Mike came to me and I got involved,' continues Miranda. 'We were not sure about the significance of the labels, but they seemed to be genuine. Mrs B had never lied or tried to mislead us over all the years we'd known her.'

'So, on you go,' guesses Mary. 'Front page?'

'No – were not a national tabloid,' says Mike pointedly. 'We decided that the right thing to do was to give Keynote the chance to comment and explain before going to press with it.'

'They've got – or rather, they *had* three directors,' continues Miranda. 'An Italian bloke…'

'Giovanni Volante,' says Mike.

'Yes, together with a foul-mouthed woman and an Australian – Brett Something.'

'Correct,' confirms Mike. 'Anyway, they concocted some story about piggy bits being part of a super and incredibly valuable breakthrough cosmetic. Some sort of cream I think it was.'

'Did you believe them?' asks Pedersen.

'Absolutely not. Complete tripe. When I asked to see their chemist, they told me that he had gone into hiding and was not available for interview. Why? Well, he was worried that someone might try to kidnap him to get the secret out of him or some such rubbish.'

'Anyway, it seemed like an interesting local story, so we did a short item on it – inside page, and left it at that,' says Miranda. 'We had no idea it was going to get blown up into a national issue. It should have just faded away, as Monty said.'

'Which is where I come in,' says Mary brightly.

'Not quite, my old fruit,' warns Monty. 'Patience. You can be next in line, but only after Mr. D Higgenbottom, address supplied.'

Slight pause.

'Sorry, you've lost me, Monty.'

'Ah ha!' interjects Miranda. 'The letter in the *Informer*.'

'Mr H. Obviously an avid reader of your rag as well as mine, Miranda. His missive in our letters page. Quite amusing. Noted by me, by Mary and more importantly, by the Boss. Don't know him, Mr H, I suppose, Miranda?'

'Sorry, not a clue. I think I'd remember someone called Higgenbottom.'

'Quite. Your turn *now* Mary. So, you spotted the letter and…'

'It was Ralph, my husband actually.'

'Should have brought him with you,' says Monty. 'Likes a drop of decent red if memory serves.'

'He's minding the shop Monty, but thank you for the belated invitation. Yes, it's true. He spotted the comment about Mike's piece in the *East London*, in the letters section of the *Informer*. Ralph found it amusing so he brought it to my attention. My thought was that it could be interesting and maybe worth a bit of digging, so I phoned Monty's news desk to get more information.'

'And you got more than you expected - a nice Christmas bonus from me personally,' grins Monty. 'Not a bad job actually. Boss quite liked your piece. And response from the paying readership - those that *can* read whole sentences - spectacular! Touched a raw nerve methinks.'

'And that started a national debate?' asked Pedersen incredulously.

'Not quite, Chris. Still had some way to go. So next step…'

'Radio!' guesses Mary.

'Radio,' agrees Monty. '*London Radio Online*'s prime time hatchet man.'

'Stu bloody Edwards.'

'Say what you like about him Mike, but he has a huge following,' says Mary.

'Over two million daily listeners on average,' agrees Monty. 'Not to be sniffed at.'

'So where are we now?' asks Mike wearily.

'After the thunder and lightning, comes fire!' answers Monty. 'Is this where you come in Chris?'

'Yes,' says the patient Pedersen. 'It was a serious incident. A major fire, possible arson and attempted murder. A trapped person - the foul-mouthed director – was nearly killed. Our local branch was onto it straight away. Was it arson? If so, who started it and why? Animal Rights slogans were painted on the wall, and according to our trapped victim, they weren't there when she first entered the building. Who started the fire and closed the door on her? Animal Rights? Other Keynote directors? Was she lying? If so, what was her motive? Perhaps she herself started it and it got out of hand? They all had motives, as it turns out.'

'I don't understand...' says Mike.

Miranda agrees.

'I can see why Animal Rights might do it, given their distorted view of the world, and the Keynote crew might be after the insurance, since they had known money problems. But a fellow director?'

'Having met her, I would have some sympathy with anyone who wanted to bump her off,' says Pedersen with a grin. 'But the fact is, that Keynote had no insurance cover, and therefore no obvious motive. It turns out that at least one of them may have had *another* motive for starting the fire. But we'll come to that later.'

'One of the reasons I invited Chris here,' explains Monty, 'is to tell us about Volante. Interesting fella.'

Pedersen takes his cue. 'Actually, he's the real reason why I got involved …' But he doesn't get a chance to finish as Mary interrupts.

'Chris. If you don't mind my saying so, this is all a bit strange. I've reported on enough punch-ups between the Special Branch and national newspapers to know that they are not well-known for getting along with each other. So why would you agree to do this? Monty's not been bribing you, has he?'

'Bribing a Special Branch police officer? Now there's a thought,' smiles Pedersen thoughtfully. 'But it's strangely relevant, as it happens.'

Monty interjects.

'Fair point Mary. As a matter of fact, Chris's family and mine - long history. Served in the army with his dad and all that. Water under bridge but assume special relationship. Actually, very useful in this case. Able to help each other to sort it, Chris and I together. Combined resources. Unusual, I agree Mary. Hence the need for confidentiality. Don't want our respective bosses getting hot under their collars.'

Pedersen resumes by opening his brown vanilla envelope and, with dramatic effect, removes some typewritten A4 papers. Placing them conveniently on his lap, he adopts a story-telling mode.

'OK. Let's wind the clock back to 1978. The Italian Authorities have issued a European Arrest Warrant for a guy who has absconded with his company's finances.

Not a huge amount, but enough to ruffle the feathers of the Italian police. He'd also upset the *Camorra*, the local Neapolitan mafia, who were somehow involved with the business.'

'What sort of business was it?' asks Miranda.

'The warrant didn't say, but we subsequently learned that the absconder, a guy by the name of Benito Galasso, and his partner, Mario, made cheap, imitation versions of well-known perfumes. They were supplied with materials by Mario's brother, and *he* was a trusted member of the *Camorra*. However, we think Benito began to see signs of a cooling off. Mario was spending more time drinking with his brother than with him, I would guess – that sort of thing. Benito had probably seen what sometimes happens to owners of small, profitable companies in that part of Italy.'

'You mean the owner suddenly and mysteriously disappears and company falls into waiting hands, no questions asked?' suggests Mary.

'We can only guess. Anyway, for whatever reason, Benito decided it was time to act. So, he empties the company's bank account and goes into hiding. After some fruitless searching, the *Carabinieri* concluded that he has skipped the country, probably on a false passport, hence the issue of the European Arrest Warrant.'

'This is getting exciting,' says Mary. 'What happens next?'

'Nothing Mary. Absolutely nothing. Nothing for at least eighteen months.'

'Presumably our friend was lying low somewhere,' suggested Miranda. 'Who wouldn't, with the mafia and international police after you?'

'But then things start to warm up. So now we wind forward,' continues Pedersen, consulting the top page on his lap. 'Forward eighteen months after the issue of the warrant. It's England and the Plymouth ferry terminal. Immigration is checking new arrivals from the Bilbao ferry. One astute female officer, Susan Larkin, spots what looks like a dodgy Italian passport. I have her report here. Seems she remembered seeing the EAW issued on Galasso and became suspicious. An Italian arriving by ferry from Spain with no luggage - so let's have another look at his passport.'

'Something not quite right about it?' suggests Miranda.

'The ironic thing,' replies Pedersen, 'is that this guy was actually playing his cards right. He'd obviously been told that immigration surveillance at UK ports was less intense than at airports, hence his boat trip from Spain. Unlucky for him then that he should run into the astute Ms Larkin. I quote from her report. *'A closer examination revealed major discrepancies in the MRZ'* – that's the machine code at the bottom of your passport – *'The date of birth didn't have a control digit, and the expiry date was cited as the date of issue'*. Now that is pretty damming. At this point there can be little doubt that this was a fake passport.'

'So, she arrested him?'

'No Mary. She didn't have the power to arrest him - if she *had* then we wouldn't be sitting here now. No. What she did was to hand him over to a local Special Branch copper for further investigation. Special Branch has a base at most ports. Anyway, that was her duty done, apart filing a report – standard procedure. Interestingly, she included the name on the passport and also the name of the Special Branch officer she passed him on to.' (Pause). 'The name on fake passport was not Benito Galasso, it was Giovanni Volante!'

'Wow,' gasps Mary. 'Our dear friend Gus!'

'Or in reality,' says Monty, 'Senior Benito.'

'The immigration officer,' continues Pedersen, 'made a special note of her surprise and consternation when an hour or so after she had handed over her report, the suspect Italian, complete with his false passport was allowed to walk free! She assumed that it must have been some kind of police plot to catch a more important criminal, because it seemed so obvious to her that the Italian was travelling under a false identity. But she was mistaken. You'll begin to see the light when I tell you who the Special Branch officer she passed her report to was. It was none other than police officer Stanley Guthrie!'

Pedersen pauses to let this revelation sink in. Mary eventually spoke, slowly and thoughtfully, working out the puzzle.

'Ok… It's beginning to make sense. Crook with false passport plus bulging bank account. Bent copper with an eye on the make. Am I right in thinking that Stanley buys a new car and an expensive holiday and Gus walks free as the proverbial?'

'The EAW has a clear photograph of Benito,' Pedersen informs them, 'and there is no way that the passport photograph can be anyone *else* but him. Guthrie nevertheless gives him the all-clear. On your way sunshine, but just remember who it was that helped you out. The start of a not-so-beautiful relationship.'

'It goes both ways though, doesn't it? I mean, they each have a hold on the other. If one squeals the other one can follow suit in retaliation.'

'That's true, Miranda. And we eventually see how this leads to disaster for both of them. But over to you Monty for the next chapter.'

Pedersen takes a sip from his whisky glass and leans back in his chair. But Mike is still not happy.

'What happened to the immigration officer's report? Did Guthrie destroy that as well? If not, someone else should have seen it and acted on it. Especially if, as you say, it's was pretty damming.'

Pedersen hesitates again, then shrugs his shoulders before replying. 'Just one more report,' he says, waving his hands dismissively. 'Put it in the pile and file it along with all the others to gather dust. Flick knives, drugs, tinned meat from India, porno mags from Thailand and, oh yes, this other one about a dodgy Italian who got handed over to the SP. All dealt with. No need to read them especially.'

'Does that often happen?'

'The immigration officer had passed the suspect on, made her report and it was filed. That was the official and logical end of her responsibility, even though she clearly thought his release very strange. But if it had been done on purpose by the police authorities, she could see no point in pursuing it any further.'

Chris turns away from Mike, signifying that the topic is closed, but Mike is far from satisfied with this explanation.

'Just one more report? Excuse me Chris, I don't mean to be rude, but are you telling us that nobody bothers to even *read* reports of immigration breaches by border staff, let alone *act* on them? Where the hell do these reports go to? How many terrorists are we letting in because nobody can be bothered to follow up on a false passport?'

'Steady Mike,' warns Monty. 'Chris is not personally to blame.'

'Forgive me, but I thought Special Branch was supposed to protect our national security.'

Pedersen's voice changes to a lower but more intense level.

'OK Mike. Yes. Border security was then far from perfect – and if I'm honest, it still is. Before you ask why, I'll tell you, but don't quote me. It's basically down to stretched resources, and also, I suppose, weak management. Where do the reports go? All reports go to the Border Agency Executive, but usually in the form of a summary. I also discovered that, at the time, there was no effective oversight of fake IDs reports and consequently, no effective follow up to reports such as this one. If you're telling me that this is totally unacceptable, I can only agree with you.'

'I know we're pushing you into places you don't really want to go, Chris,' says Mary, 'but out of natural concern, how does Special Branch fit into this – this lack of professionalism?'

Pedersen frowns before replying.

'I guess I have to say that Special Branch doesn't come out of this very well either, because of one rogue officer.'

'You mean you've only got one of them?' asks Mike, re-polishing his glasses vigorously.

Monty's intervention is more strident this time.

'Come on Mike. This is getting a bit out of hand. Let's give Chris some room. Are there no rogue journalists?'

Mollie suddenly appears pushing a coffee-laden, cup-clattering trolley. It could be a happy co-incidence, but

Miranda is sure that Mollie had been listening and decided to make a strategic entrance.

'My main function in the household is the waitress,' she says cheerily. 'We used to have an au pair girl from Slovakia, but she could never understand anything Monty said to her, so she left in exasperation.' Then turning to the occupants of the couch. 'Monty! What are you thinking of? Look at our guests all squashed together. I'll get another chair.'

Mike leaps up with heartfelt relief.

'Let me give you a hand Mrs Meyer.'

He and Mollie leave the room. A few moments later, Mike returns carrying a large, hand-carved wooden chair, fitted with arms and a soft cushion,. He places it next to Miranda's end of the couch and enthrones himself on it.

The conversation has moved in a direction Pedersen was not prepared for and he feels a natural obligation to protect the reputation of his organisation, especially as he is talking to a bunch of journalists. He needs to be careful about what he reveals. On the other hand, a cover up is against his instinct and anyway, he's going to have to reveal a fair amount if they are to understand his relevance to the discussion. He continues with a preparative sigh.

'The answer to your last question, Michael, is that we have a lot more than one bent copper in the force. And it's my primary job to wheedle them out and deal with them. Officially, I'm part of the Internal Section of the

Met Police colloquially known as *The Ghost Squad*. We investigate police corruption whenever it shows its ugly head.'

'You have a special section just to investigate police corruption?' asks Miranda. 'So how much of a problem is it? Is police corruption *that* common then?'

'Whoa! Slow down folks. Chris is not here to defend the entire Met Police force – he's doing us a favour by coming here,' says Monty.

But Pedersen is prepared to answer.

'Look, I'm a pragmatist. I live in the imperfect, real world. We will never uncover all the coppers who are soliciting or accepting minor bribes – we don't have the resources to do that. But as a matter of fact, on this occasion, I feel we haven't done too badly. Guthrie was not under investigation at the time that Volante entered the country, but he was subsequently put on the 'suspicious' list.'

'Meaning?'

'Meaning Mike, that there had been some minor whistleblowing from staff that worked with him. Nothing strong enough to confront him or charge him with, just a nod and a wink. Enough for us to keep a wary eye on him – on our radar if you like – with the aim of collecting enough evidence to confront and charge him. And that's where we were before the next element in the saga burst onto the scene.'

He pauses yet again to give them time to think. Mike is the first to figure it out.

'You mean the fire?'

'Precisely. The Keynote fire. This was the moment that things started to get serious. No longer just a silly story about a little-known cosmetic company and what it was putting into its products, this was possibly attempted murder.'

'The fire was handed over to you?'

'Not initially. The investigating officer was strongly of the belief that it was started deliberately, which is what made it a possible attempted murder. In a case like this there's an obvious need to investigate the backgrounds of all possible suspects and look for motives. Naturally, the board of Keynote were included. Volante's past was re-scrutinised – a bloody awful task I can assure you. But it came to a dead stop in July 1988. Not a trace of any Giovanni 'Gus' Volante before that date. He suddenly appeared in 1988 as if by magic.'

'And that raised your suspicions?'

'It did more than that, Mike. It caused us a real headache, but with the help of the Port Authority and with a bit of luck we managed to uncover Susan Larkin's report from the archives.'

He holds it aloft like Neville Chamberlain.

'Bingo!' cries Mary. 'You've got your connection. Guthrie and Volante.'

'Yes, but we wanted more. Scum bags like Guthrie deserve everything they get, but we needed to ensure that the case against him was bullet-proof. Just think about this for a moment. Let's go back to the deal between Volante and Guthrie – was it just a simple money transaction? Here, take the cash and goodbye? Hope I never see you again? Or was there something more?'

'You mean some kind of… ongoing commitment?' asks Miranda.

'I think I get it,' claims Mary. 'Guthrie reads the papers and sees that Volante might be on the brink of some money-making. He still has a hold over Volante and he could use that to cash in to whatever profit Keynote might be in the process of getting.'

'Possibly more than that. It's likely that part of the original deal was that Guthrie should get a cut of whatever Volante managed to earn.'

Mary is getting quite excited.

'So, Guthrie comes onto Volante and threatens to squeal on him if he doesn't keep to their arrangement and cut him in. Perhaps he thinks that Gus is being tricky over Patterson - that they know where he is and they are going to make a fortune. Should Volante refuse to co-operate, Guthrie, I assume, is not the kind of guy who's going to let them screw him out of what he sees as his fair share. Gus then issued a counter threat – you fuck me and I'll fuck you.'

'The rash thinking of greedy men,' agrees Pedersen. 'Guthrie has a history of gratuitous violence and is obviously going to demand his pound of flesh from Volante – and this is the point where my imagination begins to run riot. What better way the scare Volante into submission than to burn his factory down to show the Italian he means business?'

'The fact that Beverly Curtis came close to losing her life must have scared him.'

'Sure. But to be fair, we don't have definite proof that Guthrie did start the fire,' admits Pedersen.

'And scrawled that message on the wall to deflect the blame onto animal rights... Clever!'

'Presumably Curtis and Kander don't know Gus's background or his link with Guthrie,' guessed Mary.

'I always wondered why they didn't get the police involved to help find their missing chemist,' mused Mike. 'Seems the obvious thing to do. Now I think I understand. Volante must have been terrified by the possibility they would discover his true identity.'

'And he wouldn't have found it difficult to persuade the other two, considering the illegal way they were running the company,' agree Miranda.

'To be fair,' suggested Mary, 'the police did discover who Volante really was, thanks to Chris and the Met.

'Finally,' says Pedersen grinning. 'A scrap of praise! Now things begin to happen quickly. Bear in mind: Volante is now frantic. He is being threatened by Guthrie, hassled by Brett and Curtis, and is in mortal danger of losing everything – including his life, if Guthrie carries out his threat to tell the Italian mafia where he is. He desperately needs help and in his tiny mind, the only source he can think of is his missing chemist, George Patterson. But where the hell is he? The only route to him must be through his son. Surely Simon knows where he is. But where is Simon? Has anyone bothered to go back to the Patterson house to see whether he might now be at home? Well of course, nobody had. Everyone knew the house was empty. But Volante was willing to try anything – and he got lucky. That is exactly where Simon *was* hiding – you might say, hiding in plain sight.'

Monty decides that this was the time to take the reins. He stands up, grabs the whisky and circulates, filling everyone's glass with a generous measure, speaking as he did so.

'Refreshments needed. Excitement at fever pitch! Last piece of the jigsaw in sight. Be prepared for violence and bloodshed. Chris?'

'Violence and bloodshed indeed. Fortunately, we were now watching Guthrie very carefully and we were pretty sure that he could get violent. But we needed to catch him in the act. Our chance came when one of our staff caught Volante – who we were also watching - making his way to the Patterson household. Then, I did a naughty.' Pause for effect. 'There's a way to do things by the book. And then there are ways to actually get things done.'

'Are you sure we should hear this, Chris?' asks Mike.

'Mollie might need help washing up. Kitchen just through the door,' offers Monty.

Mike sits back in his chair and folds his arms, head down, looking over the top of his glasses by way of response.

'Go on,' encourages Mary. 'I'm sure all our lips will be sealed. Won't they Mike?'

'End justify means comes to mind,' suggests Monty. 'Go on Chris. What naughty did you do?'

'I set him up,' confesses Pedersen, obscurely. 'I got my desk sergeant to tell Guthrie that Volante was on the way to the Patterson's residence. I knew that Guthrie would follow – in fact, I told the sergeant to make sure he did.'

Mike can't resist asking the obvious question.

'You must have been aware that Guthrie might get aggressive with Volante. Is that what you were expecting to happen?'

Pederson turns to look directly at Mike.

'I hope you're not suggesting that I was willing to put either of those two worthy gentlemen purposely at risk, Mike. That would be a very serious offense. These two honourable gentlemen had every right to expect protection from the law, and I was determined to give it to them. That is why I followed on with two police cars and an ambulance as quickly as I could. Unfortunately, as I mentioned in my report, a certain amount of blood had already been spilt by the time I got there, and young Simon Patterson had very sensibly decided to temporarily retire to his bedroom upstairs so as not to become contaminated with it. Further, it seems that one of the kitchen knives had been misplaced from the kitchen rack but luckily, one of my officers spotted it and took it into safe custody before anyone could accidently get hurt with it. OK?'

Mike, crushed by the heavy sarcasm, remains silent.

'Mike is passionate about the way the law is administered in this country, Chris. There has to be some means of keeping the excesses we sometimes see in check, don't you think?' says Miranda, protectively.

'I agree,' says Mary,' but the fact of the matter is that both Guthrie and Volante are now locked up and awaiting justice.'

'Yes,' says Pedersen, 'and Volante, or should we use his real name, is not going to have a good time in the nick. He's going to need some protection, even before he comes out of prison.'

'Well, that was an interesting ride,' says Mary, attempting to bring the saga to an end by standing and grabbing her whisky glass, almost as though she was about to propose a toast. 'Can anyone guess what happens next?'

'What I'd like to know is what's happened to those containers. Are they still missing?' asks Miranda.

'No, we've got them,' says Pedersen, 'and they've been sent way for analysis. It'll be very interesting to know what's actually in them.'

'Interesting?' repeats Monty, 'Yes. Music to my ears. Page two I think – maybe even page one. The big reveal. Below the picture of Lynne Cooper in her undies.'

'That poor girl,' said Mollie, who had just returned to collect empty cups and plates. 'I'm really ashamed of some of the things you put into your papers, Monty.'

'I wouldn't worry too much Mrs Meyer,' advised Mary. 'Having met that young lady, my guess is that she'll be delighted to be on the front page with almost nothing on. It's the others that I'm more concerned about, especially Mrs Beresford and, of course, Simon. He still doesn't know where his parents are. He seems such a nice young man but he's going to need more protection until this silly chase is over.'

'Well, we tried, Mary,' Monty reminded them. 'Did your bit – you and hubby. Lead a horse and all that. I suspect more can be done but he'll need to ask. Mrs B? Should be able to get a story out of her. Modest but useful sum for her piggy bank I should think.'

'And the other two directors?'

'I think they'll be let off with fairly short term suspended sentences,' suggested Pedersen. 'I don't think they ever intended any real criminal offenses.'

'So, that wraps everything up then,' insisted Mary, helping herself to yet another whisky. 'Now we await the results of the analysis on the content of those gruesome little bottles. I can imagine Monty's centre page now...'

# 23

The Laboratory of the Government Chemist rightly considers itself to be an important institution, dealing, as it does, with such weighty matters as animal health, pharmaceutical research, the setting of chemical standards for universal use, pesticide analysis and the global promotion of 'Science for a Safer World'. So, if anyone had dared - had the nerve - to ask the Director of the LGC where the two jars of questionable cosmetic goo stood in their priority list, his terse answer would have been that the LGC tackled issues in strict, chronological order: first in, first out unless there was some kind of emergency. At this moment, no such emergency seemed to have arisen, so the analysis of jars' contents would have to take their turn. If he had he been more aware of the background to the question, he might have added that the LGC would not be hurried or harried by the popular press.

Privately – that was a different matter. The very same Director would have given a less formal, measured reply to his close acquaintances. For example: *'Why the bloody hell do we get lumbered with such irrelevant, bleeding minutiae when there were so many other vital uses for our valuable time and resources?'* But then, being a scientist, the Director would not have been aware of the now widespread interest in the two "Pigs in Castor oil" containers, since no sign of it had appeared in the scientific press or literature. We also need to consider the viewpoint of the chemist who had been lumbered with having to do the analysis. It was clearly going to be a nasty, tricky, messy job and there were plenty of other, more straightforward and interesting things he ought to finish first. This is known as human nature and it is comforting to know that even scientists, in spite of their assumed cold objectivity, are not immune to it. Thus, it can be seen that the masses awaiting the analytical result were, frankly, kept waiting. This did nothing to quench their thirst, however. In fact, it had entirely the opposite effect.

In view of all this, we can imagine his surprise when the Director received an irate note from a senior government minister asking when the hell they could expect the analysis to be done. This was sufficient to create the emergency required to push the analysis to the top of the priority list. In fact, fear of further chiding and possible damage to career and reputation prompted the Director seek an urgent consultation with his chemist, after which he was able to announce that the result of the analysis would be made available in one weeks' time (Monday) at 10 am.

## 24

Since her successful handling of the PICO Project, Mary Ellis had thrown herself into a frenzy of new activity. The message from the Director of the LGC announcing the date and time of the "piggy bits" disclosure had provoked a further article, gratefully accepted and approved by Monty Meyer for publication in the *Informer*. This had involved working all afternoon without a break in her study with the door closed.

### COSMETIC BREAKTHROUGH – OR PIG-IN-A-POKE?
#### By Mary Ellis

The Keynote Cosmetic company's 'piggy bits' containers are about to reveal their secret. A scientist at the government's labs will tell us exactly what the gruesome red stuff in these mysterious plastic containers actually consist of. Unpleasant as the thought might be, most people expect that the contents are just mashed up bits of animal. If so, just what did the long-lost George Patterson (Keynote's missing chemist) intend to do with them? The ex-directors of the fire-damaged company insist that Mr Patterson was on the brink of an extremely valuable cosmetic breakthrough. This is why we need to know the precise nature the containers' contents. So, what if the analyst finds other ingredients in the bottles – maybe secret ones, along with the mashed-up pig? If so, can these extra materials be identified without giving valuable trade secrets away? And to whom would such trade secrets belong, given that Keynote has now been put in the hands of a receiver and all three directors have been charged with various offenses? Maybe the government chemist will have to be muted or even muzzled in his Monday morning report. That will only increase interest still further. Is there to be no end to this cosmetic mystery play? Roll on Monday – we can hardly wait!

Ralph was a little ambivalent about the effect that his wife's accumulating success was having on her. On the one hand, he had witnessed an incredible increase in her self-confidence. Much to his relief, they no longer had to worry about dire consequences arising from their loss of Simon Patterson – they had not been scapegoated. His main concern was that she might be over-egging it. Not just in relation to her increased work schedule, but also in terms of an over optimistic assessment of her current capabilities and her new status and influence within newspaper circles.

Nevertheless, standing outside her closed door carrying a tray with coffee and biscuit, he felt constrained to knock before entering.

'How's the print princess doing?'

Mary didn't look up before answering.

'Thanks Ralph. Just put it on the table, please.'

Ralph moved to look over her shoulder, much to Mary's clear irritation.

'What are you working on?'

'Just re-editing a piece I did on cosmetics some time ago but never got printed. Time to drag it out again.'

'I guess the public haven't got tired of the cosmetics theme yet then.'

'Nope. The animal-free cosmetics mob are having a field day. Even film stars are jumping on the band wagon. Shock and disgust that poor little piggies are ending up in their expensive face creams. All the major brands are going to produce animal-free ranges I hear. Monty is beside himself with joy over the increase in sales.'

Ralph moved away and sat down in the only armchair.

'It's frightening isn't it, the power of the press? One tiny story blown up into a major international crisis.'

Mary looked up.

'Not a crisis exactly. And it's not just any old story – it took a newspaper genius to see the potential in it.'

'You mean Monty?'

'Christ no! I mean Corbet. *Sir* David Corbet - and the "Sir" is, in my view, is clearly merited.'

'You think he was the *only* one behind this?'

'I'm certain of it. Monty was against it from the beginning and made it clear. Boy! Was he wrong?!'

## 25

In an office far, far away that no ordinary human may enter, sits a man hunched over a computer screen. His concentration is intense and nothing distracts him except an occasional glance at his desktop clock. This is a superior man, a man at the very top of the corporate pyramid. Here is the leader of a great industrial empire doing what all great leaders do best. Each click of the mouse represents a tactical advance, the rapid movement of resources from one place to another, the cold calculation of changing odds as new information comes flooding in and he moves instantly to deal with it. He has a crystal-clear vision of his ultimate goal and he moves relentlessly towards it. Industry depends upon these few great individuals who are blessed with such insight and ingenuity that we rightfully place them on a pedestal so that we ordinary mortals can admire them.

The telephone rings.

'Yes?'

'Your visitor is here, Sir David. Shall I send him in?'

There is slight hesitation.

'Yes. Thank you.'

The great man curses to himself. Blast! And he closes down his half-completed game of solitaire.

His visitor has a familiar face.

'Come in, Monty. What news?'

Even Monty Meyer, in the presence of such royalty, feels inclined to bow slightly before he takes a comfortable seat.

'How are you, Sir David?'

The great man smiles.

'You answer one question with another, eh? Does that mean the news is bad? Knowing you, if it were good, you would have blurted it out already.'

This was the tricky bit.

'Could be either - good or bad.'

With a deep sigh, Sir David removes his spectacles and reaches for the inevitable whisky decanter. Even this early in the day.

'Isn't this where you say to me 'do you want the good news first or bad news first?''

'Not that simple. If I had to, I would say the PICO Project is good news. Substantial increased paper sales. Spot on, as usual, Sir David. Brilliant.'

'I love the flattery. Are you after a pay rise?'

'To be honest, I was against making it big at first. Dodgy company. Dodgy bottles of goo - what's in them? Ridiculous fairy-tale cosmetic story. Still, you saw the light. That's not flattery. Fact.'

Sir David hands over a glass.

'Well, I put it in your hands Monty, so you deserve some of the credit for making it work. From what I saw, it was handled satisfactorily. In fact, having thought about it, I only have one question.'

'All ears, Sir David.'

'Can we be sure that with all the hype, we never actually speculated about what was *actually* in those containers? We never gave an opinion?'

Monty looks shocked.

'Why do you ask?'

'Another question answered with a question. Come on Monty. Stop this fucking about. Tell me what you've come to tell me and then piss off. I'm busy.'

Monty reaches into his inside pocket and produces a folded A4 paper.

'This arrived earlier. Thought you'd want to see it straightaway.'

He unfolds the paper and offers it across the desk. Sir David reaches for his glasses again.

'What is it?' he asks unnecessarily.

'The analytical report.'

'On those containers? I thought that wasn't going to be available until Monday. How did you get your hands on it?'

Monty answers by tapping the side of his nose with his finger.

'Best not to ask. Could put me in the Tower.'

It doesn't take long for Sir David to read the report. It's very short.

'Well-well-well,' he says, laughing. 'Why the hell didn't someone think of that before?'

He spreads the report out on his desk.

'I'm relieved,' admits Monty. 'Not sure how you'd take it. Are we happy, or embarrassed?'

Sir David gives this some consideration before answering.

'We'll get some flak from our rivals, that's for certain. A lot of flak... but it won't be the first time. If you think about it, we created a storm and gave our readers an interesting ride through it. Yes, I'm happy. Put it in a frame and hang it up on a wall...'

...

The rest of the world had to wait. The avid readers of *GLOCOM* newspapers waited. Gus Volante, aka Benito Galasso waited, in dire fear and trepidation, in his prison cell. All the other participants in the saga waited, sitting in front of TV screens or besides their radios. And in the shadows? In the shadows, hidden in the bushes, lurked the predators.

It was John Humphrys, with greying hair and a smart business suit to match on the TV who finally revealed the much-awaited content of the analytical report on that fateful Monday morning. The BBC's science editor, sat beside him to help interpret its meaning.

The reaction to the revelation was instant. No interpretation as really needed. The world gasped. The world laughed. The world mocked. The rival newspapers rubbed their inky hands together. Mary, Miranda and Mike became red-faced. *Damned George Patterson and his bloody shorthand!* But they would eventually see the funny side of it. And each of them would be presented with a framed copy of the report to display (or not) in their home and office, just as it was now displayed on the TV screens.

---

**Laboratory of the Government Chemist**
Report on the contents of two HDPE containers.
Issued 10th October 1983.

**Container 1** labelled R6:20-001BTR
Castor oil 90.3% w/w
Pigment D&C Red Ba Lake (*CI 15850*) 9.7% w/w

**Container 2** labelled R7:10-001BTR
Castor oil 95.0 w/w
Pigment D&C Red 7 Ca Lake (*CI 15850:1)* 5.0% w/w

**Summary:** *The content of both containers seemed to be a dispersion of* **cosmetic pigments** *in* **castor oil** *of the kind frequently used in waxed based cosmetic products.*
D.B. Brown B.Sc., Senior Analyst.

---

'What it means, essentially,' explained the Beeb's science correspondent, 'is that the flasks contain cosmetic pigments which have been mixed or dispersed into liquid castor oil. I've checked with some cosmetic companies and they tell me that this is a standard procedure. You see, these kinds of pigments arrive in the form of a powder from their supplier. But they are commonly used as the colour ingredients in wax-based cosmetics such as lipsticks – which also contain castor oil. So the usual procedure is to pre-mix the powder into the oil to make a liquid paste. This can more easily be added to waxes make the lipsticks. The coloured contents of the containers were simply these ready-mixed colour pigment pastes.'

'"Pigs" being short for *pigments*, in castor oil?'

'Precisely.'

'So they are a bit like oil based paints, for the face and lips, then?'

'Well, I wouldn't put is in quite that way, but yes. In essence, yes.'

'Thanks for that explanation. Now on to the weather…'

…

The feeding frenzy started the very next morning. The front pages of the Tuesday editions of the co-inhabitants of the newspaper jungle were laid out on Ralph Ellis's dining table. Tooth and claw, they fought with each other to inflict the greatest possible injury to the *GLOCOM* empire. The table should have been stained blood red – and very nearly was, with the rival Red Tops leading the charge.

Most of them had pictures of cute piglets on their front pages. *"YOU'RE SAFE, LITTLE PIGGIES!! The Big Bad Wolf has egg on his face so won't be rubbing you onto the hair of his chinny chin chin"* shouted one of them, with slightly obscure logic. *"HOGMILIATED! Have you been told porkies?"* inquired another. Others confronted the *GLOCOM* owner more directly *"Hogs and kisses, Sir David. Seems like yesterday's pig is today's burnt bacon!"* and *"You can put lipstick on a pig, Sir David – but it's still a pig!"* Pushing dodgy headlines to the limit, was *"This is your TueSTY Reckoning!"* There was also much use of fairly obvious words and expressions such as *hamming it up, telling porkies and squealing* on the readers.

On a more serious note, one of the "quality" papers, under the heading *"It's a curly tale,"* provided a thoughtful analysis of the moral and practical implications of what *GLOCOM* had done. Was it guilty of publishing "disinformation", which it defined as information that turned out to be false? This accusation upset Mary when she read it.

'That's so unfair', she complained to Ralph. 'We never said the containers actually contained any pig – in fact, we were careful not to say anything about what we thought was in them.'

'All's fair in love and newspaper war, Mary, as you well know. You just don't like being on the receiving end for once.'

'Yes, but you can't argue that we deliberately *misinformed* anyone,' she protested. 'We just reported what was going on – truthfully and accurately.'

Ralph read the piece again before responding.

'What they're saying is that it may have been *disinformation*. You implied that something was true, without actually saying it, but the implication was clear and deliberate. In any event, you can't dodge the impact it has had on people's lives which, in some cases, has been devastating.'

'Yes, I can't deny that. I'm particularly worried about young Simon. He's a damaged teenager with missing parents and no supporting family and he has just suffered a horrible, violent experience. Does anyone know what has happened to him? Or even where he is now? Does anyone care?'

But Mary needn't have worried. Simon had at last found the comradeship and the discipline that he so badly needed. He was in a place and in a position where he was too occupied to worry about parents and Keynote. At the very moment that Mary was expressing her concern, he was fully engaged in week two of an intense, eight week British Army training course. His ambition, should he survive the course, was to become a military policeman!

## 26 – Epilogue

George Patterson thought he might be in Heaven, but he wasn't sure. His eyesight was not as good as it used to be. Everything seemed to be hazy and unclear nowadays. He was aware of the person or creature in flowing white robes who was gently adjusting his pillows to make him more comfortable. Was she an angel? He knew it wasn't Penny, because she was beside him and holding his hand. Everything in the distance seemed to be blue and green and… golden. Surely these were Heavenly colours? He felt no pain. His head didn't hurt any more. He felt at peace. Wonderful but strange. Perhaps things would become a little clearer after he had had another little sleep…

Penny was in floods of tears as she watched her drugged, sleeping husband.

'Help me, Sister Rosa. How can I ever forgive myself for what I've done to him. He was such a lovely man and now… well, just look at him. How can I make it right? I keep going over it all in my mind. If only I hadn't thrown that heavy glass decanter. What made me do it? I was angry, but I never, *ever* wanted to hurt him – not in the slightest. But now, just look at him. I deserve the pain, but I want to ask him for his forgiveness, but how?'

Sister Rosa took her hand – the one that had been holding George's. It was shaking. Penny had not had any alcohol for weeks.

'You have accepted the difficulties and suffering you have caused, but you must realize that God can bring good out of everything. George is probably happier now than he has ever been. Forgive yourself Penny, and thank God by prayer for His forgiveness.'

'But it's not just George that I have damaged, sister,' sobbed Penny, 'He had a life, a job.' Then with another deep sob. 'And a son.'

Sister Rosa gave Penny's hand a squeeze.

'It will be hard, but as long as you stay in this place, our *Sanctuary of Tranquil Grace* monastery, you will have to accept complete isolation from the outside world. This is the way of our Carmelite religious order. While you are here, what happened to George's job and your son will remain unknown to you.'

Penny gave some thought to this before responding.

'Perhaps that's just as well, Sister. Perhaps that is just as well…'

## *Acknowledgements*

I acknowledge with gratitude the help and patience of my wife, Gwynneth and my brother Stephen, who is a successful self-published author of eleven 'Brother Walter' novels. His advice has undoubtedly improved the quality of this book.

Printed in Great Britain
by Amazon